Advance praise for *End of Story*

"With its unique setup, *End of Story* had me hooked from the first page. Scott's winning recipe blends top-notch banter, a hunky hero, and the charming enigma at the core of the plot into a dish both sweet and spicy. I couldn't wait to find out what would happen!"

—Anna E. Collins, author of *Love at First Spite*

"I am in awe of Kylie Scott's ability to create heroines I'd love as a bestie, a hero to fall head over heels for. I devoured *End of Story* and adored every page of this hilarious, emotional page-turner. *End of Story* has shot straight to the top of my favorite list! It's the perfect balance of wit, steam and heartwarming romance with a dynamic cast of characters that pop off the page. A must read!"

—Helena Hunting, *New York Times* bestselling author

"Angsty, addictive, warm, and loving! Lars is my new man. A HUGE recommendation from me."

—Tijan, *New York Times* bestselling author

Select praise for the novels of Kylie Scott

"*Fake* kept me up late reading because I could not put this story down. I adored Patrick and Norah, the fun, the banter…all the sweetness. Kylie Scott delivers again!"

—Carly Phillips, *New York Times* bestselling author

"Kylie Scott has been one of my favorite authors for years. Her way with words, and her ability to make me fall in love with men I know I shouldn't but do anyways, has always been the recipe for the perfect read for me. I couldn't put this book down once I started and know everyone will feel the same."

—Aurora Rose Reynolds, *New York Times* bestselling author

"Kylie Scott proves once again why she is one of my auto-buy authors. *Fake* is an absolute delight…for every woman who wished her celebrity crush would fall madly in love with her. *Fake* is romance gold from one of the genre's best!"

—Naima Simone, *USA TODAY* bestselling author

Also by Kylie Scott

END OF STORY
BEGINNING OF THE END (a prequel novella)

For a complete list of books by Kylie Scott,
please visit her website at www.kyliescott.com.

KYLIE SCOTT

END OF STORY

GRAYDON
HOUSE

GRAYDON
HOUSE®

Recycling programs
for this product may
not exist in your area.

ISBN-13: 978-1-525-80479-3

End of Story
Copyright © 2023 by Kylie Scott

Beginning of the End
Copyright © 2023 by Kylie Scott

Graydon House
22 Adelaide St. West, 41st Floor
Toronto, Ontario M5H 4E3, Canada
www.GraydonHouseBooks.com
www.BookClubbish.com

Printed in U.S.A.

For All The Unapologetic Romance Readers.

END OF
STORY

One

"This is awkward."

The big blond man standing on my doorstep blinked.

"How are you, Lars?" I gave him my very best fake smile. "Nice to see you."

"Susie. It's been what...five, six months?" Setting down his toolbox, he gave me an uneasy smile. It was more of a wince, really. Because the last time we saw each other was not a good night. Not for me, at least.

"Something like that," I said.

"This your new place?" He nodded at the battered arts and crafts cottage. "The office said you had some water damage you wanted to start with?"

"Yeah, about that. I was told Mateo would be doing the work."

"Family emergency."

"Oh."

He gazed down at me with dismay. The man was your basic urban Viking marauder, as his name suggested. Longish blond hair, white skin, blue eyes, short beard, tall and built. I was average height and he managed to loom over me just fine. In his midthirties and more than a little rough around the edges. Nothing like his sleek and slick bestie. An asshole whose continued existence I'd prefer to be reminded of never. But we don't always get what we want.

I took a deep breath and pulled myself together. "Why don't you come in and I'll show you…"

"Okay."

"Don't worry about taking your boots off. The shag carpet isn't staying."

Heavy footsteps followed me through the living room and into the dining room, where we turned left to enter the small hallway. From this point we had two options, the bathroom or the back bedroom. We headed for the latter.

"The water was getting in through a crack in the window for who knows how long," I explained. "I only inherited the place recently. There were all these boxes piled up in here. No one could even see it was an issue."

He grunted.

"I spent the first month just sorting through things and clearing the place out."

Beneath the window frame, a large stain spread across the golden-flecked wallpaper. As if it weren't ugly enough to begin with. That was the thing about my aunt Susan; she wasn't a big fan of change. The two-bedroom cottage had belonged to her parents and everything had pretty much been left untouched after my grandparents passed. Apart from the addition of Susan's junk. Which meant that while the wallpaper and carpet were from the 1970s, the bathroom was from the 1940s, and the kitchen cabinets from the 1930s. At least, that's what I'd been told. The place was like an ode to twentieth-century interior design. The good, and the bad.

He got down on one knee, inspecting the damage. "The bottom of this window frame is warped and needs replacing."

"Can you do that?"

"Yeah," he said. "I need to have a look behind here. You attached to the wallpaper?"

"Heck no."

He almost smiled.

"The sooner I can repaint and get new flooring down, the better."

Nothing from him. A knife appeared from the toolbox, sharp-pointed with jagged teeth. He punched the blade through the drywall with ease and started cutting into the wall.

"How is he?" I asked the dreaded question. Curiosity was the worst. "Enjoying London?"

"Yeah," was all he said.

"And how's Jane?"

"We're not together anymore."

Not a surprise. Lars went through various girlfriends during the year I'd been with what's-his-face. Neither he nor his friend were down with commitment. Which was fine if you just wanted to have fun. But Jane was a keeper, smart with a wicked sense of humor. Lars definitely had a type. All of his girlfriends were petite, perfect dolls who behaved in a ladylike manner. The opposite of buxom, loudmouthed me.

He pried a square of drywall loose. "You thinking of living here permanently or flipping and selling the place, or what?"

"Haven't decided."

"Great location. A bit of work and it'd probably be worth a lot of money," he said, keeping the conversation on the business at hand. As was good and right.

Using the flashlight on his phone, he inspected the cavity. The man was all handyman chic. Big ass boots, jeans, and a faded black tee. All of it well-worn. And the way his blue jeans conformed to his thick thighs and the curves of his ass was some-thing. Something I hadn't meant to notice, but oh well, these things happened. Maybe it was the way his tool belt framed that particular part of his anatomy. For a moment, I couldn't look away. I was butt struck. Which was both wrong and bad. It would not be smart for me to notice this man in the sexual sense. Though it was nice to know my thirst meter wasn't broken.

I don't know if Lars and I were ever really friends. We had, however, been friendly. Though that was romantic relation-ships for you. One moment you had all of these awesome extra people in your life and the next moment they're gone.

I tugged on the end of my dark ponytail. An old nervous habit.

"At this stage, it looks like the damage is only superficial," Lars said. "These two sections of drywall have to go. Once I've done that, I'll have a better idea of what we're dealing with."

"Okay."

"But it wouldn't surprise me if some or all of that one needs replacing too." He pointed to the wall the bedroom shared with the bathroom. "See how there's bubbling along the joins of the wallpaper there?"

"Right."

"Do I have your approval to get started?"

I nodded.

None of this was exactly unexpected. Old buildings might have soul, but they could also have heavy upkeep. Renovations cost big bucks. While my savings were meagre, lucky for this hundred-year-old house, my aunt left me some money. Which was a point of contention for a few of my family members. Like any of them had time for Aunt Susan when she was alive. Besides being my namesake, she was also the black sheep of the family. A little too weird for some, I guess. But weird has always been a trait that I admired.

"I'm going to make myself coffee," I said. "Would you like some?"

"Yeah. Thanks."

"How do you take it?"

"White. No sugar."

"You're sweet enough, huh?" And the moment those words were out of my mouth, I knew I'd made a mistake. Talk about awkward.

He snorted, then said, "Something like that."

Lars didn't mess around. By the time I returned, he'd removed the first two panels of drywall. Hands on hips, he stood staring at the interior of the wall with the problematic window. Mostly it looked like a lot of dust and a couple of cobwebs. But then, I'm not a builder. When I handed over his mug, he gave me a brief smile before taking a sip.

"How is it looking?" I asked.

"Your house has good bones."

"Great."

"As long as the damage on that wall is due to the moisture spreading from the window and not a leaky bathroom pipe, this should be pretty straightforward," he said.

I'd taken over the main bedroom, but this room still held a lot of sentimental value for me. Whenever Mom and Dad were busy or needed a break from us kids, my brother would stay at a friend's house and I'd be packed off to Aunt Susan's—to this bedroom in particular. Which was fine with me. Andrew was an outgoing jock while I'd been kind of awkward. In this house, I was accepted for who I was. A nice change. With my parents divorced, growing up between three households and living mostly out of a schoolbag sucked. But Aunt Susan gave me the security that was lacking elsewhere.

"Is the floor okay?"

"Let's pull up some carpet and see." He set his coffee on the windowsill. Then, knife back in hand, he got busy with the shag. It was impressive how the tool became a part of him. An extension of his body. "You've got good solid hardwood under here."

"Ooh, let me see."

He tugged the tattered underlay back farther. "Oak, by the look of it."

"Wow. Imagine covering that beauty up with butt-ugly brown carpet."

"No sign of water damage. You were lucky."

I smiled. "That is excellent news."

"Now let's see what's behind this."

I took a step back so he could start removing the next section of drywall. He had such big capable hands. Watching him work was pure competence porn. As a mature and well-adjusted thirty-year-old woman, I definitely knew better than to have sexy times thoughts again. The best friend of my ex is not my friend. Confucius probably said that.

"Looks like there's something back here," he said, setting a panel of drywall aside.

"Something good or something bad?" I winced as a big hairy spider scurried out of the cavity. "Ew."

"It's just a wolf spider. Nothing dangerous."

"But there might be more."

Without further comment, he reached down and picked up a piece of paper. It looked old. Which made sense. Lord only knew how long it had been in the wall. It was kind of like opening a time capsule.

"What is it?" I asked, more than a little curious.

His gaze narrowed as he scanned the page, his forehead furrowing. Next his brows rose and his lips thinned. His expression quickly changed from disbelief to fury as he shoved the piece of paper at me. The open hostility in his eyes was a lot coming from a man of his size. "Susie, what the fuck?"

"Huh?"

"Is this your idea of a joke?"

"No. I…" The paper was soft with age and the writing was faded but legible. Mostly. *Superior Court of Washington, County of King* was written at the top. There was also a date stamp. This was followed by a bunch of numbers and the words *Final Divorce Order.* "Wait. Is this a divorce certificate?"

"Yeah," he said. "For you and me. Dated a decade from now."

I scrunched up my nose and ever so slightly shrieked, "*What?* Hold on. You think I put this in there?"

"No," he said, getting all up in my face. "I know you put it in there, Susie."

"Take a step back, please," I said, pushing a hand against his hard chest.

He did as I asked, some of the anger leaching from his face. Then he grumbled, "Sorry."

"Thank you."

"Why would you do that? Actually, it doesn't matter. Find someone else for the job," he said, gathering up his tools. "I'm out of here."

"Can you just wait a second?"

Apparently the answer was no. Because the man started moving even faster. "I don't know what game you're playing. But I'm not interested in finding out."

I took a deep breath and let it out slowly. "I did not put this in the wall, Lars. Think about it. You're a builder. Had any of the wallpaper or drywall been disturbed in the last forty or fifty years?"

"You could have accessed it from the other side. I don't know."

"I didn't even know you were coming here today."

He grunted. "Only got your word for that."

"And I've only got your word that *you* didn't put this in in the wall for some stupid reason," I said, thinking it over. *How did that not occur to me?* "Of course you put it there. I wasn't the first one to have access to that space. You were. A quick sleight of hand is all it would have taken. This is so unprofessional."

"Very nice. I'm sure you prepared that speech at the same time you planted it, knowing I'd inevitably be the one who first touched it."

"And I'm sure *you* prepared that speech at the same time you planted it, knowing I'd suspect you."

He glared at me. "Why the hell would I, Susie?"

"Why the hell would *I*, Lars?" I bellowed. "This is ridiculous. I just want my house fixed. That's all. And I specifically asked who would be doing the job because I didn't feel the need to see you again."

With his back to me, he paused.

"No offense. But I knew it would be wildly uncomfortable."

"Why'd you use the company I work for then?"

"Because I know they're reputable and do good work. You yourself said that's one of the main reasons why you've stuck with them. Because they don't encourage you to cut corners or use shoddy materials and they treat their staff well. Also, they pretty much do everything. These things matter." I raised a finger. (No. Not that one.) "Take car repairs for instance. Because I know little to nothing about cars, I get ripped off by repair shops—I'm sure of it. I didn't want that to happen here."

Another grunt. What an animal.

"I wish neither to marry nor divorce you, Lars. And I'm pretty sure the feeling's mutual. So this piece of paper I'm holding in no way benefits me. Look at me. Am I laughing?

No, I'm not. Nor am I enjoying all this drama. Confrontation stresses me the fuck out," I said, my shoulders slumped. "I don't know what else to say. This is ridiculous."

"You already said that."

"It's worth repeating."

He gave me a look over his shoulder. "If you're messing with me…"

"I'm not. Are you messing with me?"

"No."

"Then what the hell is going on?" I asked the universe.

Without another word, he got to his feet and strode out of the room, heading straight into the bathroom next door. There he made quick work of checking everything. The tiling and paintwork, around the white pedestal basin, inside the mirrored cabinet set into the wall, and the end of the claw-foot bathtub. Then he turned around, face set to cranky. "Access point for the attic?"

"Hallway."

In no time flat, he had the ceiling hatch open and the ladder down. Then up into the darkness he went. His cell phone doubled as a flashlight again.

"Lot of stuff up here," he commented.

"That does not surprise me. My aunt was kind of a hoarder. Not as bad as the people on those TV shows, but…yeah."

He sneezed. "A lot of dust, too."

"Bless you. I haven't even been up there yet," I said. "Cleaning and clearing space out down here has taken all of my time."

His big boots disappeared up the last rungs of the ladder while I waited below. After all, I'd only be in the way. It had absolutely nothing to do with my fear of creepy-crawlies. Someone had to wait below with the weird ass document. The sounds of him stomping about and things being shifted came next. Something heavy was pushed aside. Something else fell and glass broke.

"Sorry," Lars called.

"I'm sure it was nothing valuable. Hopefully."

Then his face appeared in the dark hole overhead. "Looks like they built the attic to use as another bedroom or office at some stage. The floorboards and everything are tight. No real access into the walls below."

"Mmm."

"Plus there's about an inch of dust on the ground and no sign of any footprints other than mine."

"Good work, Nancy Drew," I said. "Is the basement next?"

He gave me a flat, unfriendly look. "Yes."

Maybe I'd be better off finding another builder. In fact, I knew I would be. Though it would only be trading one peace of mind for another. While Lars would no longer be in my face, I wouldn't be able to trust the new builder's work to the same degree. Which would be anxiety-inducing and possibly costly. Talk about a no-win situation.

Back into the dining room then through to the kitchen at the back of the house, we went on our not-so-merry adventure. I opened the door to the dingy staircase. "I like to call this the murder room. Dark, dank, dangerous. It's got it all."

No response from him as we made our way down. Tough crowd. It was just a basic concrete room with a boiler, laundry area, and more assorted crap. But the old boiler, the one before this one, used to make creepy noises. Hence my childhood fears of the basement. Helping with the laundry was always an ordeal. I usually avoided it by offering to do the dishes instead.

Lars began examining the ceiling.

"When did you find out you had this job?"

"Around eight this morning. The office called," he said. "Mateo's boyfriend got hit by a car riding to work."

"Is he okay?"

"A few bumps and bruises and a sprained wrist."

"Phew."

"Yeah," he said. "The job I was on was close to finishing and they could spare me, so they asked me to come here."

"What gets me is that the paper looks old. I mean, the way the text is faded and everything." I carefully turned the certificate over in my hands. "I wonder if we could get it tested, somehow."

He scoffed. "You don't actually think it's real?"

"I honestly don't know," I said. "What I do know is, if you didn't put the certificate there to mess with me—and I guess I believe you when you say you didn't—then I can think of no rational explanation for how it got there."

He frowned harder and kept right on inspecting the ceiling. Even he had to admit that it was highly unlikely I'd put the decree of dissolution in the wall. Surely.

"Does your middle name start with *A*?"

"Alexander. Yes."

"So the details are right, at least. No money judgment is ordered. No real property judgment is ordered. This marriage is dissolved. The petitioner and respondent are divorced. Not much information there to go on." I chose my next words with care. "You know, my aunt, she was kind of eccentric. She was always burning candles and buying crystals."

Looking back over his shoulder at me, he raised a questioning brow.

"The thing is, she used to talk to the house sometimes," I finally said. "Like it was an actual living breathing entity. And yes, maybe she was lonely or a little strange. Please don't say anything mean or dismissive about her."

"I'm not going to say anything about your aunt."

"Thank you."

He didn't even blink. "But it's not supernatural, Susie. This was no ghost or spirit or whatever you're suggesting."

"Okay. Fine. I just thought I'd put that out there," I said. "Did you find anything down here?"

"No."

"So now what?"

Face set, he walked over, staring into my eyes as if he could read my soul.

"Susie."

"Lars."

"I want to believe you when you say you had nothing to do with it. You always seemed like a pretty honest person to me," he said. "A bit too honest, sometimes."

"How so?" I asked, only mildly annoyed—although I was exercising great restraint.

"Some of the stuff you come out with sometimes is...unnecessary."

"Let's agree to disagree," I said.

He shook his head.

"I would point out, however, that I'm not brutal. Ever notice how people who say they're *just being honest* usually are?"

His nostrils flared on a deep breath. How that was in any way attractive I had no idea. Something must be wrong with me. Guess my vibrator was getting a little boring. Maybe it was time for me to get out there and meet some men. Then again, not dating for the rest of my life would also be great.

"For the last time," he said, speaking nice and slow, "did you put that piece of paper in the wall?"

"No. I swear."

"Fuck," he muttered.

"Fuck," I agreed.

He sighed. "Someone's messing with us."

Two

"Correct me if I'm wrong, but I thought you just said that you couldn't find any way for someone to slip the certificate into the wall," I said, confused.

"I've got to be missing something."

"Like what?"

"I don't know," he said, voice thick with frustration.

"Let me think." I took a deep breath and let it out slowly. "Why don't we go pull off the other panels on that wall? See if they left anything else for us to find."

He gazed off at nothing for a moment before nodding. "Good idea."

Nothing about this made sense. I couldn't think of anyone who might have put the divorce certificate in the wall to mess with me. The other thing was, I'd made the choice to not get married a long time ago. My parents divorced when I was five. They'd given up on having children about a decade before, when my brother arrived out of nowhere. They then compounded the problem by having me. I read a study once that showed that children of divorced parents are almost seventy percent more likely to have their marriage end in divorce. While I dreamed of finding the One, there would be no big white dress for me. And I didn't need one. If love and commitment weren't already present in the relationship, then a marriage certificate wasn't going to fix a damn thing.

It took no time at all for Lars to remove the next section of drywall in the second bedroom.

Nothing. Just more dust and cobwebs. But as for the third…

"There's a hole down at the bottom of this one," said Lars, bending to inspect the drywall. The hole was about the size of his hand and cunningly hidden behind a flap of wallpaper.

"Notice how the carpet is darker?" I asked, pointing. "There used to be a set of drawers here. No one would have even known the hidey-hole was there."

He cut into the drywall once again, revealing the house's insides.

"Bingo," muttered Lars.

"What is it?"

He brushed off the front of the magazine. "Porn."

Sure enough, a blonde hippie wearing a sheer floral dress contemplated her toes on the cover. Bet she had natural bush and everything. And good for her.

"*Playboy*. April 1972." I inspected the thing. "Oh, good God. Do you know what that must be? My father's teenage masturbation material!"

He bit back a smile. "Probably."

"Gross!"

"At least the pages aren't stiff."

"That's not funny," I said, tossing the magazine onto the ground. "I need to go bathe in bleach."

He returned to the wall. "The drywall is well-attached to the studs. Not much room to slip anything through."

"Studs are the pieces of wood making up the frame of the house?"

"That's right."

"Even if you could get your arm in the hole, I don't see how you could get a piece of paper past the first stud, across the space between, then past the second stud to place it where we found it."

"No." He scratched at his short beard. Or maybe it was long stubble. "I'm out of ideas. How about you?"

I shrugged and slipped the folded-up certificate out of the pocket in my black cotton dress. Because in a right and good world, dresses should have pockets. "I can't think of anything."

"Why don't I get back to work?"

"You're really going to stay?"

His turn to shrug. Then he picked up his now-cold coffee and downed half of it.

I smiled. "Okay. I'll leave you to it."

While the sawing and hammering commenced in the bedroom, I got busy with my own work. First I responded to comments on today's posts. Defused an angry customer with a twenty-dollar gift card. Then I started working on future promotions. Such was the joy of being a social media manager. I got to work from home the bulk of the time. But I had to be friendly, funny, creative, a problem solver, and available just about around the clock. My main clients were an organic and recycled-clothing company, a fleet of coffee trucks, and an online menstruation products store. I loved my job.

By the time I took a lunch break several hours later, I was ready to return to solving this whole mystery-divorce-certificate thing. I was also ready to eat. "You hungry?"

Lars gazed up at me. "Starving."

There was a certain satisfaction in seeing a man on his knees. Too bad it was only renovations-related. But I digress. "BBQ?"

"Let's do it."

Thanks to the magic of delivery, we were soon sitting on the front porch with our food in hand. It was a typical pleasant summer's day. Blue sky, birds, the usual. The sun was out, which meant you could see Mt. Rainier. Always a good thing. While Seattle was known for its rain, we do get some good weather. And all of the wet meant the grass and trees were a shade of green I'd never seen anywhere else. The plot of land the cottage sat on was about the size of a postage stamp, but there was room for a small garden in the front and back. I'd killed more than my fair share of houseplants. Perhaps this was my chance to develop a green thumb.

"Thought of a few questions," Lars said, piling up his fork with coleslaw. "Who's visited since you moved in?"

"Didn't we already establish that there was no way someone could have hidden the certificate without the drywall being removed?"

"Humor me."

"Okay." I took a sip of water. "It's not like I've been throwing parties or anything. The place isn't ready for that yet. My friend Cleo has been over a few times."

He gazed out at the quiet street for a minute. "Don't think I ever met her."

"No, I don't think you did either. And leaving that in the wall isn't something she would do. It's not even like I would have mentioned you to her."

"Harsh."

"You were the best friend. Not the boyfriend."

"Women only talk about relationships?"

I wrinkled my nose in disgust.

"What?" he asked.

"That question was just so stupid I honestly don't know how to answer it."

He gave me a dour look.

"Women talk about a lot of things, Lars. I just didn't particularly talk about you."

"All right," he said. "Who else?"

"Just my family."

"Do they know about me?"

"Maybe I mentioned you in passing," I said. "But certainly not to the degree that they'd feel the need to pull a stunt like this."

"Is there anyone in your life who would?"

"I have an uncle who put fake dog poop in my shoe once. I was twelve at the time." I wiped my mouth with the napkin. "But that's about it as far as tricksters go."

"What about neighbors?"

"What about them?"

"Do you know any of them?"

I shook my head. "Aunt Susan knew some of them, but..."

We ate in silence for a moment. Then he held up his half-eaten plate of brisket, coleslaw, and cornbread. "You want to swap?"

I passed over my pulled pork, mac 'n' cheese, and collard greens. No idea how it started, but swapping meals was something Lars and I used to do when we all went out to dinner. Double dating or whatever. We had similar tastes and this meant we could sample more of the menu. After all, who wouldn't want to try two different desserts?

I tapped my fork against my lips, thinking deep thoughts. "Just to reiterate, no one knew you were coming here today before eight o'clock this morning?"

"Right," he said.

"This is so bizarre. It's like something out of a movie."

He took a bite of cornbread and nodded. After he swallowed he said, "This isn't the first time we've found stuff behind walls during renovations. Newspaper for insulation, tools that got dropped when the place was being built, old bottles from Prohibition, even."

"Wow."

"One job I heard about, they found a gun and some money."

"Wish we'd found money."

"What would you have done with it if we had found ten grand?" he asked.

"Something frivolous. Like go to Paris or buy a pair of Prada heels." I smiled. "What about you?"

"Nothing. Your house, your walls, your porn collection. The money is all yours."

"Say we'd have split it down the line."

"In that case, add it to the fund for my business startup."

"How sensible and mature."

"You say that like it's a bad thing," he said. "We're old enough, we should have our act together."

"I have a house."

"Not because you saved up and worked for it."

"Ouch." I opened my eyes painfully wide. "I'll have you know, I've been building up my business for years."

"Sounds like I hit a nerve."

"Oh, you think?"

He cocked his head, and didn't say a word.

"You make me sound like some profligate," I said.

"I didn't mean—"

"Yes, you did. And it's true, I enjoy pretty things, but I work damn hard for them. I invest back in my business often and my credit card and car are paid off in full."

"Okay," he said.

"Men like you do my head in. You know, you call yourself nice guys. So laid-back and easygoing. But then you sit back and judge the absolute shit out of people. And more often than not, those people are women."

For a moment he just stared at me, then he sighed. "I'm sorry."

"Are you?"

"Yes," he said. "You're right. I was out of line."

"I'm glad you see that."

"You and I have a bad habit of rubbing each other the wrong way. Always have."

"Guess we do."

He shoved an agitated hand through his golden hair, pushing it back off his face. He had a nice face. High cheekbones and a sharp jawline. Too bad he could be an utter jerk. The Ex had a tendency to see things in black-and-white too. As if the world were full of absolutes. Small-minded people terrified me. Imagine thinking you already knew everything there was to know. That you were never wrong. How the hell would you ever learn anything new?

"I'm no longer wondering why we got divorced, at least."

Lars did the raising-one-eyebrow thing again. "It's not real, Susie."

"I know, I just..." I watched a butterfly fluttering around the lavender plant by the front steps. "We don't even have any chemistry."

He paused. "I wouldn't say that."

"Wouldn't you?"

"No." And he said it so matter-of-factly.

My eyebrows all but kissed the sky. "Huh."

"Not that it matters," he said. "You dated my friend so there's no way."

"Ah, the bro code."

"That's right."

"You dudes, you're so principled. I love that about y'all," I drawled.

The hint of amusement was back in his gaze. "Susie, in another life, if we actually got together, I honestly think we'd be lucky to last five minutes. Don't you?"

"Probably."

And then he smiled. He had a great smile. Dammit. So maybe there was something there. Just not anything that would ever be acted upon. That much was certain.

"That's *wild*," said Cleo later that night on the phone. She was a photographer, and a kindred spirit. We met years ago through work.

"Right?"

"Do you think the house is haunted?"

"I love that you ignored logic and jumped straight to that conclusion."

She laughed. "There's a reason we're friends."

"I was thinking that the hole is a split in the space-time continuum."

"That would work," she said. "Though that would also require you to marry and divorce him at some point in the future."

"Not if it was from a parallel dimension."

"Okay. I'm buying it. Carry on."

"You know, I tried to tell him it might be supernatural and he wouldn't listen." I lay back on my bed, staring at the ceiling. Plain white, thankfully. Unlike the walls and floors, it had escaped any ugly interior trends from bygone eras. The certificate lay on the mattress next to me. I had carried it around all day. As if the strange thing might disappear if I took my eyes off it. "Though the house isn't haunted, that I'm aware of. I mean, it creaks now and then. But all old homes do that, right?"

"Mmm."

"It's not like I've sensed Aunt Susan's presence or anything," I said. "I think I'd like to see a ghost, but I'd also be terrified to see a ghost."

"Agreed."

"Maybe we should have a séance."

"Knowing our luck, we'd accidentally open a portal to hell," she said. "And my mama would be appalled we were messing with that sort of thing."

"Right. No séance."

"It's certainly a very odd discovery."

"Lars is convinced someone is screwing with us. Which is the most likely conclusion," I said. "I just can't imagine why."

"You definitely don't think he put it there when you weren't looking?"

"No, I don't." I frowned. "At first, he was baffled like me, but then he was furious. Like I was playing a game or stirring up trouble. He was ready to walk out until I talked him down. Not that I actually want him here. I've only just gotten over his idiot friend dumping me in front of everyone that he knew. Having Lars around is not my idea of a good time. Too complicated. Too many memories. He basically called me fiscally irresponsible and immature today."

"What a poopy head."

I laughed.

"And if you wanted payback against your fool of an ex you'd do it in a mature and sensible manner."

"Exactly."

"Like egging his house or something."

"Actually, that sounds fun. How are you doing in the condo on your own?"

"I'm turning your old room into my office," she said.

"Good work."

"Josh wants to move in with me."

"Oh, yeah?"

"It would help with the rent," she said. "And I don't mind him."

"Aw. True love."

Cleo laughed. "Maybe. I don't know. It's a big step and I'm enjoying having the place to myself. After the divorce I didn't think I'd want a man in my space again. Of course, I didn't think I'd ever want to date."

"There's no rush."

"No." She sighed. "Guess we're both divorcées now."

"Sure. Sort of. Though mine is still out there lurking in the future, apparently."

"You better have asked me to be your bridesmaid."

A plaintive meow had me turning my head. "There's a cat sitting on my bedroom windowsill staring at me."

"Little pervert," she joked. "Are you dressed?"

"He's gray with pretty green eyes. I wonder who he belongs to," I said as the animal sat back and started cleaning its belly. "Oh, he's a she. Thanks for the view, friend."

"Probably belongs to a neighbor," she said. "What did you find in today's boxes?"

Cleo helped me unpack the first few weekends after I moved. We scrubbed and vacuumed and sorted. With Mom in Michigan with her new husband, Dad having moved to head office in Florida, and my brother in a state of woe over having been left out of Aunt Susan's will, Cleo's been a life-saver. Now that I'm on my own, I've been going through a box of Susan's junk a day. Separating the important from the trivial, from the puzzling. Making way for the future by clearing out the past. That's how I tried to look at it. The idea of this task had quietly terrified me for years, but now that I'm neck deep in it, it's been bigger than I ever imagined.

"The one I opened had holiday and birthday cards from the eighties. A stack of projector slides from the seventies documenting family holidays. A pair of cracked white leather knee-high disco boots, some cool and colorful plastic bead necklaces, and the ashes of a dog named Rex."

"Rest in peace, Rex."

"Amen. I wish she was here to tell me the stories behind some of this stuff."

"Mmm."

"At least now the main floor of the house is clear," I said. "Anything that still needs to be sorted has been put down in the basement. Though there is the attic. I may just pretend it doesn't exist."

"That's not a bad idea. We still on for lunch on Thursday?"

"Absolutely," I said. "How are the shots for the florist shop coming along?"

"Should be finished with the final edits tomorrow. The client was happy," she said. "You know, maybe whoever left the fake certificate in the wall will come forward. Point and laugh at you. That sort of thing."

"At least then I'd know what was going on."

"I watched this courtroom TV drama one time where they had a forensic document examiner," she said. "They gave testimony about a birth certificate being falsified. Maybe that's the sort of person you need."

"Maybe. Or maybe one of the ghost-hunters from those TV shows."

"Keep me updated," she said. "I love a good mystery."

★ ★ ★

To my great disappointment, no one came forward to claim responsibility. Though it's only been one day since we found it. And no more documents appeared while Lars continued working yesterday. Which was probably for the best. Sandra Bullock and Keanu Reeves might have been cool with sending messages through time in that movie, *The Lake House*, but I found the experience to be less romantic and more of a mind fuck.

Lars arrived bright and early the next day. He immediately got busy fixing the warped window frame. The man said few words, but whenever our paths crossed he gave me sideways glances. Super sketchy ones. And if he wanted to go back to doubting me about the divorce certificate then there was no way I would be making him coffee. We ignored each other until it was time for my lunch break.

Any other contractor/handyman I could have largely ignored and left to their own devices. But Lars existed in a gray zone. He sort of felt like a guest in my house rather than a worker, but not really. It was complicated.

"I'm making lunch," I said. "Would you like a sandwich?"

"No."

"Fine," I snapped.

You don't mess with a woman when she's premenstrual and hungry. Everyone knows that. Lars, unfortunately, was an idiot. Because he gave me another of those dubious-as-all-hell sideways glances. The bastard.

"I can't believe we're back to this again," I said, hands on hips. "Do you have something you'd like to say?"

"No."

"You're sure about that?"

"Yes."

I smoothed down the front of my black tank top, and

straightened the waist of my cropped jeans. The black polish on my toes shone bright, which did wonders for my confidence and looked great with my strappy flat leather sandals. "Let me guess, you went home last night and your little brain started working overtime. *Where could the divorce certificate have come from? I didn't put it there. Susie was the only other person present. It must be her. Burn the witch!*"

He gave me a dry look.

"Well?"

"No one knew I was going to be here," he growled. "It's the only thing that makes sense."

"Give me strength. No one, including me, knew you were going to be here. And this leads you to believe I must have planted it. Where's the logic in that?"

"It's like they say on that TV show. If you rule out the impossible, then whatever's left, however improbable, must be the truth."

"If you really believe that, then pack your shit and get out," I said. "Ask your office to bill me for the work that's been done. We're through here."

He froze. "Are you serious?"

"You bet your ass I am. I don't need this tension in my life. In *my* home while I'm trying to work. If you honestly believe I'm up to something, that I'm trying to mess with you, then go."

Today he wore a faded Pearl Jam tee, which was kind of the uniform in this town. And he wore it well. "It's like you said yesterday. Another builder might rip you off. Not do the work right."

"What do you care?"

For a long moment, he just looked at me. Then he sighed. "I always liked you."

I didn't know what to say.

"Not like that." He hung his head. "I just… This shit is ridiculous. It makes no sense."

"I agree. But how about instead of turning on each other, we do something constructive?"

"Such as?"

I crossed my arm and leaned against the doorframe. "A friend gave me an idea about how best to ascertain if the document is real."

"It's not."

I shrugged. "Fine. So we send it to the forensic document examiner and rule out the possibility."

"But it's not real. There's no point."

"Do you have any better ideas?"

"No," he admitted, eventually.

"I already called them and got a quote. I'm doing it."

"All right then." His expression spoke clearly of the suffering he endured at the hands of womankind. "Whatever you want, Susie."

"Good answer, Lars." I gave him two thumbs up. "In the future, why don't you just lead with that?"

In response, he cracked his neck. "I lied. I would like a sandwich."

"Of course you would."

"What are your plans for out here?"

We sat out back in the two old Adirondack chairs beneath the Japanese maple to eat lunch. The area consisted of a patch of grass and a collection of bright ceramic pots filled with various herbs, a tomato plant, green onions, beans, and lettuce. I hadn't managed to kill them yet. Fingers crossed.

"I'd love a small fire pit," I said. "Make it a nice space to hang out at night."

He nodded. "What about the exterior?"

"It definitely needs a fresh coat of paint. I was thinking some shade of blue. That way if I do decide to sell, it has broad appeal."

Another nod.

"Don't look now, but we're being stalked." I nodded to the side of the house where the gray cat sat watching us.

Lars smiled and took a bite of his sandwich. Roast beef, mustard, cheese, tomato, and lettuce. Comfort food was the best. Then he tore off a bit of meat and tossed it to the feline. I've never seen an animal move so fast. Or look so happy.

The messenger from the forensic document examiner had already picked up the document. But it would be two weeks before her report on the divorce certificate would be ready. A bummer since patience had never been my thing.

"What's the plan for removing the wallpaper and carpet?" I asked.

"Mateo and Connor will be on-site tomorrow to help with those jobs. This afternoon I'm going to measure some of the siding that needs to be replaced. Maybe take a look at that front step that's a little loose."

"You're a useful man."

A grunt.

"So what have you done with your life in the last six months?"

"What have I done?" He raised a brow. "Let me think… worked on this cool houseboat that a friend bought. That was fun."

"Nice."

"And I've been doing some hiking."

"How athletic of you."

"Went on a winery tour the other weekend. That was okay."

"That sounds like a date," I said. "Who'd you go with?"

"Just a friend."

"And you're such a friendly guy."

He gripped the back of his neck. "I forgot how much you like to bust my ass."

"Oh now, don't feel special. I do it to everyone."

"I don't know. Seems like you were always pretty sweet to—"

"Do *not* say his name."

For a moment, he said nothing. "What about you? What have you been up to?"

"My aunt passed soon after the last time I saw you. That was hard."

"I'm sorry," he said in a low voice.

I nodded. There were a lot of things you could say about losing a loved one. But there wasn't a single word that would bring them back. "Work has been good. Busy. This place has taken up most of my time."

"Must be strange, dealing with all the debris from someone else's life."

"It is," I agreed. "There's a lot of history here. I'm the third generation of our family to live in this house. No one but me is really interested in any of it. Guess that makes it easier in some ways, deciding what to do with it all. What to keep and what to rehome. But it's sad too, you know?"

He just watched me.

"Are you close to your family?"

One side of his mouth turned upward. "Yeah. I'm the oldest of three. My sister's married with two kids down in San Diego. I share a condo with my brother."

"You live with your brother? I didn't know that. Are you enjoying it?"

"I am." He gazed around the little yard. "We have a couple of investment properties together. It's all part of a business plan we've been working on for a while. Eventually we'll get sick of living in each other's pockets. But for now everything's good."

"That's great. I'm glad."

"Me too." Something started buzzing and he pulled out his phone. The expression that crossed his face... I couldn't read it. "Excuse me."

"Sure."

Then he was up and out of his chair, walking away. "Hey, man. How's London? What time is it over there?"

I stared at him as he wandered around the side of the house out of listening range. Not that I wanted to hear a damn word. Shame on me for relaxing for a moment and forgetting. Lars and the Ex were tight and had been since he moved in next door at the age of eight. No way could I ever trust someone who had such appalling taste in besties. It was a fundamental flaw in his character. There was no getting past it. Therefore there was nil chance I would ever marry or divorce him. Guess Lars was right about getting the document examined, after all.

A total waste of time and money. End of story.

Three

I was sitting on the porch with a cup of coffee when two pickup trucks arrived the next day. The cat was crouched at the other end of the porch with the bowl of milk I'd left for her. It seemed rude not to offer her something to drink too. We discussed the weather for a while, but she didn't have much to say. She mostly flicked her tail, watched the occasional car go past, and kept an eye out for birds. Despite the early hour, I'd already styled my hair in loose waves, done my makeup, and dressed in black linen shorts and a black knit top with a square neckline and cap sleeves. Why else had God given me boobs if not to use them?

"Susie," said Lars. "You look nice."

"Thank you."

"Damn nice," enthused a young white man with spiky hair and dimples.

Lars turned a frown on him. "Way to be professional, Connor."

"What?"

"This is Mateo and Connor." Lars introduced the two new arrivals. "Like I told you, they'll be helping me out today."

"Hello," I said with a smile.

Mateo was a handsome man in his forties with dark hair and brown skin. He gave me a brief nod before beginning to unload the truck. This was it; I'd at long last be rid of the gruesome gold wallpaper and brown shag carpet. Hallelujah.

"I moved as much stuff as I could into the basement." I picked up the abandoned milk bowl. The cat bolted as soon as she heard new voices.

"Great," said Lars. "We'll deal with the rest. You heading out?"

"Got a meeting with a client then lunch with a friend." My smile was the perfect balance of friendly and boundaries. I knew this because I'd practiced it in the mirror the night before. "Thought it would be best if I got out of your way."

Connor strolled past me and headed into the house. That he managed to leer at my legs while balancing a variety of tools forever silenced the debate about men's ability to multitask. Bless the little creep.

"Keep your eyes to yourself," barked Lars.

Mateo shook his head and muttered something in Spanish.

"Sorry about Connor," said Lars. "He's the owner's kid."

I just nodded. "Better grab my bag and get going. I'll be back before you finish for the day. If you need me for anything, you've got my number."

Lars tipped his chin.

We hadn't talked much after he received the call from the Ex yesterday. Which was fine. I needed to remember to keep my distance. The Ex wasn't my first mistake. But I was determined that he'd be my last. And Lars was tainted by that association. It was best for everyone if we kept things on a professional level.

★ ★ ★

Aunt Susan's house was in the heart of Ballard, an up-and-coming Seattle neighborhood with plenty of bars, restaurants, and cool little shops. There was a nice park nearby and plenty of trees. I liked going for walks, and working in cafes was a fun change of scenery.

I met with my client then joined Cleo at a place near the water. She wore a white denim outfit that complemented her dark skin. If I attempted that color, I'd have spilled something on myself within the first five minutes. Guaranteed. But Cleo was far more graceful than me. We ate fried oysters with a pea vine salad and semolina cake for dessert. Good food and company went a long way toward making up for the fact that my uterus not only chose violence this morning, but committed wholeheartedly to the cause. A couple of Advil didn't hurt either. Once we established there'd been no update about the mystery divorce certificate, conversation moved on and I didn't think of Lars once. Twice, maybe. But definitely not once.

Confusion was my predominant emotion when it came to Lars. He annoyed me, but he also made me laugh. What perplexed me the most, however, was how someone who seemed like a semidecent human most of the time could be best friends with someone like the Ex. A male for whom the term *raging asshole* had been created. Which raised the question of why I even dated him?

Lars and the Ex both had a lot of forward momentum. Lars with his plans to start his own business, and the Ex busy climbing the corporate ladder. He was all about getting that fancy condo downtown. I just never thought he'd try to upgrade me too. Guess the girl who was fun could easily turn into a distraction. Especially when you had your eye on the prize.

When I arrived home, Lars was sitting on the front steps

waiting. A whole lot of tired, dusty, and sweaty, but he was smiling. Impossible not to smile back at him. "Hey."

"You're finished?" I asked, flustered. "You should have called me. I would have come home sooner."

"The other guys just left. You're fine." He rose to his feet. "Let me take those."

I handed over my grocery bags. "Thank you."

"I think you're going to like what we've done."

I followed his broad back into the house. Whoa. The white walls of the living room were a bit battered and marked, but no longer covered by ugly gold-flecked wallpaper. Honey-colored wooden boards covered the floor instead of that insult of a carpet.

"It feels totally different," I said, setting my purse down on the floor and turning in a slow circle. "Like there's room to breathe."

"We thought it was going to take a couple of days, but another job got postponed so we had extra help." He placed the grocery bags on the dining room table. "You're happy?"

"I'm happy."

Without all of the dark colors and unfortunate patterns, the place seemed more open. I hadn't kept much of the original furniture. Just the round mahogany midcentury dining table and chairs that had been a wedding gift to my grandparents. The old floral couch had been on the verge of collapse and the beds peaked sometime in the last century.

Cleo owned most of the furniture in the condo we shared in West Seattle. The only thing I had was a king-size bed. Because being able to sleep spread-eagle is important. Since moving here, I'd been sitting on the floor in the living room and storing my clothes in either a suitcase or the built-in closet, which was all hanging space. And with the last of Susan's boxes relocated to the basement, the house was next to empty. A jarring change from just a month ago.

"What's wrong?" he asked.

Sure enough, the smile had fallen off my face. I stuck my head into the front bedroom. Everything seemed bigger—the room, the windows. While this was what I wanted, it was a strange journey to undertake. "It doesn't look like Aunt Susan's house anymore."

"That's because it's not her house, it's yours," he said. "And that's not being disrespectful, it's just stating a fact."

"Yeah."

He crossed his arms and leaned against the wide curved entryway into the dining room. In silence, he watched me wander around like I was lost.

"I still have plenty of pictures and mementos."

He nodded.

"You know, even she hated that wallpaper and carpet," I said. "She just…didn't like change. It was like it was too big of an idea for her to grasp. There were too many things that could go wrong. So she kept adding stuff instead."

"The attic and basement are full of her things. The bathroom and kitchen are still pretty much original. You haven't changed everything."

Grief was a bitch. Just when you thought you had a handle on it, the sudden lack of that person in your life slapped you upside the head all over again. "I need a beer. Do you want one?"

"Please."

"What comes next?"

"Prep the walls so they're ready to paint, and refinish the floor."

Out of the grocery bags, I retrieved two cans of Dawn Patrol Pale Ale and passed him one. My inner peace returned with my second swallow. Everything was fine. There was no need for anyone to be freaking out. Change was both good and natural, etcetera. And I would keep telling myself that until I believed it.

Which was about when my phone rang. I rushed over to my purse, setting my beer on the floor.

"It's the forensic document examiner," I said, putting the call on speaker. "Hello?"

"This is Nisha Singh. About the certificate you sent me…"

"Yes?"

"I had a quick look when it arrived yesterday and it's…very unusual," she said. Which definitely won understatement of the year. "At first, I thought it was a joke."

Lars and I exchanged glances. "I know exactly what you mean."

"I have other jobs ahead of yours, but I couldn't resist taking a closer look," she continued. "Whoever created the document appeared to have done a good job of simulating the effects of age on paper. I was curious to know how they did it. So I put it under the microscope then tried looking at it with different light sources, and ran some other tests."

"It is fake, isn't it?"

The woman took a deep breath and let it out slowly. "After a thorough examination, I've decided I'm unable to write a report on the document. I won't be charging you for my time."

"Wait," I said. "Why?"

"While I cannot disprove the document's authenticity, I also cannot confirm it given the details it contains."

My mouth gaped. "You're saying it's real."

"I'm saying I cannot help you, Miss Reid," she said. "I've been in this business for almost thirty years and my reputation is important to me. Your property will be returned to you by messenger tomorrow morning. Goodbye."

And the call ended.

★ ★ ★

My ass met the floor with a thump. Which hurt. As for Lars, who'd heard the conversation, he just kept staring off at nothing. Half a can of beer later, I still didn't know what to say. This was beyond unexpected. While my imagination might have been somewhat charmed by the idea of receiving missives from the future, this was something else entirely.

"We'll find another expert," Lars finally said.

"O-okay."

"Because she's clearly on drugs or something."

"Really?" I asked. "She sounded pretty sober to me."

"Then she's lying."

"Why would she do that?"

"I don't know." His laughter held a definite edge. "All I know is that it cannot be real. That's impossible."

"'Sometimes I've believed as many as six impossible things before breakfast.'"

His forehead furrowed. "What?"

"It's a quote from *Alice in Wonderland*," I said, climbing to my feet. "Did you know Lewis Carroll wrote books on mathematical logic?"

Even more furrows appeared. He'd be running out of forehead space soon.

"Never mind. Beer isn't strong enough for this occasion."

Hot on my heels, the man ranted on, "Be realistic, there's no damn way it can be real. Otherwise, how the hell else would you explain it?"

"I can't."

A bottle of silver tequila, a bag of limes, some salt, and two shot glasses later, things felt much more under control. Or spiraling out of control. Sometimes it was hard to tell those two apart. I poured out the drinks and passed one to Lars.

"We're doing shots?" he asked, sounding less than impressed.

"Yes." I raised my glass. "To us."

"That's not funny."

Oh, yeah. The citrus, salty goodness, and hit of alcohol made everything better. I leaned against the kitchen cupboard with a sigh of relief. Then I remembered the groceries still sitting on the dining table. Ice cream and frozen dinners didn't do well in the heat.

"Fuck, fuck, fuck," I said, by way of making conversation.

Lars watched in silence as I started unpacking and putting things away. Then he poured out another two shots of tequila. "I'm still not used to hearing you swear."

"Your friend didn't like it. He'd get this little line between his brows every time. But I don't want to talk about him." I sighed. "We may never be able to explain this."

"And you're okay with that?"

I shrugged and set the loaf of bread on the counter.

He picked up the knife to slice more lime. What was it about his hands that fascinated me so? Those thick calloused fingers and the muscles shifting in his arm as he moved. "I don't accept that. There's got to be an explanation. Something that makes sense."

"Maybe we should talk to a psychic," I said.

"I ask you to make sense and that's your reply."

I laughed. It was mostly not hysterical. Go me.

"Shut up for a minute and drink the tequila," he said. "Please."

I did as told. More alcohol was definitely the answer to this conundrum.

The big brooding male carried his beer to the dining room table and took a seat. He slumped his whole heart out. "Your cat is back."

"Hmm?"

He nodded to the stray sitting in the open front doorway.

I grabbed a bowl and the milk. Then added some small pieces of leftover roast beef to another dish. A fine dinner. While she watched with intensity as I approached, she didn't run away. She meowed as I set down the dishes.

"You're welcome."

Lars brushed his thumb back and forth over the smooth wooden tabletop. "I like fixing things."

"That makes sense. It's your job."

"So I don't like that this situation is so..."

"Yeah," I agreed when he didn't continue. This was a whole world of unwieldy.

"I don't believe in aliens or ghosts or fairies or any of that shit."

"Fair enough. It's not like there's any conclusive evidence that they exist."

"Exactly," he said. "And I wouldn't betray a friend. That's how I know it's not real."

"What you're saying makes sense."

"If you believe all that, then why the hell did you suggest a psychic?" He waved a hand around in an aggrieved fashion. Men. Such delicate creatures. So emotional.

"We're back to that again?" I asked. "You know, I can support your beliefs without adhering to them. You have your way of thinking about things and I have mine. Guess I'm okay with not having all the answers. With seeking alternative points of view."

He shook his head.

"How do you do that, frown and smile at the same time?"

"Huh?"

"Your mouth is grumpy, but your eyes are amused."

He just snorted.

I finished unpacking the groceries. "Aunt Susan always said that life was an adventure."

Another grunt from him. He really was more animal than man sometimes.

"My point is, you're still in control of yourself, Lars. You can walk out right now and never see me again. Never talk to me. Have absolutely nothing to do with me for the rest of your life," I said. "And the universe or fate or whatever will not be able to stop you. That divorce certificate, fake or otherwise, doesn't get to decide your future. Only you can do that."

"I thought the whole point of fate was that it was predetermined."

"Eh. I don't believe that."

He raised a brow. "No?"

"There is no fate but what we make."

"Are you quoting *Terminator*?"

"I never claimed to be deep, just to have fantastic taste." I opened the fridge and stared with wonder at the unusually well-stocked shelves. It was the little things in life that made me happy. I put on some music and started swaying. "We need snacks."

Lars watched, amused. "Can I help?"

"Just sit there and look pretty. You've already worked your butt off today. Want another beer?"

"Thanks."

I passed him a can and thought more deep thoughts about food. As you do after a few drinks. Out of the fridge and pantry came prosciutto, cheese, crackers, those cute little tomatoes, green grapes, and hummus. All of it was then artfully arranged on a pretty old cut glass dish. An excellent charcuterie board. At least, that's what I told myself. And what better accompaniment than more tequila?

Once everything was on the table, I passed him his shot glass and lime. "We're making a party of it, huh?" he asked.

"It's not every day you find out you probably really are divorced."

"My folks would be so disappointed," he said, before downing the booze. "They've been happily married since the dawn of time."

"Wow. What's that like?"

He shrugged. "It's just home."

"Nice," I said. "I find it interesting that I was the petitioner. But it doesn't necessarily explain anything. Maybe I gave up. Maybe you were long gone. Who knows?"

He grunted.

"Thing is, we're opposites."

"Aren't those supposed to attract?"

I scrunched up my nose. "Not sure if I entirely believe that. I mean, for example, what did you want to be when you grew up?"

"Rich." And that was all he said.

"There you go."

"Why?" he asked. "What did you want to be?"

"A princess in a fairy tale with a happy ending. But like one with great style. No pastel dresses."

He just blinked.

"The way I figure it, you left me for another woman."

His brows drew together. "You calling me a cheater?"

"All right. Fine, not that. How about we were fundamentally incompatible?"

"In what way?"

"Didn't we just discuss this?" I asked.

"I'm still not convinced."

"Um. We fought about money."

"This is about me giving you shit the other day, isn't it?"

he asked. "About spending any money we found on fancy shoes. I already apologized for that. I learn from my mistakes. It won't happen again."

"What if in this hypothetical future we reached an agreement regarding what we each contribute to household expenses and what we do with the rest is our own business?"

"Sounds good," he said.

"Okay. How about...religious differences?"

"Mom used to drag me to Sunday school, but that was a long time ago."

I cut a piece of cheese and put it on a cracker. "I'm sort of an atheist. Probably. Haven't really made up my mind."

"So unless you suddenly decide to run off and join a cult, I'm not really seeing religious differences as being a big deal."

"No," I agreed. "What about children?"

"As in, do I want them?" He thought it over for a moment before nodding. "Yeah. You?"

"One or two would be okay."

He tapped out a beat against the tabletop with his fingers. "This one couple I know is always arguing about family. Where they're going to spend the holidays. Every year it's a big fucking drama. She doesn't get along with his mom and he doesn't like her dad and then there's the drunk uncle who got handsy at Thanksgiving."

"Ugh. That would be awful. But your folks sound nice. Let's go there."

He gave me an amused smile. There was even a tipsy twinkle in his eye. Lord knows, I had a buzz going on. But tequila had definitely loosened Lars's tongue.

"Mine suck," I said. "Just take my word for it."

"All right."

"What else could it be?"

He pointed a finger at me. The rude man. "When we go

out you're always flirting with the waiter or bartender. It's disrespectful and it drives me nuts."

"That's weirdly specific."

He let his head fall back so he could stare at the ceiling. "Jane used to do that."

"Really?"

"Yes," he grumbled. "It's why we broke up."

"That's sad. I'll be sure to observe the boundary between friendly and flirty, so you don't feel dismissed and or uncomfortable."

He downed some more beer. "Thanks."

Over on the doormat, the cat had finished her meal and was busy giving herself a bath.

"You spend too much time on your phone," he said.

"A large part of that is my job so I'm afraid you're going to have to suck it up. I will, however, do my best to minimize screen time whenever possible. Though I use it to read books too. You're really going to have to suck this one up."

"Fair enough." He gave me a brief smile.

"What else? Oh, I've got one." I dipped a little tomato in the hummus. "Household duties. You never do your share. You're always forgetting to take the garbage out."

"I'm on garbage duty? Okay. I'll set an alarm so I don't forget," he said. "What are you doing when I'm taking out the trash and whatnot?"

"Ah. Loading and unloading the dishwasher. I can't handle the chaotic style some people have, just shoving things in wherever. It's not okay. There's a system and it must be observed."

"Fair enough. I'll take the laundry. Then you won't have to go down into the spooky basement or murder room or whatever you called it."

"That's very considerate of you. But will you separate the colors?"

"If it's important to you then yes."

"And you'd want to live here."

He picked up a couple of grapes. "It's your house so that's up to you. What about cooking?"

"I like to cook."

"That's great because I like to eat. Why don't I do the grocery shopping and the yard and car maintenance?" he asked. "That way mechanics won't rip you off anymore."

"I like to shop, too."

"So we share the grocery shopping. Do it together or whatever."

"Okay. Well, this is surprising," I said, once I finished my mouthful. "I honestly thought it wouldn't be that hard to identify the source of our relationship going boom. But here we are, a functioning fictional couple."

"You finished that?" he asked, pointing at my can of beer. "You want another?"

"Thanks."

"Of course, you know it's still all bullshit."

"I know." I laughed. "But you have to admit our communication skills right now are stellar. Being pragmatic and problem solving everyday aspects of a relationship apparently works. Who could have guessed?"

"Easy when there's no sex or emotions."

"True." I accepted the can and took a sip. "Thank you. But I made a decision a long time ago that I was never getting married. And that's how I know on an intellectual level that the divorce certificate will never come to fruition. Though it continues to make for an intriguing mystery."

"You're *never* getting married?"

"That's right. I'm not against relationships, obviously. But taking vows is a big no for me."

"I always figured I'd be ready around forty, in five years' time," he said. "Give my brother and me a chance to establish the business."

"If you're with the right person then, of course."

"Of course."

"What if you meet someone sooner?"

"It's a matter of priorities."

"Ouch. I hope whoever you settle on to be your life partner is understanding." I wrinkled my nose. "I'm still sticking with never."

Lars said nothing, just scratched at the stubble on his jawline. He had rough edges. An air of unkempt. While the Ex was as dapper as could be. He wore his handsome face like a mask to hide his narcissistic insides. It took me so long to see. There's nothing quite like disappointing yourself. Of course, the Ex had never minded that I had no wish to be married. It suited him perfectly since he'd never been open to getting serious with me in the first place. Yet again, I'd been the girl they played with then put aside. Some men were the worst. And now I had this weird divorce certificate confirming I was right to distrust love and marriage all along. What a kicker.

"It had to be sex," said Lars, out of nowhere.

"Sex?" Something about that word coming out of his mouth stalled my brain. Probably just the alcohol. "Wait. What?"

"We broke up due to sex. It's the only thing left I can think of."

"Right," I drawled. It did make sense. "I mean, it was probably fine to start off with. It usually is in most relationships. It's fun and new and thrilling. But then over time..."

For a moment he gazed at me, then said, "Guess we'll never know."

Four

"This is where you found it?"

I nodded.

Miss Lillian took a deep breath and placed her palm flat against the drywall. Her extensive collection of silver bangles jingled with each movement.

"Hey. What's going on?" asked Lars, appearing in the second bedroom doorway. His gaze was a whole lot of wary.

Unlike me, he didn't require a tube of concealer to cover the dark circles beneath his eyes this morning. Though his eyes were tinged red. He had a car take him home sometime after our sixth or seventh shot of tequila. Our conversation had deteriorated into exchanging embarrassing anecdotes from our college days. That he omitted any mention of the Ex was appreciated.

Mateo arrived at the usual time, but Lars stopped at another job site first. Hence his late arrival.

"Miss Lillian, this is Lars," I said.

"He has a kind face." The older lady stared into his eyes. "Hello, Lars. It's nice to meet you."

"Ma'am."

"Miss Lillian was a friend of my aunt's," I explained. "When I told her about the situation she insisted on coming over right away. Wasn't that good of her?"

"Very."

"She's a psychic."

Lars's eyes widened ever so slightly.

"I prefer clairvoyant and intuitive counselor," said Miss Lillian.

I smiled. "Of course."

"It's great that you could stop by." He was so lying. And he wasn't even good at it.

"There's definitely a strong connection between you two. A lot of sexual energy." Miss Lillian's gaze narrowed as she examined the air around us. "It doesn't surprise me that there's a romantic entanglement in your future."

"We're not getting together," said Lars, voice adamant. "That's not going to happen."

"I second that," I confirmed.

Miss Lillian gave a knowing smile. "Whatever you say."

"I thought maybe Miss Lillian could tell us if there were any other walls we needed to look behind."

"You really think we're going to find something else?" asked Lars.

"Who knows?"

Head cocked, Miss Lillian moved closer to the big man. "You have a blocked heart chakra, dear. You might want to try working on that. It makes it difficult for you to recognize trustworthy people when they come into your life."

Lars blinked.

"Now then," she said, brushing her fingertips against the wall. Ever so slowly, she walked around the edge of the room. Then the bathroom, main bedroom, living room, dining room, and kitchen. At last, she stopped and nodded to herself. "There are no other messages here for you two."

"Are you saying there are things there, they're just not for us?" I asked, wildly curious.

"We're only custodians, dear. Spirits passing through. This house won't always belong to you," she said. "One day, you'll pass it on to your nearest and dearest. Just as Susan passed it onto you. By the way, I love what you've done with the floor."

"Oh, thank you. That's all Lars and his helpers."

"Speaking of which, be extra careful today. I have a feeling," she warned Lars.

"Right," said Lars, with a frown. Messages from the great beyond were really not his thing. "I better get to work."

Miss Lillian waved her fingers at him.

Once he was gone, I asked, "Is this house haunted?"

"Have you experienced anything that would make you think that?"

"No," I said.

She looked around the kitchen with interest. "Major changes like this can certainly stir things up. Restless spirits and echoes from the past. But I don't get the sense that anything here means you harm."

"That's not a no."

"It's not a yes either, dear."

"What do you suggest we do about the divorce certificate?" I asked. "Are we doomed if, on the off chance, we do get involved?"

Her smile was gentle. "The future is a fluid thing, Susie. Little is definite. We're born and therefore one day we'll die. That's unavoidable. As for everything in between..."

"But what about fate?"

"What about it?" She patted me on the hand. "Just do your best, dear. That's all any of us can do. But I will say, you're going to need a lot of patience."

Suddenly we heard Lars yelling out a curse in the living room.

"What?" I yelled back.

More swearing, followed by a begrudging "Hit my thumb with the hammer."

"Are you okay?"

"Yes," he grumbled.

Miss Lillian just shook her head.

It wasn't funny and I shouldn't have laughed.

"It's not like Miss Lillian didn't warn you."

Lars sat on the front steps with a bottle of water. "Have I ever happened to mention that you talk too much?"

"No. You did say I'm overly and somewhat unnecessarily honest."

"That's the polite way of saying you talk too much."

"Maybe you listen too little," I said. "Have you ever thought of that?"

Silence. Which meant I won.

Since the house stank of primer and plaster, it was more pleasant outside. I'd been sitting on one of the porch chairs and working on my laptop for hours. Mateo already left for the day. The cat wandered out from behind the lavender bush and peered up at Lars. Then she climbed up the steps to sniff at his boot. Happy with whatever scents she picked up, she commenced rubbing her face against his jeans-clad leg. What a hussy.

The divorce certificate had been returned and was in my pocket. For some reason I felt better having it with me. Like it had become a touchstone or something.

"Hello," he said.

I smiled. "She likes you."

"I'm a very likeable person."

"Sure," I agreed. "Among other things."

He snorted and reached down to scratch behind her ears.

"I'm having a few drinks with friends tomorrow for my birth-day. Nothing big. I was wondering if you'd like to come."

"Really?" I asked, surprised. "You want me there?"

"Yeah." He shrugged. "Why not?"

"I don't know. It wouldn't be weird?"

"No."

Not quite sure that I believed him, I um'ed and ah'ed for a minute. "Well, not that I want to willingly admit that I don't have Saturday-night plans, but I'd love to."

"Great."

"Are we becoming friends?" I asked, bemused.

"Weren't we already friends?"

I took a moment, choosing my words with care. "If we were friends, we'd have made some effort to keep in contact after I broke up with he-who-shall-not-be-named. But we didn't. We were more like acquaintances."

"Right."

"It's nice that we've started talking this week. That we're getting along independent of...all that."

"Yeah." He held up his thumb, inspecting the poor bruised thing. "She had a *feeling*."

"And she was right."

He gave me an indulgent smile. "She saw that I was hung-over and distracted. That's what people like that do, they read body language."

"Are you saying she was correct when she said we're horny for each other?"

"There's no way in hell I'm answering that."

"You're smarter than you look."

"Thanks." He laughed. "Why are you always picking on me?"

"Why are you always picking on me?" I asked. "It's like that old nonsense about how the kid in third grade who pushes you over is secretly crushing on you. They're not. They're just an asshole. And yet, we cannot seem to stop poking at each other."

He grinned. "Maybe we're both assholes."

"Maybe," I said. "Isn't it nice that we have things in common?"

The birthday drinks were held at a whiskey-and-meat joint near the water downtown. I wore a black silk tank, blue jeans, and black leather slide sandals with a high heel. My hair was in a messy bun, my lips were shiny, and I felt good about myself. It was great to be out and about. The last six months mostly involved hunkering down and hiding.

At first, I was dealing with the emotional and mental fallout from the breakup, then with Aunt Susan's sudden passing, and then with the house and the overwhelming amount of work it required. It would be interesting to see what the rest of this year held for me. Happier times would be great. Though love wasn't necessary. Single was good. I liked it for me.

I once read that you get a month of grief for each year you've been in the relationship after it falls apart. So in theory one month should have been enough for me to move on. And I was, in a way. But to risk being with another person is a big ask. That sort of thing took more time. Especially when I'd chosen so disastrously with the Ex. Nothing shakes your confidence like getting your heart publicly stomped by a paramour.

The party wasn't an intimidatingly large group. Lars invited a couple of work friends including Mateo and his partner James, who had a bandaged wrist, Lars's current lady friend Amie, a beautiful brunette wearing a Givenchy sheath dress I'd have killed to own, (though they didn't make it in my size), and hiking buddies by the name of Brandon and River. And of course, Lars's brother, Tore, who made a point of sitting next to me. Tore was every bit as big as Lars, but with dark hair. He watched me with a vaguely suspicious smile, which wasn't strange or off-putting at all.

When everyone was busy listening to James tell the tale of

his bike accident, Tore leaned in and said, "Never had a sister-in-law before."

"Oh good, you've heard about that."

"Very strange."

"Very."

"How do you think it got there?" he asked.

"I can't explain it," I said. "I've given up even trying. It was hurting my head."

He looked at me expectantly and nodded.

"Let's just get it all out into the open," I said. "I don't want anything from your brother and I'm not interested in any drama. Nor do I have plans to get married or divorced in this lifetime to Lars, or anyone else. Does that answer any questions you might have?"

He smiled though his gaze was wary. "Lars said you were a straight shooter."

"I find it saves time. So continuing on in that theme, it strikes me that if I were a protective younger brother, I'd be very suspicious of strange documents lurking in walls with my sibling's name on them."

"And what might you say to allay those suspicions?"

"Honestly, I've got nothing. Lars and I have been over it a hundred times. There's no plausible way either he or I could have faked it. And there's no third party we can think of who could have done it or who would benefit from it. It just *is*. That's all I've got."

"Fair enough." He raised his glass of bourbon. "To family."

I snorted and tapped my vodka mule against his drink. "Sure. Why not?"

Later that night, Tore and I were midway through a debate on the usefulness of psychics, what even was fate, and did ghosts really exist—when Lars called out from the other end of the table, "Susie, you ready to swap?"

"Hmm? Oh. Yes."

He rose from his seat and wandered down our way with his plate of pork shank in hand.

I handed over my roasted chicken. "You got black-eyed peas as your side. Yummy."

Amie was only eating a salad. Guess that's how she managed to fit into that dress. I dreamed of having that sort of discipline. But they had pecan pie on the menu.

"You two aren't afraid of sharing germs," said Tore.

I loaded up my fork. "Nope."

And Lars was hovering for some reason. "You guys are getting along well."

"Yes, we are," confirmed Tore.

"What?" I asked. "Are we not supposed to?"

"See," said Lars, "she takes everything I say the wrong way. Disagrees with me constantly."

"I do not."

Tore winced. "You kind of just proved his point."

"You're both imagining things."

"What are you two talking about, anyway?" asked Lars.

I cocked my head. "Are you aware you asked that in a somewhat cranky tone of voice?"

"It's his birthday," said Tore. "He can grump if he wants to."

I giggled my ass off. So I may have been on my third cocktail. I was having fun.

"It was just a question." Lars fake frowned. "You two need to be separated."

"Boo," I said.

Tore just smiled. "And the marriage didn't work, you say? I'm shocked and stunned. You get along so well."

"Shit." Lars's gaze jumped to Amie. "Don't talk about that here."

"I like your brother," I said. "He's sarcastic. It amuses me."

"Great. Be good." Lars ambled back to his end of the table.

After dinner, we moved to a rooftop bar a couple of blocks away. It was a perfect night, with a cool breeze coming in off the ocean and the stars burning bright above us. I took a shot of the view for social media. And all the while, Tore stuck to my side. But it didn't feel like a sexual-attraction thing. Just more of that initial curiosity.

"I don't understand how you fit into my brother's life," said Tore, out of nowhere.

"Well… I'm his friend, I guess."

"That's the thing I don't understand. Lars has had plenty of girlfriends. But not girls who are friends."

"They all dude bros, huh?"

"Yeah."

"Then this is a growth thing for him."

"I'm not sure my brother believes in growth. Pretty sure he emerged from our mother's womb fully formed and ready to work hard and succeed," said Tore. "He tends to be set in his ways and ideas. How everyone fits into his life."

"And I don't fit into his life?"

Tore just shrugged.

"I don't know what to say to that. What does he want for his birthday?" I asked, watching Lars talk to Amie.

They looked good together. Though Lars had a more laid-back style in his black jeans and pale blue polo. Both of them were attractive. I had to work at being alluring, but Lars just breathed and it happened. So annoying. Same went for how he seemed to live rent free in my brain these days.

He caught my gaze for a moment. Such an odd expression on his face. I couldn't read the man for love or money. Then he turned back to his date. Even at his ease among friends he didn't seem to smile much. Whoever did wind up marrying him would have a job on their hands. The man was so serious. Which was just another sign that the divorce certificate was a fake somehow. I wanted someone with a sense of humor. Lars and I together would be a disaster. Though he had laughed with me the other day on the step...

Tore shrugged. "Just buy him a drink."

"Will do."

His phone chimed and he pulled it out of his pocket and scowled at the screen. Then he sent off a quick text.

"Everything okay?"

"Yep," he said, studying the tiled floor for a moment. "So Lars was telling me about the place you inherited. Said you might be thinking of selling."

"I haven't decided," I said. Though the thought of letting the house go soured my stomach.

"Let me know if you decide to head in that direction. Lars and I are looking at buying another investment property."

"Sure. Be back in a minute," I said before heading for the restroom.

Music pumped out of the speakers as I checked my phone and answered a text from Cleo about how the night was going, and saw to business. When I came out to wash my hands, Amie was at the mirror reapplying her lipstick.

"Hey," I said.

She smiled. "We haven't really gotten a chance to talk. Lars mentioned he'd been working on your house."

"Yes, he has been. He's doing great work."

"But you used to date his friend?"

"That's right. I like to think of it as ancient history, but it actually only ended about six months back."

"Well, it's great you could come tonight. Lars is kind of a closed book so meeting his friends is a nice way to learn more about him."

"I can see that," I agreed.

She smiled again and retrieved mascara from her purse, moving on to the next stage of her touch-up.

"Later," I said, heading for the door.

After taking approximately eight steps outside, Lars grabbed my elbow and tugged me behind a potted palm. Which was weird.

"Did you see Amie in there?" he asked. "You didn't tell her anything about the divorce certificate, did you?"

"No."

"Are you sure?"

"Yes, I'm sure," I said. "It's not really something I want to explain to people. Which I've already had to do once tonight with your brother, by the way. The fewer people who know the better."

"Exactly," he said, then narrowed his gaze on me.

"What?"

"Nothing."

"Whatever," I said. "I'm getting a drink, do you want one?"

"I'm good for now." He smiled. "Thanks."

When I returned from the bar, Tore once again had his cell in hand and was scowling at it. I didn't bother asking why. Tonight seemed to have taken a turn. People were acting strange. Maybe it was the full moon or something.

One thing tonight had taught me, was that I definitely did not miss dating. I was happy on my own. I could do what I wanted and talk to whoever I wanted without worrying about anyone else. Free and easy was the way.

"Holy shit," Lars said suddenly, all excited. "What are you doing here?"

"I couldn't miss your birthday," answered a smooth male voice.

Oh no. I knew that voice. I hated that voice.

And sure enough, there he stood...the Ex. His dark hair was slicked back just so, his white shirt and black slacks were pressed to perfection, and his loafers shone. Such handsome packaging. It was a shame about the contents. At his side was a redhead who surely just stepped off the runway. Even Amie, in her awesome designer wear, couldn't compare.

This sucked. However, it was also sort of useful. I now knew without a doubt that I didn't miss him, didn't want him, and my heart no longer hurt because of him. I'd wasted a year of my life trying to please him. Being a lesser version of myself on the off chance it might make him happy. But now I was free. The spell had been broken. And I'd sure as hell learned my lesson.

"Susie," said Tore. "Why don't we go get another drink?"

My shoulders were high enough to touch my ears. Like I was in hiding. "I just got one."

"This is a hell of a surprise," said Lars. "It's good to see you, man. I thought you were in London."

"It didn't quite work out. I'm back home for now. Let's talk about it later." The Ex stuck out his hand. "You must be Amie. Lars told me all about you. Pleasure to meet you."

Amie gave him a pretty smile.

The Ex's beady little eyes took in the group. It was like the world slowed down as the inevitable happened. His head turned and, at long last, he saw me. The way he scrunched up his nose as if he'd stepped in dog shit was a singular delight. But it was there and gone in an instant, his good-guy persona back in place. "Susie? What are you doing here?"

I forced my shoulders back down where they belonged. Because fuck him anyway. There was a lot to the old saying that you get what you settle for. And I was done settling for anything less than I deserved. "Hello, Aaron."

"She's here because I invited her," said Lars.

"We were just going to get a drink." Tore placed a light hand at the small of my back.

"Hang on," Aaron said with a fake ass smile. "Are you two together?"

Before Tore could answer, I said, "You haven't introduced

your date. You know, the woman standing next to you. That's sort of rude."

A muscle popped in his perfect jawline. "This is Hannah. My fiancée."

"Fiancée. Wow."

"There's no need to make another scene," muttered Aaron.

Tore opened his mouth to say something, but I got there first. "Oh, I'm not."

"You are. You can't help it. It's always got to be about you."

I shook my head. "The lack of self-awareness in that statement."

"Hey," said Lars, being all conciliatory. "Let's just—"

"What are you even doing here?" asked Aaron. "Really? Is this some twisted sort of revenge or what? God knows I wouldn't put it past you."

"Go fuck yourself," I said with a smile.

And the way he flinched. "Real nice language, Susie."

I turned to the birthday boy. "Thank you for inviting me, Lars, but I'm going to go now."

He just nodded.

There's a special kind of person who treats the people they've slept with like trash. As if having been intimate and vulnerable with them is demeaning. They're the sort who sees a female's righteous anger and labels her the mad woman. Though Aaron was a jerk throughout our relationship too. He was just more subtle about it. Making the kind of comments that seem helpful on the surface, but are really pure fuckery.

I quickly got my ass out of there. Because life is too short for that sort of thing, and playing the woman scorned didn't suit me. I had better things to do with my time. I blinked a couple of times to get rid of any unfortunate moisture. Most likely caused by hormones or something. Smoke in the air. I don't know. Should have just stayed home. This whole need for human connection was such a bummer. Given half a chance, I really think I would have made an awesome hermit.

I'd just stepped into the elevator when Tore joined me.

"You heading home?" he asked. "I'll wait for your car with you."

"That's not necessary."

"Yeah, it is." He said nothing for a minute. "I'm sorry."

"You didn't do anything."

"I knew he was coming and I didn't warn you," he explained. "It was supposed to be a surprise for Lars. That's why I didn't say anything. I knew you two had broken up, but I had no idea—"

"How messy it was?" I sighed. "I probably should have just left when I saw him."

"He's always been an entitled prick."

"Wait. You don't like him?" I asked, delighted.

"Not even a little."

I grinned. "That makes me feel so much better."

Tore laughed. Then he sighed. "All we can hope is that Lars wakes up one day and sees the asshole for what he is. But the denial is strong."

"They've been friends a long time."

"Yeah."

I smiled up at him. "Thanks for checking on me, Tore. You're just like Prince Charming, but taller."

"Thanks," he said drily. "Of course, it should have been my brother."

"It's his party and he has a date to look after, and a bestie to catch up with. I'm fine." And it was the truth, I was fine. The reasons for Lars not running after me were likewise valid. At least, the rational part of my brain thought so. Feelings, on the other hand. Ugh.

Five

On Monday, I greeted Lars with a smile. "Morning."

"Hey. Listen, about Saturday—"

"I think it would be best if we don't talk about that."

He paused and frowned. "You're mad at me."

While I hadn't dressed for war, I had dressed for work. Slim black cotton pants and a matching sleeveless top. I wore a lot of black. It not only made my curves look great, but it was my happy color. My father firmly believed that females were pretty ornaments. Dressing like I was constantly on my way to a funeral had been my way of pushing back as a teenager. Then it had become my normal. Today my hair was up in a ponytail and my lips were matte red. I wore flat leather slides. Though heels might have been better. But no matter how Lars loomed over me, I would not back down. I'd given the situation a lot of thought and decided a professional approach between us was best. His taste in friends made anything else impossible. This had now been proven beyond a doubt.

"I'm not mad at you, Lars," I said. "He's your best friend. I get it. But for me, he's a horrible mistake that I want to never be reminded of ever again. On the bright side, I think it's now obvious what caused the divorce. Don't you? Having your loyalties divided between the two of us would be impossible."

Nothing from him.

"At any rate, I think it's best if we just keep things on a professional level."

His frown deepened.

"I'll be out today. Is it okay if I leave you with a spare set of keys in case I'm not back by the time you're finished?"

"Sure." And he said no more.

The day was spent at the offices of my client who produced clothing from organic and recycled materials. Cleo was shooting their winter collection while I handled the behind-the-scenes shots and discussed some online marketing ideas with their owner and manager. A long day, but a productive one. And leaving with a selection of samples made for an awesome perk. My job required a solid social media presence and having new things to post about was great.

Cleo and I wound up going out for dinner afterward and I didn't get home until dark. Finding the house still open and a couple of lights on was strange. Guess Lars decided to work late. I wandered through, dumping my purse (with the certificate safely inside) and other things on the dining room table. The plaster work on the walls had been completed. It might not look like Aunt Susan's house anymore, but it was starting to look like my home. Though a couch would be nice. Something comfy to lounge on at the end of the day.

Lars wasn't inside, but I could hear the soft sound of his voice coming from out back.

A fire burned in a big black metal bowl and old-style party lights were strung up between the maple and the house. Pale blue cushions now sat on the Adirondack chairs gathered around the fire pit. A collection of stone pavers had been laid beneath the bowl to protect the ground. He must have had help from his crew. Because the small backyard had been elevated into a magical space. Just like I'd imagined it could be.

And there stood Lars with the cat winding around his ankles. Guess that was who he'd been talking to. Shadows danced along the hard lines of his face and it was so wildly unfair how attractive this man was. Life would be so much simpler if he were easy to ignore.

"I didn't know what you had in mind exactly," he said when he saw me, tone almost hesitant. "But I thought this would get you started."

"It's beautiful."

He gave me a brief smile. Very brief. "I don't like it when you're mad at me."

"I wasn't mad."

"You kind of were," he said. "Anyway. How he talked to you...it wasn't right. You were my guest and..."

"Yeah," I said. "Though I guess I did sort of start it. Sort of."

"Tore really gave it to me yesterday."

My brows rose. "Oh."

"He was right. I wasn't a good friend to you. I let you walk away alone, and upset. I'd like the chance to try again."

"Wouldn't it just be easier not to?" I asked.

"It might be easier, but I don't think it would be better."

I didn't know what to say. Nor did I need all of these emotions. Seriously.

Then he scratched at his beard and said, "My brother and you... Is there something there?"

"No."

He nodded.

"Your girlfriend seemed nice," I said, for reasons.

He turned his face away. "Yeah."

"What you've done out here is amazing."

"It's not a big deal," he said. "They were getting rid of the fire bowl at another job and the pebbles were left over from something else. Mateo helped."

"You decorated, Lars. You bought soft furnishings."

He shrugged, all embarrassed like. "I better get going."

"You *really* want to be friends?"

"Well...yeah."

"Okay," I said. "Thank you, Lars. It really is beautiful."

If he were someone else, I might have hugged him in thanks. But we kept a careful distance between us. Without another word, he gave me a nod and left. And that was that.

I sat in one of the chairs, the cat settled in the other, and we both watched the flames. So soothing. Pity about the mess in my head regarding a certain handyman. Otherwise now known as my friend, apparently. I'd had male friends before, but for some reason this felt different. In the year I'd been with Aaron, I'd received a wilted bunch of flowers. Talk about ignoring the signs. Not that I couldn't buy things for myself. But showing some appreciation now and then was a good thing.

Finding the divorce certificate raised about a billion questions. But it also made Lars and me look at each other in a new, different, and unwelcome way. It brought hearts, flowers, and sexy times to mind, rather than a *you're an okay human being whom I don't object to spending time with* mind-set. The idea that someone might be your everything was a lot. Same went for finding out in advance that a relationship would fail. Messages from the future weren't as helpful as you'd think.

As for actually being friends with Lars, I had no damn idea whether that was possible. Time would tell. Meanwhile, the firelight flickered and the chair was comfy and my backyard rocked.

★ ★ ★

I leaned around the side of the house and called out, "Lunch is ready."

After decorating my backyard yesterday, Lars was now busy pulling off the house's old siding. And the way the muscles in his arms were bunching and working while the sun graced his sweat-dampened skin, it was as if he were a summertime god. All virile and large and shiny. Wait a minute. That was not me getting poetic about a male. Heck no. Wash my mind out with soap.

"We're eating inside," I said, averting my eyes.

"You don't have to keep making me lunch."

"It's nothing."

Things had been off since his arrival this morning. We were now uneasy around one another. I blamed it on the makeover out back. Lines had been crossed. Not that there'd been any clear delineation previously. But in my experience, a dude didn't buy cushions and party lights for just anyone. His apparent determination for us to be friends was...surprising. Though now that I thought about it, maybe he just felt bad about how his birthday night ended and wanted to make it up to me. In which case, I was definitely making more out of this than I should be. Overthinking things was such a joy.

Once he'd washed up, he sat opposite me at the round mahogany dining table. Then, without preamble, he picked up his fork and dug into his bowl of cauliflower gnocchi with semi-dried tomatoes, chicken, basil, and a creamy parmesan garlic sauce. A simple enough dish. Not a big deal at all.

"This is nice," he said between bites.

My smile was more of a wince.

The other half of the table was taken up with my laptop and assorted paperwork. One of the issues with having a floating office was the tendency for things to become strewed about. And that was good. It meant I hadn't completely lost my fucking mind and gone overboard trying to impress Lars with my domestic skills or anything.

"Do you think we'd be sitting here together now if not for the divorce certificate?" I asked.

He stopped and pondered the thought. "I don't know. I really thought someone would have come forward by now. Said that they forged the certificate and placed it in the wall somehow."

"Yeah."

"I mean, it's fake. We both know that. It has to be. It would just be nice to know how they got it in there. 'Cause I still don't have a clue." He stared off at nothing for a moment. "You're probably right, though. Without it, we wouldn't have made this weird connection or whatever it is."

"I think if the certificate hadn't appeared we wouldn't have had any of these conversations," I said. "You'd have done the work on the house. It would have been awkward having you here. And then you would have finished the job and gone on your merry way. The end."

"Mmm."

"We wouldn't have gotten to know each other on a different level separate from days of yore and therefore we wouldn't have become friends. That's my theory, anyway."

He nodded.

"Did you know that there are three types of friends according to Aristotle?" I asked. Just making conversation. "Friendships of utility, friendships of pleasure, and friendships of the good."

Lars blinked.

"Utility is when you're useful to each other. Say, a neighbor or a coworker or a client. While friendships of pleasure are when you enjoy each other's company. Like you and your hiking buddies, for example. You enjoy doing certain activities together," I explained. "Whereas friendships of good are based on mutual respect and admiration. Shared virtues and goals. You may not have many actual interests in common, but these people are your closest friends just the same. Isn't that interesting?"

"Sure."

"Just thought I'd share that."

He cocked his head. "Nothing in particular made you mention that today?"

"Well, it's just that you could say we're friends of utility because of our current professional relationship. What with you working on my house."

At this point, he set his fork down, giving me his full attention.

"Or a case could be made that we're perhaps more friends of pleasure. Because we enjoy dining and sometimes drinking together."

"Okay."

"But friends of good is the ultimate goal, right?" I asked. "Building long-term relationships with people you can trust. You might not necessarily feel like you have room or a need for someone like that in your life, however."

"Are you asking what kind of friends we are?"

I shrugged. "There's every possibility I'm overthinking things. But I like to know where I stand with people. And this situation between us can be confusing."

"Because of the divorce?"

"Because of everything."

"Is that what you need?" he asked with a frown. "Labels?"

"I guess it is. As cute as confused looks on me, I can't say I enjoy it."

"Okay." He took a sip of water and stared off out the window for a moment. "Give me a minute."

I sat quietly and waited for him to speak.

"In all honesty, I didn't miss you when you two broke up. You crossed my mind now and then, but it didn't really bother me that you weren't around. It would bother me now, though. We've been getting to know each other separate from that situation and it's different." He turned back to me. "Does that answer your question, Susie?"

"It does. Maybe Aristotle just needed another category or something. Thank you."

He held out his drink. "Friends?"

I tapped my glass against his with a smile. "Friends."

The best way to get over awkward feelings for a friend is to hit the town. Everyone knows that. Which was how I came to be sitting opposite Cleo on a Thursday night in a tiki garden bar near the water listening to a woman sing and play acoustic guitar. And she was damn good. Another reason to love Seattle. The music scene in this town was mighty.

"I'm thinking about upgrading to the new Canon EOS. Also, Josh wants me to meet his parents," she said, taking a sip of her frozen alcoholic slushy. "Sunday dinner with the family."

I finished eating my dumpling before answering. "You work damn hard and deserve a shiny new camera. And by the tone of your voice I'm guessing this invitation does not make you happy."

"You guessed right." Cleo frowned. "It's too soon."

I opened my mouth and then shut it. Because I'm smart like that.

"I know I've been seeing him for almost a year, but..."

I nodded. "Do you think this is about him or your past bad experiences or both?"

"I don't know." She wrapped a braid around her finger and tugged on it. "He's a great guy, but…"

"But…"

"Insert segue here. Someone's watching you from over by the bar," she reported, perking up. "Casual business attire with a beard. Designer watch and nice shoes. I would rate him as being not only attractive but showing visible means of being able to financially support himself."

"Is he groomed or hirsute?"

"The facial hair is under control."

"Probably has mommy issues."

"Don't they all?" she asked drily.

I took a peek over my shoulder. "Eh. Not feeling it."

"Neither of us want what we can have." Cleo popped a roasted corn nut into her mouth. "Why is that?"

"Either we have exacting standards or we're difficult bitches. I can never quite decide."

"In all honesty, they both sound about right." She smiled. "The weather's not looking good for the Friday shoot. Postpone or move?"

"Postpone," I said. "We can't shoot the coffee vans inside. The message is all about great caffeine and personalized service while you're out enjoying the big wide world."

"I'll see what my calendar's like for the next few weeks and get back to you," said Cleo. "Did you get a sample box of eco-friendly sex toys?"

"No."

"It'll be on its way. I name dropped you to a new client."

"Thank you. That sounds fun." I smiled. "Speaking of which, I need you to read this monster porn Romance novel so I can discuss it with you. It's very important."

Her brows rose.

"Trust me. You want to read it."

"Okay."

I grinned.

Which was when it happened. Amie walked into the bar with another man. And his arm was wrapped so tightly around her, it was like they were trying to meld.

"Holy shit," I mumbled.

"What?"

Amie's gaze met mine, paused for a moment, then she quickly looked away. She was going to pretend she hadn't seen me. Might be for the best. Less awkward than exchanging greetings. Then she sneaked another look at me over her shoulder and was most definitely not wearing her happy face. Awesome.

I nodded oh so discreetly toward the couple now standing at the bar. "She was with Lars at his birthday last weekend. Introduced herself to me as his girlfriend."

"She's wearing the wide-leg one-shoulder jumpsuit I wanted," said Cleo, turning to look. "But they'd sold out of my size."

"It would look better on you. Beige people shouldn't wear beige. It's about the only useful thing my mother taught me. That and to always carry breath mints." I took a long sip of slushy. "Do I tell Lars about this?"

"Yes."

"Really? Ugh. What do I tell him?"

"The truth."

I frowned. "Maybe they're not exclusive."

"Maybe. Or maybe not. Either way, as his friend you have to tell him."

So my nod was a little hesitant.

"What would Aunt Susan tell you to do?"

I stirred the straw around in my drink. "She'd ask me if Oprah would be proud of the choices I'm making. Which would then be followed up with, what would Dolly Parton do?"

"I always did like your aunt."

"I would still really rather not be in this situation. If Amie could just not cheat in my neighborhood that would be great." I sighed. "Wonder why she felt the need to go a-wandering?"

"Self-esteem, low commitment, emotional needs not being met…could be lots of things. You know, this might be what leads to your inevitable divorce," suggested Cleo. "You console the poor brokenhearted man so good he has to put a ring on you."

"I don't want to get married. I don't even really want to be in a relationship. Things are fine as they are."

"But you do want to console him."

"If by *console* you mean sex then the answer is no."

"Oh, girl." She laughed. "You are such a liar."

I did not blush. It was just the lighting. "It's complicated."

"Isn't it always?"

"Wow," said Lars as he walked into the living room.

"Yeah," I agreed glumly.

Outside, the morning sunshine shone bright, the birds were singing, and the bees were buzzing. The whole world seemed in a good mood. And why wouldn't it be? Friday was an excellent day of the week. Hooray for the oncoming weekend. The vibe in Aunt Susan's house, however, was less than cheerful.

Lars set down his toolbox. "Did you intend for it to be that color?"

I nodded from my position sitting cross-legged on the drop cloth covering the floor.

"And, ah, how do you feel about it now?"

I stared at the wall behind the fireplace mantel. It was probably the most offensive thing in the room. The original fireplace was pretty, surrounded with gray tiles. Then there were the big polished built-in bookcases on either side. And above those sat the ugliness. A blight upon such a charming scene.

"It was supposed to be this cool chartreuse that would look great with a navy blue sofa and chairs," I said in a despondent tone. "I knew it wasn't quite right. But I thought, just keep going. It'll all come together and make perfect sense once the whole room is painted. But, Lars, it doesn't. It just doesn't."

"Right." He crossed his arms. "You're looking a little wired. How long have you been awake?"

"All night. I couldn't sleep. Thought I might as well get a start on painting."

With a sigh, he knelt in front of me. "It's not that bad."

"It looks like Kermit the Frog exploded all over my walls."

Lars pressed his lips together tightly. "That's a surprisingly apt description."

"It's okay, you can laugh. I would laugh, if I wasn't about to cry from sheer exhaustion and the pain of having my eyeballs assaulted by the heinous color."

His big ass hand encompassed my shoulder and delivered a comforting rub. "It's okay, Susie. We can fix it."

"Another shitty choice to round out my year of brilliance."

"Hey," he said, voice stern. "Do not put yourself down."

"But the money I wasted."

"No renovation goes a hundred percent smoothly. There's always some bumps along the way. I can get you a deal on new paint."

"Thank you." I took a deep breath and let it out slow. "There's something I need to tell you."

"Okay."

"This would be better if, um… Can you sit?"

"Sure." He mimicked my pose opposite me. "What's up?"

"The thing is, I don't want you to think that you're not a great person, Lars, because you are. But sometimes people disappoint us and do the wrong thing. And it's no reflection on us, it's just them being a fundamentally flawed human being. You know what I mean?"

"What are we talking about?"

"Life, really." I blew out an exaggerated breath. "Can I hold your hand?"

"You want to hold hands?"

"Yes, please. This isn't romantic hand-holding, just to be clear. It's the other reason people hold hands with someone."

He frowned, though he seemed more confused than worried. And he reached his hand forward. His palm was warm and his fingers calloused. I wrapped up his hand in both of mine and mentally and emotionally shored myself to continue. "The thing with men like you is, you're so great at hiding your emotions. I honestly have no idea how you feel about most things. So I'm just not sure how you're going to take what I have to tell you. But I suspect there's a warm and sensitive heart beating beneath that big chest of yours. Just because you act all tough and you're built all brawny doesn't mean that you don't feel things. And I want you to know that I care about you and I'm here for you. You matter to me."

"Thanks," he said, tone bewildered.

"You're welcome."

"Is this about us being friends?"

"No."

His thick brows rose. "Okay. Continue."

"The thing is, last night when I was out at a bar with Cleo, Amie walked in with another man. And, Lars...they were all smooshed together. There was no doubting that something was going on."

"Oh," he said, eyes wide with sudden understanding.

"Please understand that I take no enjoyment from this. I'm deeply sorry to have to be the one to tell you." I gave his hand a comforting squeeze. "You deserve better, Lars. I'm not calling her a ho, but...actually yeah, I'm calling her a ho. Because cheating is not okay. If she wanted to see other people then she should have sat down with you and had an adult conversation about both of your expectations and what it is you're after in a relationship. And if ending it was the right choice, then—"

"We did," interrupted Lars. "Monday night."

"Y-you did?"

"Yes."

"Huh."

His gaze softened, but his smile was pure amusement. "We're no longer seeing each other. Amie's free to date who she likes."

"Right." I swallowed hard. "In that case, first up, I would like to apologize for calling her a ho. That was out of line."

He gazed down at the firm grip I had on his hand. Which I immediately gave up. "Is this what kept you up all night?" he asked. "Worrying about telling me this?"

"You could say that."

"Sounds like you practiced that speech for a while."

"Mmm." I stared at the Kermit-splattered wall. "I've had male friends before, but not close ones. Not ones that might be my husband in a parallel universe. You know?"

"I know."

"And I wasn't sure how hard you'd take the news. I mean, I've seen female friends through breakups, but...anyway."

"You think maybe paint fumes and lack of sleep has gotten to you?"

"That's a distinct possibility."

"C'mon," he said, rising to his feet. "Let's get you cleaned up and into bed. Mateo and I can get a fresh undercoat on this and have it ready for you to pick out a new color when you wake up this afternoon. Sound good?"

"Yes." I took the hand he held out to me and let him pull me up. "Thank you."

"No problem. You have some Kermit on your cheek. And on the side of your nose." He grinned down at me. "Thank you for holding my man feelings in such high regard, Susie."

"You're welcome, Lars."

Six

Our second attempt at socializing came that weekend. And given Aaron was busy, I was free to attend. The condo where Lars and Tore lived was an older four-story building close to Fremont at the top of Queen Anne. It had a heated outdoor pool available from May to September. What better way to celebrate summer?

Mateo and his partner, James, were there, along with Austin, a musician (very cool tattoos), who had gone to school with Tore. And their neighbors, Shu, an interior decorator who lived on the first floor, and Isaac, a nurse from the second floor.

"That's the thing with bold colors like chartreuse," said Shu, "a little can go a long way."

I added my Caprese salad to the offerings already set out on the table. I decided this would be my contribution because the tomatoes and basil looked awesome and cheese was life. "I see the error of my ways now. The walls are going to be navy blue with a chartreuse sofa to add a pop of color."

Isaac smiled. "I'm sure that'll look great."

Of course Lars had told everyone about the exploding-Kermit incident. At least he seemed to have kept his big mouth shut about my dramatic cheating speech. He gave me a wink and passed me a beer.

"Thank you."

"You're welcome," he said before inspecting my face with much care.

"Fear not. I got the last of the green off during a deep cleanse last night."

With a grin, he took a seat at the long wooden outdoor table. "Just checking."

Mateo and James threw a ball around in the pool while Shu, Isaac, Lars, and I sat at the table and Austin hung out over by the BBQ with Tore. It was a perfect day and a pretty place. Asters, ferns, and ocean spray grew in the garden. A large umbrella shaded the table, but what the heck. You couldn't go to a pool party and not get out in the sun and get wet. And why else would Baby Jesus have invented waterproof mascara if he hadn't intended for us to get in the damn pool and enjoy ourselves?

Pool parties were fun for voyeurs young and old, but especially me. Because Lars's chest was spectacular. Miles of muscles and golden tanned skin. Not that I dribbled or stared. But I did appreciate how his cargo shorts rode low on his hips when he'd stood up to offer me the beer. How evolved of me that I could ignore all of these lustful thoughts and just be friends with the man.

I leaned his way and lowered my voice. "Your bestie is definitely not coming?"

"Definitely not," said Lars.

"Phew." My whole body relaxed. "Does he even know I'm here?"

"Does it matter?"

A good question. And the honest answer was, I didn't know. Lars's usual woodsy fresh scent was complemented with cologne today. There was a hint of sage and a dash of sandalwood, along with something more elusive. Something I couldn't quite make out. Sticking my face in his neck to take a sniff would be too much. Swooning over Lars was the height of bad manners, because I knew it wasn't what he wanted. Though at least he was single now. Which was still no excuse to crush on a friend.

"Lars has been telling me how great your place is," said Shu. "It's hard to find old houses with all of the original features."

Lars nodded. "It's solid with a lot of character. You'd love it."

"Decide if you're selling yet?" asked Tore.

"No," I said. "Not yet."

He saluted me with the tongs. "We can wait. Whenever you're ready. Just be sure to call me first."

I nodded.

"Be great if I could do a walk-through sometime, though. If that's okay?"

"Um, sure."

As usual, the whole idea of selling filled me with… I don't know. What's the opposite but sort of the same as butterflies in your stomach? Selling the house would set me up financially. Then there were the feelings of nausea to consider. Anytime I thought about letting go of the place, I kind of wanted to puke. I don't know. The best thing to do would be to ignore it all. End of story.

I toed off my flip-flops, unbuttoned my denim shorts, and pulled my black tee off over my head. Of course my tee caught on my ponytail and I had to struggle to get free. Such style and grace. When I finally liberated myself, Lars was staring at my face with his jaw set and lips in a thin straight line. The man seemed to almost be in physical pain.

"What's wrong?" I asked.

"Nothing."

After checking that my black halter-neck one-piece swim-suit had all of the essentials covered, I turned to Tore, who gave me a wide grin. This time he waved a spatula at me. I checked my swimsuit once again, just to be sure. The neckline did plunge, but it was nothing especially risqué. And yet I had the strangest feeling that it was neither the round of my stomach nor the cellulite on my thighs that had drawn Lars's attention. Nope. It had to be the boobs.

And still, his gaze continued to remain glued to my face. Interesting. Perhaps I wasn't the only one who had occasional issues ogling my friends. At least I had the social skills and subterfuge to keep it on the down low.

"You got sunscreen on, Susie?" asked Tore with an even wider grin. "Just yell if you need a hand. I'm sure Lars would be more than happy to help."

Lars's gaze jumped to his brother and narrowed with a look that promised all sorts of violence. Fratricide, it seemed, was the word of the day. Their heated staring competition continued on for quite some time.

"I'm fine, thanks." The "idiots" that I added at the end was almost silent, but not quite.

Shu snorted and picked up her glass of wine.

Isaac bit back a smile and pulled out a vape.

"Lentil patties are done and looking delicious," said Tore. "Steak is up next for the carnivores."

Mateo and James were getting out of the pool as I was getting in. We exchanged greetings as I waded into the shallow end. Oh, so good. Cool and refreshing after the warmth of the sun. I drifted my fingers over the sparkling water before swimming the length to hang out at the deep end. Which was where Lars joined me. Of course he was even more attractive with his wet hair all slicked back and water beading on his skin. Any hard nipples on my part were fortunately hidden below the waterline. That was the problem with noticing someone in a sexual sense. It was so hard to stop. The libido should really come with an off-and-on switch.

We rested our arms on the edge of the pool side-by-side.

"Sorry about that," he mumbled.

I looked down my nose at him. He deserved all of the judgment in all of the land. Because if anyone was going to embarrass me publicly, it would be me. Thank you very much.

"He's been giving me shit about you for days now. He calls you wifey and brings you up constantly. He won't stop."

"I agree that's a terrible nickname. But surely you can rise above his nonsense. You're five years older than me, Lars. How are you not more mature?"

He frowned. "I honestly don't know. I thought I was until this."

"Are you saying I'm your weakness?"

The growly noise he made in reply was a total turn-on.

I decided to just cut to the chase. "Is there something wrong with my swimsuit?"

"No."

"Shu is sitting at the table in a string bikini looking like a snack. But it's my side boob that's the issue?"

For a long moment he stayed silent. Then he gritted out, "Yes."

"Why?"

"Because there isn't a part of me wondering if Shu's destined to be my future spouse."

"Holy shit." I stared at him stunned. "You think the divorce certificate might be real now? When did this happen?"

"I don't know, I just... I can't explain it. How it came into existence. How it got into that wall. None of it."

"Me neither."

"I keep going back and forth in my head and...fuck."

"Yeah."

"We always got along fine, but we never used to pay each other that much attention," he said. "Then I started working on your house and we found that thing. It's like it's changed how I see you. How I think about you. Even if I don't actually believe it's real."

"Like a self-fulfilling prophecy."

"Exactly."

I thought it all over for a minute. "Oh my God. You lied to me."

"What?"

"You don't just want to be friends. You want to be more than that."

"Susie, no." He sighed. "I do just want to be friends. I've given this a lot of thought and even if I could get past you being involved with my best friend—"

"Ugh. Don't remind me. Such a lapse in judgment."

"—I still believe that we're better off as we are. Hanging out and enjoying each other's company without a whole lot of fuss. This works, right?"

"It does." I smiled. "And you've obviously thought this through and I respect that. Though I would like to point out that I wasn't in fact suggesting we start dating."

"Noted."

"All of this open and honest and free flowing communication feels very healthy and I'm sure we have a long and happy friendship ahead of us," I said with a smile. "Out of curiosity, have you ever had a female who was just a friend before?"

He thought it over for a moment. "No, I haven't."

"Truly these are challenging times. I'm just sorry that my side boob distracts you."

"You're enjoying this way too much. Isn't there something about me that distracts you?" And the man totally flexed his deltoids and biceps. What a show pony.

"No," I lied, pushing back from the edge. "I'm good. Thanks."

Monday came around along with the rain. Lars and I painted the living room in mostly companionable silence. Mateo and Connor were away at another job.

I had found an old Pioneer record player in the basement behind a stack of boxes, and Ray Charles and Bing Crosby were now taking turns crooning, and all was well. It was possibly the best thing I'd found in the house so far. Apart from Aunt Susan's debutante photo. Eighties formal dresses were the definition of extra. But her smile in the shot was sublime.

"Best to paint from top to bottom. That way you catch any drips and work them in as you go," said Lars, watching me with a practiced eye. "Maybe just a bit less on the roller."

"Okay."

He got back to work on the wall above the fireplace.

"What'd you do yesterday?" I asked.

"Caught a Mariners game." A frown crossed his face right before he spoke, leading me to believe that it would not be in my best interest to ask who he'd gone to said game with. "What about you?"

"Work and more sorting of stuff." I stepped back and looked at the wall. "This navy blue is so much better than the frog skin."

"Glad you like it."

My phone buzzed in the back pocket of my old paint-splattered jeans. A picture of my father flashed on-screen, which was odd. We were special-occasion communicators. Usually just birthdays and major holidays. For a second I froze. Then I set down the roller and headed into the kitchen for a little privacy. "Dad, is everything okay?"

"Yes, yes. Just thought I'd give you a call."

"That's nice. How are you? How was Mexico? Though that was a while back now, wasn't it?"

"It was wonderful, honey," he said. "But it was a company retreat. Lots of meetings and team-building exercises. There wasn't much time for playing tourist."

"That's a pity."

"Listen, I haven't got long. I just wanted to ask if you had a chance to consider what we talked about last time."

"Um." I rubbed my damp palm down the side of my dodgy painting pants. "About investing in stock?"

"No. About sharing the inheritance with your brother."

"Hold on," I said. "As I recall, you said it was a pity Aunt Susan hadn't felt as benevolent toward Andrew."

"That's right."

"I was supposed to deduce from that that you wanted me to give my brother money?"

Dad cleared his throat. "He's looking at branching out and starting his own business and could use the cash. It's the sisterly thing to do."

"Because Andrew was such a help to me when I started my own business."

"Susie, sarcasm does not suit you."

As if to prove the inherent idiocy of his statement, I doubled down. "And he was always so good about visiting Aunt Susan and wanting to be a part of her life. I'm sure not leaving him anything was just an oversight on her part."

"There's no need for that, honey. He made his mistakes and he regrets them now."

"Oh my God." I laughed. "Are you actually suggesting Andrew should have sucked up to Aunt Susan in the hopes of landing some money when she died? That's awful. She's your sister."

"Of course I don't mean it that way," he snapped. "Don't be ridiculous."

"If he's so desperate for funds why don't you donate to the cause?"

Silence.

"Oh. You already did. Which is funny, because when I was starting out with my business you told me it was too soon and questioned whether I even knew what I was doing. Which, between you and me, was kind of the opposite of being helpful, Dad."

"That was different."

"Did you know that Mom and her new husband sent me flowers when I landed my first client? I mean, they're busy people with their own lives, and yet they still manage to meet the baseline of familial support."

"You're hardly a child to need your hand held, Susie."

"Neither is my brother. You know, I used to think if I was quiet and good that you'd love me. But it just made me easier to ignore. Is that all you called about? Money for Andrew?" I asked. "Ugh. Don't answer that. Of course, it is. Tell my brother he'd have had a better chance approaching me directly than attempting this bullshit."

"Susie!"

"Though he still owes me an apology for giving me crap about inheriting the house at Aunt Susan's funeral. Which is why we haven't talked in months."

Dad started to splutter something, but I was done. I liked to be liked. It was a failing of mine; being a people pleaser sucked. But at some stage, you have to accept that for some people you are never going to be enough. No matter what you do.

"Sorry, Dad. I've got to go. Bye."

I slumped against the kitchen counter and just concentrated on breathing for a minute. In and out. In and out. Everything was fine. My dad had never been overly interested in filling the role of father in my life. This was nothing new. My brother was a jerk. Also old news. At times like this, the connection between the faulty male folk in my family and my awful taste in boyfriends seemed obvious. It might be time to schedule an appointment with the therapist Cleo recommended. And I would. Any day now.

Lars appeared in the archway with a concerned expression. That was the problem with this house: the living room led into the dining room, which led into the kitchen. It was all very open and had great flow. And the music had stopped. When you're listening to vinyl that happens more than you'd think. Lars must have heard everything.

"You okay?" he asked.

I gave him something between a grimace and a smile. "Yes."

"I didn't mean to listen. It's just…it's a small house."

"Yeah."

"You sounded upset."

"I was." I nodded. "But I'm okay now."

His tongue played behind his cheek. "I feel like I should offer to go punch someone for you. Not sure if that's a suitable response, though."

"Oh, that's sweet. It means a lot to me that you'd be willing to fly to Florida and assault my father. But it's really not required."

He shrugged.

"I did warn you that my family was less than great."

His smile was empathetic. "Holidays will definitely be held with my folks."

"I'm almost willing to marry you for that alone." I grabbed the old glass cookie jar out of the pantry. The first chocolate chip cookie got shoved in my mouth, but the second I passed to him. Sugar was my friend. Sort of. Once the cookie was finished, I happy-sighed and said, "That's better."

The usual amusement filled his gaze. Though it soon turned serious. "Can I ask you a question?"

"Sure."

"Why don't you just tell Tore you're not going to sell?"

"Because I haven't made up my mind."

"Susie." The smile he gave me was gentle. "You're not

going to let go of this place. You love it. Just tell him you're not interested and he'll stop asking you."

I didn't know what to say.

"Of course, then you'll have to actually commit to the place and buy some furniture and get settled."

"Whoa there, my oversize friend. Are you suggesting I have commitment issues?"

"How many months have you been living here now?"

"A few," I hedged.

He shrugged.

Huh. I actually hadn't thought of my lack of furnishings as having deeper meaning. Apart from it seeming smart to wait until after the renovations. Though not having a sofa was annoying. But what if I chose wrong again? Maybe I'd throw my money away on a chair that made perfect sense in the moment, only for it wind up a mess. The fear was real.

"You're not still worried about replacing your aunt here, are you?" he asked. "Because she obviously wanted you to have the place."

My shoulders slumped. "No. It's just…"

"You feel like you don't deserve all this?"

"Eh," I said, still hedging. "I don't know."

"You're worried about making another bad call?"

"Tell me, Lars. Since when do you think you know me so well that you can finish my sentences?"

"Since you started wearing that sad face," he teased. "It's the pout in particular that does it to me."

"Great." I pondered the existential horror of it all. "Aaron would say take the money and run. He'd be aghast at the idea of settling down and living in the suburbs."

"Who gives a fuck what he thinks?"

My mouth fell open. "Oh my God. Lars. You blasphemed

against the bestie. Do you need to sit down? Say a few Hail Marys?"

"I'm being serious. This is your place and it's your choice."

"True."

"And you're happy here, aren't you? I mean, you seem happy. It's like you're more relaxed now than you used to be."

"That may be because of the company I'm keeping. Or not keeping," I said. "But yeah, I mean…this is really the only home I've ever known. At least, it's the place where I was the most wanted and welcomed. But enough about my childhood trauma. Nice weather we're having, isn't it?"

He just waited.

So I took a moment and thought over what he'd been saying. This was the kitchen where my aunt taught me how to bake. How to roast and fry and other things. The same as what her mother taught her when she was little. And out the back door was the small yard and Japanese maple. I don't know how many hours of my youth I spent staring up at the colors and the play of sunlight through the leaves of that tree. Often with music blasting in my ears and a book sitting forgotten on my lap. Then there was the back bedroom where I slept. Tales of dinosaurs had morphed into middle school worries and then high school woes. Aunt Susan had listened to it all with patience and love.

I knew I'd been lucky to have her. But I don't think I'd ever quite realized how lucky. Maybe she wasn't the only one who'd been afraid of change. There was every chance I'd inherited some of the trait myself. I wish she was still here. I hadn't asked her nearly enough questions about her opinions on life and love and everything. What would she have thought of the divorce certificate?

"Fine," I admitted. "So maybe you have a point or two about me and the house."

"Are you actually agreeing with me?"

I groaned. "Yes."

He smiled. Then his expression turned serious once again. "Have you told any of your family about the divorce certificate?"

"Hell no. Have you?"

"Just Tore. My sister's busy with her own stuff."

"What about your parents?" I asked. "How do you think they'd react?"

"I honestly don't know."

"Hmm. Well, as was just displayed, I'm not particularly close to any of my family. Sharing our discovery with them hadn't really crossed my mind."

He just looked at me.

"On the plus side, if the certificate is fake, overhearing that conversation is the closest you'll ever have to come to dealing with any of them, you lucky thing."

He gave me a half smile. "It's fake. It's got to be."

"Yeah. Want to go furniture shopping later?" I asked. "And I'm not just asking because you're strong and can lift things and you drive a truck. You actually seem to have a knack for picking out soft furnishings."

"And you like having me around."

"That too," I admitted. "What will I do when you finish work on the house this week?"

"Why don't you throw a party? Have a housewarming?"

"Hmm. I don't know. An intimate gathering of friends, maybe," I said. "Furniture shopping, yes or no? And how do you feel about stopping by Biscuit Bitch for lunch?"

"Whatever you want, Susie."

Seven

"You're out of gin," said Cleo.

I unwrapped a wheel of brie and set it on the charcuterie board. The fourth such arrangement I'd made this evening. Snacks were my bitch.

"I can't wait for your ex-husband to arrive so I can finally meet him," she said. "Though I guess he's currently your pre-husband."

"You should definitely call him that. He would be delighted to hear it," I joked. "Did you check the bar cart in the corner of the living room for more gin?"

"On it." Cleo swept out of the kitchen in her yellow maxi dress.

The house party was indeed happening. Lars and his crew finished painting the interior and exterior of the house and were packed up and gone by Friday. It all transpired scarily fast. I couldn't help but wonder if that was it for us. If perhaps our friendship would fade once we weren't in each other's faces five days a week. In the same way that school and work friends tend to drift away. Time would tell.

In the meantime, the house was now mostly furnished. Because once I get an idea in my head, I tend to fixate. And Cleo, who needed a distraction after breaking up with Josh, embraced the furnishing and housewarming party idea whole-heartedly. Lars hadn't been available for all of my furniture-shopping needs, sadly. This might be due to some dithering and repeat visits to stores on my part. Now everyone was here, eating my food, drinking my booze, and admiring my home. Along with giving me presents, which was awesome.

The cat, however, was horrified by all this and hiding under my bed. Poor baby.

"You're not going to sell, are you?" asked Tore, appearing in the kitchen.

I smiled. "Hello."

"I love it." He looked around with wonder. "You're so cruel."

"Sorry."

"No, you're not." He held up two bottles of wine. "I bought white and red since I didn't know what you drink."

"Thank you very much."

Lars wandered in behind his brother. "I thought you said an intimate gathering."

And I did not feel better just knowing he was there. Some wound-up part of me did not relax at the sight of him. That would be too weird. Oh, fuck. He looked fine. Black linen shirt, blue jeans, and black sneakers. Though it was the man in the clothes that smacked me upside the head. The sheer size of him just got to me. How his wide shoulders and broad chest tapered down to a slim waist and... That's where I had to stop for sanity's sake.

Lars frowned. "Susie?"

"Hey," I squeaked. "Hi."

"You okay?"

"Yep. Yes. Just a lot going on, you know, hostessing."

What with me running around making purchases and both of us working, we actually hadn't seen much of each other during the last few days. The interior was finished so he, Mateo, and Connor had been outside dealing with the exterior. Seeing him now hit me harder than expected. Which was stupid. The man should not matter this much to me.

He shoved a big hand through his golden locks in a move that was pure porn and asked, "What can I do for you?"

"Um."

My knowledge of the English language…was gone. None of the other males at this party had thrown me. Just him, dammit. Since when had my mind gotten so sex addled? And the condition was only getting worse. Why, I'd given myself three stern lectures about rude thoughts with regards to him just this week. I was a weak-willed woman.

"Susie," he said again. "Focus. How can I help?"

Tore grinned.

So I pointed my cheese knife at Tore first. "Put the wine on the sideboard in the dining room and go see if Cleo needs any assistance."

"Will do. Who's Cleo?"

"Best friend. Yellow dress."

"Got it," he said and disappeared.

"What about me?" asked Lars.

"I need the tzatziki and grapes out of the fridge and more crackers and cashews from the pantry."

He did as told. "Who are all these people?"

"Business acquaintances and assorted friends."

"You're popular."

"Does this surprise you?" I asked somewhat archly.

"No. It doesn't."

Lars smiled at me and I smiled at him as he set the asked-for items on the counter. Which meant we were standing close together as he finally took in the fully glory of my appearance. And the man didn't just frown, he scowled.

I didn't understand his reaction—given that my lips were a demure matte rose pink and my hair was classy and sedate in a sleek low ponytail, I was practically dressed like a nun. If a nun wore a black leather pencil skirt with matching organic cotton ribbed tank top and plain kitten heels.

He took a mighty step back from me and said, "I was thinking, maybe you should introduce me to your friend."

"You want to meet Cleo?"

One thick shoulder lifted in the most tentative shrug of all time. "Might be an idea. A way to fix our…problem."

"Is this something to do with the self-fulfilling-prophecy theory?" I asked. "The illicit thoughts regarding each other's bangability?"

"The unwanted-attraction thing. Yeah."

"Huh."

"Because the way you were just looking at me leads me to think maybe I'm not the only—"

"Stop. Say no more. Please." I hung my head in shame. The truth sucked. "This is so humiliating."

"It's okay."

"No, it's not," I said. "What do you call an unrequited crush when it is requited, the person on the receiving end just really and truly doesn't want it to be?"

Lars sighed.

"It's even worse than the person not knowing you're into them. You acknowledge being attracted to me and you *hate* it."

"Hate is a strong word."

"I mean, is this how we wind up married?"

His jaw firmed. "The divorce certificate isn't real. You know that."

"Do I?" I asked. "Don't answer that. So you want me to introduce you to my best friend so you can be into her instead of me. Okay. I get where you're coming from." I sighed. "I mean…it's a valid idea. And at least you'd be dating within the extended friendship group."

He nodded. "There is that."

"Guess I should go have a drink with Tore."

"Wait. What?"

"Give that connection more of a chance. I do really like him. He's smart and funny and kind of hot."

"You said there was nothing between you and him." And the growl in his voice was nothing less than thrilling. The sheer depth and crankiness it conveyed.

I blinked big innocent eyes up at him.

He leaned down until we were almost nose to nose. "Are you fucking with me?"

"I would never."

He glared at me. "Susie, he's my brother."

"That's right. And, Lars, she's my best friend." I gave him my very best smile. "Maybe we should both give this a bit more thought. What do you say?"

More glaring.

"By the way, my graphic designer friend, Hang, wants to talk to you about renovating her place at Madison Park. Why don't you take these snacks out for me and go socialize?"

He grabbed the board and stomped off to enjoy the party.

Because I'd invited people I knew professionally, I didn't get to kick off my heels, have a strong drink, and stop being my best self until after midnight. The crowd had thinned out by then. I'd just seen Miss Lillian to the door (she said it was good karma to be one of the last to leave a party) when Lars sat beside me on the gray velvet sofa. I still planned to have it reupholstered. Though there was something about the colors of a storm, being surrounded by grays and blues. They were moody and comforting at the same time.

Many of the pieces I managed to acquire were vintage thanks to the cool secondhand shops around town, and a local estate sale. The mahogany sideboard was an antique. But the round mirror above the mantel and the silver-and-glass bar cart were brand-new. And the battered midcentury coffee table had been discarded by someone up the street so it was perfect for me to put my bare tired feet up on it now.

"Hey," he said.

I wiggled and stretched my toes. The kitten heels had been seriously uncomfortable. "Did you have a nice night?"

"Yeah. I was out in the back keeping an eye on the fire pit and talking to your friend Hang and her husband for a while."

"They're good people."

He nodded. "Then Mateo and James arrived. It was kind of you to invite them."

"I like them. Besides which, you and Mateo and that little creep are the reason this place looks so good."

"But you didn't feel the need to invite the little creep?"

"Hell no," I said. "I'm not that nice."

The windows were open to let in the cool night breeze and Jimi Hendrix played softly on the turntable. There was a stillness in the small hours that you couldn't find at any other time. With Lars there, it felt even nicer. And for a moment, I set my issues and worries aside and let myself enjoy it. It didn't matter that the house was a mess with empty glasses and dishes strewed about. It didn't matter that our feelings for each other were equally muddled. Everything was good.

Right up until he opened his mouth and said, "Thought Tore might be in here with you."

I took a sip of my vodka and soda with lime. "I'm not interested in your brother. And I have no idea about his current whereabouts."

Nothing from him.

"I thought Cleo might have been out back with you," I said, not sounding like a jealous shrew in the least.

"No." A slow smile curved his lips. "I haven't met your friend yet. Figured you must have hidden her somewhere. But I get the point you were making earlier in the kitchen."

"Oh?"

"Whatever this is…we're just going to have to work it out between us. Wait it out, I guess," he said, tone contemplative. "I have no idea where that divorce certificate came from or what the hell it all means. But it's like you said, we're still in charge of the decisions we make."

"Yes, we are. No one can force us to get together, let alone marry and then separate. Regardless of any stray weird and unwarranted sexual feelings we may be experiencing." I nodded in full agreement with myself. "Because you'd be breaking the bro code and I'd be rushing into a relationship, and probably making another mistake and inevitably everything would go to shit. Which neither of us wants."

"Exactly. But dating each other's brothers or friends right now would be stupid. And possibly hurtful, I guess."

"Friends don't hurt friends," I said. "At least, not on purpose. And I definitely haven't hidden Cleo from you. I have no idea as to her whereabouts. Maybe she had to leave early. I'll text her in a minute. Just as soon as my feet stop hurting."

The cat let out a plaintive meow and stuck her head out from underneath the sofa. I hadn't even realized she was there. Someone deserved a saucer of milk for tolerating all of the people. She'd been in hiding for hours. Parties were definitely not her thing.

"You're going to swipe right on a dating app, I take it?" I asked.

"I'm in no rush." He gave me a long look. "What about you?"

There was a bang as the back bedroom door opened. Lars and I both looked over our shoulders to see Cleo stumble out into the dining room giggling. With her was a very large half-dressed male busily pulling up the zipper on his jeans.

My mouth fell open. "Huh."

"Guess that answers that question," said Lars.

Cleo looked up and her eyes went wide. "Oh. Hi."

"Enjoying the party?" I asked.

"Yes."

I bit back a grin. "Excellent."

"Babe," said Tore, buttoning up his shirt. "This is the brother I told you about."

Lars lifted a hand in greeting. "Hey."

"Nice to meet you." Cleo gave him a smile before turning her attentions back to her new friend. "You missed a button. Let me get it."

"Sneaking off at parties to make out," I chided. "What are we, eighteen?"

Cleo dealt me a look. "You're just jealous, Susie."

"That's true. I really am."

Lars patted me on the knee. "There, there."

"The chaise you put in the new office is very comfortable," said Cleo.

"The fabric was okay?" I asked. "No rug burn?"

"Smooth as silk."

I gave her a thumbs-up. "Good to know."

"We have to go." Cleo led a now-blushing Tore toward the

front door. And the smile on the woman. "But I'll be back tomorrow to help you clean up."

"Right," said Tore. "You were going to show me that thing at your place. Which I'm really looking forward to. But we will definitely be back, Susie."

"It's fine." Lars waved them off. "We've got it. Go have fun."

Tore grinned. "Thanks, brother."

"Ah, young love," I said as they disappeared off into the night. It had been months and months since I'd gone to bed with anyone. Not that I couldn't provide for myself. But it was nice to feel another person's touch now and then. And there sitting beside me was Lars, all big and strong. His hands, in particular, appealed to me. Those clever calloused fingers would be capable of all sorts of amazing things. Just the thought made me clench. Which reminded me: "Thanks for following me on TikTok and Instagram."

"You're welcome."

"Though I noticed you only liked the picture of me holding the biodegradable vibrator."

"I liked your smile in that one. It was…what's the right word?"

"Salacious?"

"That'll do." His low laughter gave me feelings in my underpants.

And then I went and did it. I opened my mouth and asked, "Did you ever consider us becoming friends with benefits?"

Given the intensity in Lars's gaze, he either loved or hated the idea. A question soon answered when he spit out the word, *"No."*

"Huh. That wasn't half-hearted at all."

A look of alarm crossed his face.

"It was just an innocent question, Lars. No need to get so

upset. I was only thinking that it might have been a way for us to perhaps *manage* the hormonal effects of the divorce certificate. Just do it once to get it out of our system, you know?"

He grunted.

"No one has come forward and claimed responsibility for the thing. And neither of us has any more of a clue than we did when we found it. Maybe it's time to start managing the situation instead of looking for answers."

His cheekbones stood out in stark relief. The man was seriously feeling things. "Susie, you and I getting involved would only make things more complicated."

"Okay. I see now that it was a truly terrible notion and I'm going to stop talking about it." The truth was, I never should have asked in the first place. It was my own damn fault if my delicate little feelings got hurt. The heart was a fool and the vagina far worse. I finished off my drink and got to my feet. "Why don't you gather the dirty glasses and so on while I start on the kitchen?"

"Sure," he said, and certainly seemed relieved by the change in topic. "I didn't mean to insult you or anything. You know I find you attractive. But…"

"You're worried about upsetting your best friend."

"No. I mean, it's not ideal, but…you and me—we don't make sense." He stopped and frowned up at me. "Shit, Susie. The look on your face. I've hurt you."

"Eh. You didn't mean to. That counts for something."

His expression became pained.

I pasted on my brightest smile. "Think it might be best if we gave each other some space for a week. Let things settle. Given the existence of the certificate, all of this time together has really been a lot, you know?"

His hands flexed open and closed at his side. "If that's what you want."

"I think it is," I said. "It's late. I might just go to bed. Thank you for offering to help, but it's okay. I'll clean this mess up in the morning."

"Are you sure?"

"Yes."

But it was safe to say, even if I knew what I wanted, chances were, I couldn't have it. Not when it came to him. Such was life.

"Wait a minute." Cleo followed me down the steps to one of the lower levels of Pike Place Market. "You were going to set me up with the man you have a crush on? Susie, are you serious?"

"No. That was his brilliant idea. Which I did not entertain even a little."

"Thank goodness for that."

It was the Saturday after the party and the first time we'd had a chance to catch up. The morning after the party, I texted her and told her I had the cleaning up in hand. I hadn't been in the mood for visitors, even helpful ones, until now. And she'd been busy with her new man friend, Tore, all week. Mostly I spent the week working and trying not to think about Lars. The last one made harder due to my habit of staring at the damn certificate. Having a piece of paper attempt to dictate your future choices was a trip. Which was why I needed to know more. Nowish.

"Neither of us are stupid enough to get involved with a man a friend is sweet on," said Cleo.

"Agreed."

"So Lars is an idiot, but Tore is wonderful."

"That's the official opinion?" I asked.

Cleo just beamed. "I really like him. Though *like* is such

a tame word. I just… I'm trying not to get carried away, because I know it's early days. But damn it's hard."

"I'm so happy for you. And if he hurts you I'll hurt him. I'm thinking golf stick to the knee."

"Thank you. I think it's called a club. We've seen each other almost every day this week," she admitted. "I'm so scared we're moving too fast and it's all going to go wrong. But right now, it's so right. You know what I mean?"

"Yeah."

"It's like there's all this going on inside me about him and I…anyway. That's why I've been missing all week."

"An excellent reason." I grinned. "After we sort this stupid mystery divorce certificate out once and for all, want to go get donuts and watch fish being thrown around?"

"Yes."

We stepped inside the small shop for Madam Karen. It looked how you'd imagine. Red velvet curtains and a display of tarot cards for sale. Crystals sat on almost every surface. A bored-looking teenager glanced up at us from behind the counter before shouting, "Mom, your next clients are here."

I raised my chin. "How did you know that without asking? Are you psychic too?"

The girl just rolled her eyes.

Fair enough.

"You must be Lillian's friends," said an older woman with a neat black bob. A variety of colorful stone necklaces hung from her neck. "I'm Karen. Come on through."

A small table and chairs sat behind the curtain and we all took a seat in the dimly lit room. The walls were painted dark red and it was very atmospheric. On a shelf in the corner sat a crystal ball and a variety of spiritual books. Thank goodness I'd worn a black maxi slip dress and flat sandals. It was a warm day and the AC was not up to the challenge. Cleo took a sip from her water bottle and fanned herself with her hand.

I retrieved the divorce certificate from the plastic bag in my purse and set it on the table. "Miss Lillian said you specialize in psychometry and might be able to shed a little light on this. It was—"

"Don't tell me any more," said Karen.

I shut my mouth and exchanged a look with Cleo. Neither of us knew what to expect. Not really. But everything about the document made me nervous. Psychometry was the reading of vibrations or impressions attached to an object. Assessing the energy field via extrasensory perception. Google told me that. And if there's one thing you can always rely on, it's the internet talking about spiritual matters. Since the forensic document examiner had been a bust, it was time to look further afield. And Miss Lillian thought this might be helpful since she wasn't a specialist in the field.

Karen caressed the edges of the document before sliding her fingers over the surface. All the while, her face was a study in concentration. Then she closed her eyes and exhaled. Took another deep breath in and exhaled again. "I'm grounding my energy and setting safeguards around us," she explained. "Now I'm opening my mind to the object. There's some very feminine energy attached to this."

"I keep it either on me or in my underwear drawer. I figured that was safest. It's where I put my... Anyway."

Karen opened one eye and gave me a look.

"Sorry," I whispered.

"There's a lot of confusion in the recent contact. The people who have touched it lately have a lot of questions, but no answers." The psychic frowned. "Let's see if we can go back further. It was lost and forgotten for a long time."

Cleo watched the woman with a blank face. I tried to do the same, but my foot wouldn't stop tapping. Anxiety was a bitch.

"There's so much sadness." Karen placed her palms flat on the paper. "She feels great anguish about this fate. She's frustrated and profoundly disappointed that mistakes were made on both their parts."

"Wait. I did something wrong?" I asked, surprised. "I really thought it would have been him."

Cleo shushed me and I slapped a hand over my mouth.

"It takes two to tango," said Karen, with the one eye on me again. "The pain attached to this document is so great it echoes."

"It echoes?"

"So loudly it reached you a decade earlier."

"Huh."

"That's everything I can tell you," Karen said. "Readings tend to go better with less interruptions. They muddy the psychic waters, so to speak."

I removed the hand. "That's it? Can I ask something?"

She nodded, both eyes open now.

"How did the divorce certificate get in the wall?"

"Nothing came through about that."

"Damn. The mystery remains unresolved."

"Have your questions been answered?" asked Karen.

"Not so much," said Cleo drily. "Is there any way you can give her something more?"

"Sure." Karen picked up a pack of tarot cards and set them in front of me. "Shuffle these, please. And think about what you want to know."

I put away the divorce certificate then did as told. The cards were soft around the edges from use and age. They were also a little large for my hands and awkward to shuffle.

As agreed, Lars and I hadn't talked this week. Neither by

text, phone, nor face-to-face. The man detox had been interesting. What Karen had said so far definitely reinforced my reasons for not wanting to date. Especially not Lars. Why would anyone want to deal with this shit? Emotions were messy and males were the worst. But I missed him more than I liked to admit. Which sucked. It had been a lonely week with no Lars and Cleo busy with Tore. While I knew a lot of people, I only had a couple of close friends. Though I got ahead on my work, spent quality time with the cat, and sorted some boxes.

I handed the cards back. "There you go."

Karen dealt three cards facedown on the table. She flipped the first one.

"Death!" I screeched. "Are you kidding me?"

She tapped the card with a purple painted nail. "In most cases, the Death card signifies change. It's shown here in reverse, meaning you've been resisting this change. That there are possibly behaviors and beliefs you need to shed to become a better version of yourself. Only then will you have a chance at being in a healthier relationship with both yourself and others going forward. In other words, Susie, you're holding on to things that don't benefit you."

"Oh," I said, relaxing. "Okay."

She flipped another card. "The Knight of Cups. Which means love may be coming your way. But you could have a tendency to be in love with love and have unrealistic expectations. If you wish to succeed, you're going to need to listen to your heart, but keep the real world in sight."

I just frowned.

Karen flipped the final card and gave it a tap. "This is the Fool."

"Well, that's harsh," I mumbled.

"It's reversed, meaning that your somewhat lighthearted

nature may need to be balanced by more caution. A risky relationship could be in your immediate future. One that is possibly lacking in commitment. You'll weather it best by seeking that balance and looking to the future."

I sighed. "So basically you're saying that change is coming. That I should act like a grown-up and do my best not to make bad choices. But to especially not make the same mistakes I made before. And after all that, at the end of the day, no one really has a clue exactly how things will work out anyway."

Karen thought it over for a moment. "Basically."

"Right."

"Did you want more woo-woo thrown in?"

"I can see why you're friends with Lillian." I smiled. "What's your take on destiny or fate?"

"I believe that great things lie ahead for all of us," she said. "If we learn the lessons we need to and grow as we go through life."

"I'm sensing a theme here."

"Funny thing." Karen gathered up the cards and stood. "You can pay my daughter on your way out."

Cleo patted me on the shoulder. "Sugar and carbs?"

"Oh, yeah."

"Are you going to tell Lars about this?"

I sighed. "Good question."

Eight

Lars: Feel like drinks tonight? Be good to catch up. Cleo and Tore will be there.

Me: Will Aaron be there?

Lars: No

Me: Ok. Sounds great!

We were meeting at a pub in Ballard near Market Street that served mead and aquavit. Lars's blond head towered above the crowd near the bar. An easy point of reference.

Any nerves I had about seeing him again were hidden beneath a black camisole, black pants, and strappy heels. A little dressy, but sometimes a girl needed armor. It had been over a week since my housewarming party, when Lars and I last spoke. It would be nice to see him. I missed his dry sense of humor and the sound of his voice. We could just be friends.

The divorce certificate could be ignored. Why, I hadn't put my hand in my purse to fondle the soft paper in at least a minute. Tonight would be great. I was in a good mood and the smile stayed on my face right up until I saw the woman hanging off his arm. Holy shit. He'd brought a date. And not just anyone.

"Jane," I said. "Wow. This is a surprise."

She immediately disentangled herself from Lars and gave me a hug. "Susie! Good to see you. How have you been?"

It was like being sucker punched. My heart hurt and I hated it.

I'd always gotten along with Lars's ex-girlfriend. We'd gone on many a double date, back in the day. She was petite and perfect, which made me feel large and loud. But other people weren't responsible for my insecurities. And seeing her again was great. So great.

Lars gave me a smile and a nod. "Hey."

Cleo appeared and passed me one of her glasses of mead. "Our table's ready. Come sit next to me, Susie."

"Okay."

"Can I sit on your other side?" asked Tore with a wink.

"Just this once," Cleo teased. Then, with a meaningful look at me, she said, "We only just arrived."

In other words, she hadn't had a chance to warn me about Jane. I nodded and smiled and made myself a promise. This stupid infatuation or awareness or whatever you wanted to call it, would die tonight. I meant it this time. He was never going to give so I needed to stop wanting. Men and women could be friends without sex getting in the way. Just watch and see.

Our table was near the back, away from the hustle and bustle. We were settling in when Tore's musician friend Austin joined us. At least I wouldn't be the odd woman out among couples. He sat opposite me and gave me a very friendly smile.

And wasn't it nice that someone appreciated the time I'd taken perfecting my eyeliner and styling my hair?

"How have you been?" Lars asked me.

"Good. I've been busy. *Skol.*" I tapped my glass against his before taking a sip of mead. "How about you?"

"Same."

"Great."

"Everything's okay with you?" he asked with a frown. It was just his way. In situations where other people would smile to encourage you, Lars would instead frown with concern. He wasn't as grumpy as he seemed. But he did have a tendency to take things seriously.

"Absolutely," I said.

"The house is all good?"

"It sure is."

"Because you know I can drop by if there's anything you need help with."

"Thank you. I appreciate that." I smiled. "How's your latest job?"

"Fine."

"You and Jane are back together, huh?"

"Yeah," he said. "We, ah, yeah."

And that's all he gave me.

I looked at him and he looked at me and, ugh. Guess we weren't going to be friends and we had fuck all to talk about. Forget the divorce certificate. Ignore the unfortunate feelings. We were through. Which was kind of a relief. I rolled back my shoulders and shrugged it off. Now I knew.

Jane, who was an attorney, was busy telling Tore about a recent case she'd handled when our waiter appeared, a pretty young man with many a piercing. Suddenly Jane perked up and with a blindingly bright smile said, "Well, hi there. What's your name?"

The waiter grinned and stuttered out something.

Lars's lips thinned.

Holy shit. That's what he said she did that time we were throwing around probable reasons for the divorce. How Jane flirted with other people and he found it disrespectful. Huh.

When my turn came, I ordered the salad with grilled salmon and settled back with my mead. Lars's reasons for reconnecting with Jane were none of my business. No doubt there were benefits to the relationship. Though it didn't speak well of him that he couldn't seem to go a few weeks without a girlfriend. Talk about serial monogamy.

Jane leaned toward me. "We never got to talk after that time at the restaurant."

"Oh. Well. I, um..."

"I thought what Aaron did was complete and utter bullshit."

I just nodded.

She laid her hand on Lars's arm. "I know he's your best friend, but really. To get drunk and announce to a room full of people—including your girlfriend who organized the going-away party—that you're looking forward to all sorts of *new opportunities* overseas. And the winking was super classy. How humiliating for you, Susie. Shame on him."

As if I didn't remember it just fine. The way everyone turned to look at me to gauge my reaction. How I struggled to keep a smile on my face. Because he'd been telling me for the past few days how he wanted us to stay together. That we'd be long-distance for a year then he'd return. No big deal. Of course, after his little speech, things had gotten ugly. It wasn't the sort of situation I was going to take sitting down. Nothing like your significant other making you feel insignificant.

"Not his finest moment," mumbled Lars.

I stared at the table. "It's in the past."

"What an ass," said Jane.

"Yes, he is." Cleo gave me a rub on the back. "But like Susie said, it's in the past. Let's talk about something else."

Jane just blinked. "Of course. Sorry, Susie. I didn't mean to—"

"It's fine. Really." I smiled. "What have you been up to lately?"

Jane talked and Lars studied his hands. Austin bought me a drink while Cleo and Tore whispered sweet nothings. It was wonderful how obviously into each other they were. I hadn't seen my best friend smile that wide in a long time.

I turned when a man at the next table dropped his wallet. Jane retrieved it and they chatted. She laughed and flicked her hair and Lars frowned his heart out. Some people were addicted to attention, to the thrill of being wanted. It was harmless. Mostly. But Lars had made the choice to be with someone whose behavior hurt him and I really wanted to know why.

"Back in a minute," Lars said, rising from the table.

I slipped out of my seat and followed without a word.

When we reached the gender-neutral bathroom door, he frowned at me in surprise and held it open. "After you."

"Thanks."

It was a nice clean rest room. Dark green tiles with copper sinks. I whirled around and crossed my arms.

Lars froze. "Something on your mind?"

"Why are you back with someone who makes you unhappy?"

His jaw shifted.

"Don't get me wrong, I think Jane's great," I said. "She tells awesome stories and that Balenciaga purse she's carrying is beyond words. But her flirting upsets you. It's why you broke up with her in the first place. An issue that obviously hasn't been resolved."

"Susie…"

"Why do that to yourself, Lars?"

His gaze narrowed on me. "You know, you sound almost jealous."

"And you sound defensive." I took several steps closer. What I really wanted to do was reach out and shake him. But we never touched. Not on purpose and not if we could help it. "I see you sitting there, looking miserable, and I don't get it. Can you just not be without a girlfriend? Is that it?"

"It's none of your business." He made a growly noise low in his throat. "This is for the best, okay?"

"Not if you're unhappy."

"Leave it alone."

"No. You made me care about you. Now you can deal with the consequences."

"Get out of my fucking face, Susie. I am not talking to you about this."

"Fine," I snapped.

He grunted.

"I can't believe I wore a strapless bra for you."

His brows rose and his mouth opened and I swept out of the room like a queen. Because I was just petty enough to enjoy getting the last word. So there. Though while the shock that filled his gaze had been enjoyable, I might try to show a little more maturity in future. Maybe not mention my underwear. Let's add it to the list of shit I shouldn't say. Oh, well. Lars had a talent for getting under my skin.

Back at the table, it soon became the second-worst night at a restaurant in my life. Lars and I ignored each other while everyone else had a great time. And we didn't swap meals midway. I didn't want to try his stupid sausage anyway.

The banging on my door came after a bellowed "Susie!"
I knew that voice. I did not hate that voice. Though I was

pretty damn irritated with him for various reasons, including it being close to one in the morning. The idiot was lucky I'd been awake and reading. I unlocked the door and threw it open and there stood Lars. He was wearing gray sweatpants cut off into shorts and a pair of sneakers. His tee had been removed and tucked into the waistband and his bare chest glistened with sweat. And all the while, his thick shoulders were heaving as he sucked down some much-needed air.

I cocked my head. "Did you run all the way here?"

"Yes."

"Do you need some water?"

"That'd be good," he gasped. "But I have something to say to you first."

"Okay. I'm listening. Though you might want to start with an apology for bellowing at me. Otherwise this is going to be a very short conversation."

"I'm sorry I raised my voice. That was out of line."

"Thank you."

"Are you going to apologize for sticking your nose in my business even after I asked you to stop?" he asked.

"Can't we call it an intervention?"

"No," he said, voice flat and unfriendly.

"I'm sorry. I should have respected your boundaries. What did you come here to say?"

He scowled down at me and said with all due seriousness, "You cannot talk to me about your underwear."

I pinned my lips shut.

"I mean it."

"I can see that," I said. "And you ran all that way just to tell me that."

"Are you laughing at me?"

"No, sir. As it happens, I'd already come to the no-underwear rule all by myself."

He blinked.

"I mean, the no-*talking*-about-underwear rule." I clarified. I gave him my most pleasant smile. "Would you like some water now?"

"Yes, please."

He followed me through to the kitchen, where I fetched him a glass of ice water. And the way his throat worked as he drained the glass. How thick his neck was. I don't know—the whole man got to me. But staring is rude. The problem was, however, when I lowered my gaze the dick print on the front of his shorts caught my eye. Like the rest of him, it was sizable. And what the sight of it did to me was obscene. My toes curled, and my thighs squeezed together. It had been safe to see him half-naked at his BBQ—with other people present. But here alone in my kitchen...how dare he not manhandle me. This was outrageous.

The thing was, every time I tried to wise up and shut down my feelings, he gave me reason to hope. Because he was no better at ignoring me than I was him. And just to prove it, he glared at my cute black sleep shorts and tank. Never had my sleepwear been so maligned. The lack of a bra seemed to particularly upset him. Though maybe he just liked scowling at my boobs in general. This wasn't the first time. That my nipples chose that moment to harden, however, was not helpful.

But this whole situation was a mess. He made me angry and happy and confused and turned-on. The only positive to having a lady boner for the man was knowing I wasn't alone with this chaos and confusion. But unlike him, I at least could display a little dignity.

"Do you often go running in the middle of the night?" I asked.

"No."

"You couldn't sleep?"

"No, I couldn't," he answered.

"That happens to me sometimes. When there's a lot on my mind."

He set the glass aside and crossed his arms. "I wasn't going to come here, but…what you said about me and Jane…you were right. We broke up because I couldn't handle the way she interacts sometimes with people, and that hasn't changed Did you know the waiter tonight gave her his number?"

"No, I didn't."

"I was sitting right there and she took it," he said. "When we met up last week and decided to try again we agreed to be exclusive. I told her accepting his number made me uncomfortable and she said I was being ridiculous. That she was just being polite and it didn't mean anything."

"Maybe it wouldn't mean anything to some people. But it does to you."

"Yeah," he said.

"I'm sorry."

"Why are you sorry?"

I shrugged. "I get no joy from you being unhappy."

"Shit." He rubbed at his face. "I rushed into something I knew wouldn't work. It's my own damn fault."

"Why do you think you did that, Lars?"

His hands fell to his sides and he looked at me. The silence got awkward fast. Finally, he said, "Being just friends with you is harder than it should be."

My mouth was a perfect O. Not that the news was surprising. I just didn't think he'd actually admit it out loud.

"Talk to me about something else," he ordered, all agitated.

"Ah. Okay. Did I tell you I took the divorce certificate to another psychic?" I lifted myself up onto the counter. "A psychometry expert this time. They read objects by touch."

"That's not what Miss Lillian does?"

"Not exactly."

"What'd they say?" he asked, taking another sip of water.

"That there was a lot of sadness attached to the document."

"You expected it to be happy?"

"Some divorces are," I argued. "My father was so overjoyed after theirs came through that he went hunting and drinking for a week with his friends. Said it was the best time he'd ever had. Sinking beers and shooting bunnies."

"Your father is an asshole."

"That's true."

"What did your mother do?"

"She doesn't talk about it. Any topic involving my dad is prohibited." I crossed my arms over my chest. "My family prefers to be dysfunctional. You could say it's our chosen aesthetic."

"I'm glad you had your aunt."

"Me too," I said. "She was so funny. She used to do this thing…if she poured you a glass of water or fetched you a pair of socks she'd say, *That's it for Christmas. That's all you're getting.* It would start sometime after Thanksgiving and just keep rolling right on through until the big day. I thought it was hilarious when I was little."

"She sounds great."

"Yeah." My smile slipped. "She really was."

"Did the psychic say anything else?" he asked.

"Um, that I should not make bad choices. With an emphasis on especially not repeating previous mistakes. To be sensible and to look to the future and let go of things that don't benefit me."

Lars nodded. "Not bad advice."

"You're not going to tell me every psychic is a fraud?"

"I'm pretty sure you can make up your own mind. Her guidance sounds a bit like common sense. But maybe it's not the worst thing in the world that people get to hear some common sense."

"Very open-minded of you. So what are you going to do about Jane?"

"We agreed to disagree. So we're done. Again." He hung his head. "It lasted one whole damn week."

"Don't be so hard on yourself. That would have been a life-time in middle school."

"That is not comforting."

"We can eat ice cream and watch TV if it'll make you feel better." I smiled. "Do you think maybe you'll give being on your own for a while a try?"

He gave me a look.

"Just a thought."

He sighed. "I wasn't running scared or anything after your housewarming. That's not why Jane and I..."

I just waited.

"*You* said you didn't want to see me. I know you just needed some space, but I didn't like it."

"Okay." He shut his mouth and said no more.

"You know, I can teach you how to be single. I'm good at being alone." I hopped down off the counter. "Actually, I wonder if that's what the divorce was about. You eventually needing time on your own to grow or whatever."

"Wouldn't we have just separated for a while if that was the case?"

"Who knows?" I shrugged. "Coupledom is complicated. Trying to keep something together long-term. Finding that balance between two people. Not making the mistake of con-forming to meet someone else's expectations. No matter how much you like them. It's why my dating history is kind of spotty."

His forehead furrowed. "You shouldn't have to change for

anyone, Susie. That's not what it's about. I mean, there's compromising, but...not twisting yourself into a pretzel to make someone else happy."

"But I'm the odd girl, Lars. The mouthy one. Not the one they take home to meet Mother."

"Then fuck them. And not in the good way."

The smile spread slowly but surely across my face. "Thank you for saying that."

He just grunted.

"You know, I've never had someone run across town in the middle of the night just to have a fight with me before."

"Wasn't much of a fight."

"Guess it was more about us sorting out our difficulties. Again."

"I better go." He took a deep breath and let it out slowly. "Tell me we're fine."

"We're fine," I said, following him to the door. "Quick question. Do you talk about this sort of stuff with anyone else?"

"No." He turned away. "Think it's safe to say I talk more with you than I do anyone else. Maybe that's why this is so important to me. You and me being friends, I mean."

"Maybe," I said. "Maybe that's how we wound up married in a parallel universe. We talked ourselves into it, somehow."

"We're saying it happened in a parallel universe now?"

"Sure. One where you didn't so much mind me mentioning my underwear or showing some side boob. It's as good an explanation as any."

"TV and ice cream tomorrow night?"

"Sounds good."

Nine

Lars appeared on the front porch Thursday evening with a relaxed smile on his face and a pint of ice cream in his hand. He'd gotten it from Molly Moon's—a solid choice. I hoped it was their honey and cornbread.

His smile, however, didn't last long. First the cat raced out from underneath the dining table and climbed the man as if he was her last hope of refuge. Which he kind of was. I ran after her while Cleo stared in horrified wonder and Austin muttered obscenities. As photo shoots went, this one was a disaster.

Lars cradled the feline against his chest and said, "What the hell, Susie?"

"You." I pointed a finger at the beast. "I am extremely disappointed in your life choices."

The cat sank her claws into Lars's tee trying to hang on even tighter. Lars winced in pain. "I repeat, what the hell?"

"She peed all over Austin's guitar and its case."

"Damn."

"I know," I cried. "It's a 1960 Martin worth a fucking fortune. We were taking promo shots for him and this one decided to piddle where she most definitely should not."

The cat stretched up to rub her head against Lars's chin. She had the audacity to purr.

I again pointed a finger in her direction. "If you think I'm going to continue to buy you the expensive organic kibble after this you have another thing coming, missy."

"I think we've got all of the shots we need," said Cleo, packing away her camera and flash.

Meanwhile, Austin had fallen silent and sat staring at his beloved instrument in stunned silence. In his hand he held a now cat-pee-stained T-shirt. Guess it'd been the first thing he thought of to clean up the mess. The man had a lot of tattoos, including a tree on his back. Very cool.

"What a mess." I pulled my phone out of my back jeans pocket and started googling. "Okay. They say vinegar and baking soda. Let me just...oh, no. Peroxide is apparently better. Not quite sure what we do about the guitar case, though."

"Are you sure about peroxide?" Austin asked, worried. "Maybe that will just make it worse."

"I'm sure," I said, still reading. "This says it won't harm the wood or the finish."

"It's soaked through a crack and a couple of nicks in the varnish."

"I'll put the cat outside for now," said Lars.

"That might be best," Cleo answered.

I found the necessary items in the kitchen along with some paper towel and kneeled before the Martin. It was a beautiful old acoustic guitar.

"I'm so sorry, Austin."

He nodded glumly.

I wiped away the remaining urine with an old towel. Then

I covered the area with a clean cloth soaked in peroxide and pressed down gently. "We're supposed to let it sit for a while."

"Hey, Lars," Austin said, greeting him with a tilt of his chin.

Lars had returned sans cat. Thank God. "Hey. I didn't know you guys were working together."

"Susie and I talked about it at dinner last night. I needed some help with social media." Austin gave me a sad smile. "Didn't expect her cat to hate me on sight. If this doesn't fix it, I'll take it to the repair shop and see what they can do."

"This is all so wildly unprofessional," I said. "The least I can do is take it to the shop for you."

"Thanks. But I know the owners."

I frowned. "Right. Of course."

"I've had newborn babies pee on things at photo shoots," said Cleo. "But never a cat."

I lifted the edge of the cloth to check all was well. "I'm seriously reconsidering giving the little jerk a home at all."

"No, you're not." Lars headed for the kitchen to put the beer in the fridge. "You're just upset. Which you have every right to be."

"You would take her side," I grumbled. "She sucks up to you."

Austin removed the cloth and sighed. "This will have to wait. I've got a show tonight at North Admiral. Would you mind throwing out this shirt for me?"

"Of course," I said, accepting the stinky article of clothing. "Here, take the bottle of peroxide so you can put more on the guitar when you've got time."

"Good idea." He packed the instrument into its case. "I'll talk to you later. About the pictures and...yeah."

I gave him my best professional smile, but felt horrible about what just went down. "Sure."

"Hey." Cleo gave my back a rub. Back rubs from my bestie

got me through the worst of times. She was a good woman. "I was supposed to have a thing with Tore, but..."

"No. It's okay," I said. "You go."

"Really?"

My smile felt all sorts of wrong. "This is unfortunate, but it'll be fine."

Cleo said her goodbyes, and Lars helped her carry her gear out to her car.

Now was a great time to pace. Back and forth across the living room in a fevered fashion. Once I disposed of the shirt, of course. Every window was open to air out the room, but the horrible scent still lingered. What a feral little thing.

"You all right?" asked Lars, when he came back inside.

"No."

"Hey, it's—"

"My cat urinated on a client's fifteen-thousand-dollar guitar," I moaned.

He paused. "Susie..."

"Austin must hate me. He definitely will when I tell him I don't want to go out to dinner with him. Though maybe he's changed his mind about that and fair enough."

"Austin asked you out?"

I nodded. Still pacing my heart out. "And he's really great. He's attractive, smart, funny..."

Lars crossed his arms.

"We only turned our backs for a minute. We were just setting up the last shot by the mantel. She's never done anything like this before."

"It'll be okay."

"What if he wants me to replace the instrument? I spent all of my spare money doing up the house."

"I've known Austin a long time and he's not the kind of guy to act like an asshole. Not over something like this."

I kept right on pacing. "Did you see the look on his face when he left?"

"Yeah," said Lars. "But it'll be okay. He was upset. Not angry."

"I just have the worst feeling."

"You're fine."

"He probably does hate me."

"He wants to get into your pants, by the sound of things," said Lars. "But it's not like he's going to sue you when you turn him down."

"Oh my God," I gasped. "He could sue me. I hadn't thought of that. Maybe I should just go on the stupid date."

"What?" He frowned. "No. He's not going to sue you. I don't think going out with him is the answer. Unless you've changed your mind and *want* to go out with him."

"No, not really."

"Right." Tension eased out of his broad shoulders. "There's your answer then."

"What a mess."

"The peroxide was working, right?"

"Who knows?" I kept on pacing, tugging hard on my braid. "What if word gets around that I destroyed a client's property?"

"There's no reason anyone would find out."

"No one will hire me ever again," I said morosely. "I'll be the cat-pee lady. That's what they'll call me."

"Susie..."

"Hmm?"

Lars stepped into my path and grabbed hold of my shoulders. He'd startled me mid-doom spiral. And the frown on his face and intensity in his eyes was immense. "You have to calm down," he said sternly. "Nothing bad has happened yet."

"But it might."

"You don't think you're maybe being a touch overdramatic?"

"I don't know." I sighed. "What if I did go out with him?"

"That is not the answer," he said through gritted teeth. "As we've already discussed twice now."

"Yeah, but are you *really* sure it wouldn't help? Because right now it's not like it would hurt anything. I can smile and be friendly for the sake of my immediate economic future. It's not like he isn't a pretty man."

Lars's frown amped up to a scowl. "Wait. So you are attracted to him?"

"I don't know."

"Susie, I need an answer." He got all up in my face. His expression somewhere between confusion and rage. "Yes or no? Are you going to go out with Austin or not?"

"Um, well..."

Guess my hesitation was the last straw for him. Because he made a growling noise and slammed his mouth down on mine. Warm firm lips pressed hard against me and there they stayed for one seemingly endless moment. Truthfully, it seemed like less of a kiss and more like an act of desperation. There wasn't really any passion in it. Not of the normal variety.

When Lars drew back, his gaze was both wary and worried.

Meanwhile, my eyes felt as wide as the moon. My heart hammered inside my chest. If his intention had been to distract me from the cat-pee problem, he certainly managed that.

His fingers untangled themselves from my hair and he took a step back. Then he opened his mouth and closed it and opened it again. Finally he said, "Shit."

"Did you just get jealous, panic, and kiss me?"

"Yes."

"Is that something you normally do?"

His brows drew down. "No."

"No," I agreed.

With a groan, he deposited himself on the couch. His hands covered his face while his elbows rested on his knees. The pose of a man in much anguish. No. A confused modern male confronted with his feelings. One of those. As for me, I loved having his mouth on mine. Even if the kiss could use some work.

"It felt impromptu," I said. "Not to be harsh."

He dropped his hands and looked up at me with extreme consternation. As if I were dancing on his last damn nerve. The man certainly knew how to return the favor. With a shake of his head, he pulled out his cell to fire off a text. "We should get Tore to talk to Austin and see what's up about the guitar."

"I don't know how I feel about that."

His gaze was serious. "Tore's known Austin since they were kids. I trust my brother. I promise you he will only help. Please let us do this for you."

"Okay," I said. "But tell him to be subtle. I don't want Austin to feel like he's being pressured. We do not want to exacerbate the situation."

A nod from Lars as his thumbs moved across the screen.

"Guess if I have to take out a small loan it won't be the end of the world. It'll set me back for a while, but hey…if I can handle college fees I can certainly handle this." I rubbed my hands against the sides of my wide-legged cropped jeans. "And my reputation is solid. My clients know and trust me. I mean, this is all just a somewhat amusing horrible thing that happened. Not the end of the world."

"That's right. Everything is going to be okay." His phone chimed and he read the text. "Tore said he and Cleo will stop by Austin's show tonight. And they'll be subtle. But he's known the guy since he was fourteen and he really doesn't think you're in any trouble."

"Either way, I have a backup plan now. I feel better." And if I just kept saying it, it would definitely come true.

"Good." His brows wrinkled. "Susie—"

"You kissed me."

"I know."

"Guess we should talk about that."

He dropped his head. "Fuck."

I got comfortable in the wingback chair opposite him. Because odds were, his retreat from this situation would be legendary. The backpedaling of the century. Such shame. Much regret. I definitely needed a front row seat for the show.

But then he looked up at me and said, "We're inevitable."

"We're what?"

"You and me, we're inevitable." His hands were held open and his expression was resigned. There was no lie in those blue eyes. Just acceptance. Like he didn't love the idea, but there was no escaping it. Which was actually less of a compliment than you'd think. The big idiot.

"Is this about the divorce certificate?" I asked.

"It's about all of it."

"Please explain."

"I'm attracted to you. You're attracted to me. Obviously, you enjoy my company or we wouldn't keep winding up having these truly baffling conversations. And I honestly can't wait to hear what the hell is going to come out of your mouth next."

I just blinked.

"We've both had multiple opportunities to walk away from this and neither of us have. We're inevitable."

"Yes," I said. "You keep saying that. But what does it mean exactly when those words come out of your mouth?"

"I even tried to put some distance between us by dating other women."

I gasped. "You said that wasn't what you were doing."

"I lied."

"Well, of course. I knew it was bullshit. I didn't realize you did too. That's a level of awareness I don't often ascribe to the male species," I said. "It's just…this is really not the direction I thought you'd take."

"Fighting it hasn't worked. Staying away didn't help either. And neither of us wants to do that long-term anyway." He nodded to himself. "We're just going to have to date."

"Um, date?"

"Yeah."

My laughter was brittle. "You don't mean that."

"Yes, I do."

"No. No, you don't. In fact, I don't think you're quite seeing this situation clearly. Do you really want to break the bro code and have to tell your bestie that you and I are…doing something vaguely romantic and sometimes sexual together?"

He sat back in the chair with his ankle propped on his knee. Totally at ease for some damn reason. "I think we're past worrying about that, don't you?"

"He's not going to like it."

"He'll get used to it."

"And I don't want to be around him. Ever."

"I understand," he said in a gentle tone. One that kind of killed me. "Susie, is this your not-so-subtle way of telling me you don't want to date me?"

"I just don't think it's a good idea."

"Can I ask why not?"

"You'd get tired of me. What comes out of my mouth would cease to be charming. Trust me. Been there, done that. And let's be realistic. We can't even maintain a friendship for more than a few days at a time without something going wrong. With everything that's already happened this year I just… I can't." I picked at the seam of my jeans and avoided eye contact. "I know the mystery divorce certificate makes things weird, but I still maintain that we're better off as we are."

He said nothing for a while. Not meeting his gaze had been the right choice. Because when I did, there was a softness there that was devastating. "He really shook your confidence, didn't he?"

I shrugged.

"You really don't want anything to change?"

"Well. I mean…sex would be nice."

His brows rose. "Sex?"

"Oh, come on. This cannot be that big of a surprise. We've been lusting after each other for weeks. I'd say we're both due a little relief."

"Okay." He scratched at his long stubble. His expression now seemed to be a cross between confusion and consternation. Still handsome as fuck, however. "Let me check I understand what's happening here. I suggested we date and you counteroffered with no-strings sex."

"That's right."

"Because you don't believe a relationship between us stands a chance."

I nodded. "Basically. You think that a relationship between us is inevitable. I think that under the current circumstances a *brief* and *bad* relationship between us is inevitable."

"Can I think about it?"

"Take all the time you need." I watched him with interest. "You're not used to getting turned down, are you, Lars?"

"I'm really not," he agreed.

"Think of it as a growth experience."

"Right." His smile was bemused as he rose from the couch. "We were supposed to be doing TV and ice cream."

"You still want to do that?"

"Absolutely. *Friend*."

★ ★ ★

Patience was not my strong suit, but Lars was worth the agitation. My reasons for not falling headfirst into a romantic relationship with him made sense to me. You didn't just snap out of sorrow and rejection. And emotionally I still felt shaky. Me and my poor delicate feelings. But the Ex had fed my doubts and insecurities every step of the way. The loss of Aunt Susan also remained brutal at times. How shockingly sudden her death had been. Then there was the whole *inevitable* thing. Like the man was giving in when he offered to go out with me. Did he really want to date me or had those papers worn him down?

There was no way to be sure.

Friday evening I attended a period-proof underwear launch downtown for work. It was a huge success and finished at around nine. Lars had invited me for drinks at a bar a few blocks from the Fremont Troll, but I turned him down, thinking the work event was going to go later. However, I was feeling myself since my slick side-part hair had worked out and the bar was sort of on my way home, so why not?

The magnitude of my mistake was soon made clear.

"Susie," said Aaron, standing tall with a pool cue in his hand. His usual sneer was soon replaced with a careful blank expression. No sign of his fiancée. I found it interesting that I'd been deemed acceptable enough to date for a year. But having the audacity not to disappear once he dismissed me was obviously the ultimate insult in his eyes. Men who put women into neat little boxes were the worst. As if we could only play certain parts and had no destiny of our own. Like if we weren't an adjunct to them then we weren't real people.

Mateo and his partner, James, were sitting on stools waiting for their turn at the pool table. They gave me a smile and I raised my hand in greeting. I don't think they had much time for Aaron either. At least, they seemed to be giving him a wide berth.

How could Lars not see this?

Lars set down his beer when he saw me and there was a whole lot of *oh fuck* in his eyes. "Hey. This is a surprise. You look beautiful."

While it was true that my black, wide-leg pants, linen halter top, and ballet flats were on point, this situation sucked. Though seeing Lars did deliver that high. The man wore a pair of jeans like nobody's business. And the way his T-shirt fit was a singular delight. How the cotton stretched just so over his shoulders and embraced his biceps. Any happy, however, was soon drowned out by awkward.

"The work thing finished early and…" I downed a mouthful of the cider I'd grabbed from the bar then set it on a nearby table. "I'm going to go."

Lars picked up the drink and held it out to me. "Stay. At least until you finish this."

"I'm making your boy uncomfortable."

"He'll live." He moved closer so we wouldn't be overheard. "I only invited him after you said you couldn't come. But now you're here and that's good."

I groaned.

"We had a talk. He's not going to give you any shit."

"A talk?" I asked. "When did this happen and what exactly did you say?"

"After my birthday. I told him that I valued your friendship."

"My friendship, huh?"

"Yeah." His smile was amused. "You changed your mind and want me to update the relationship status?"

"Unnecessary. *Friend.*"

"Just checking. Stay. Finish your drink."

"Fine," I said. "I'll finish the drink."

Mateo and James got tired of waiting and headed for the pinball machine. Meanwhile, Aaron's gaze moved between Lars and me with no small amount of suspicion. I gave him my most innocent smile. Of course he scowled. And all the while, Lars stood at my side. I had to admit, it would be interesting to see how things were going to play out. It had occurred to me that Aaron saw niceness toward women as transactional. As he no longer believed I had any value and could give him nothing he wanted, there was no reason for him to bother being polite. Asshole.

"Take your shot," Lars told Aaron.

And he did, turning to me and saying, "How's your job, Susie? Business still afloat?"

"Yes."

"Great." He bent over the table and lined up a shot. "Did you ever get back that big account for the landscaper? You know, the one who disagreed with your fee structure?"

"Nope."

"Pity," he said. A ball went down and he lined up the next. "You look nice. That your take on a business outfit? You always were creative."

"Thanks," I said, somewhat drily.

"And your parents? Have you talked to them lately?"

"Yes."

"Always liked your dad."

I kept my mouth shut.

Lars frowned, but said nothing.

"I was sorry to hear about your aunt Susan," said Aaron, lining up another shot. "We didn't get on, but I know you two were close."

I drank my cider and thought about calming things. Shoe sales and walks by the water and such. Because it wouldn't be

me that blew up this time. Not a chance. I would learn from
the pain and no longer allow him to hurt me. Fuck him. I'd
been mulling over Karen the mystic's words about not repeating mistakes. My Ex knew all my buttons. That was a
given. While I couldn't control his behavior, I could control
how I reacted.

"Your aunt and I were a little like you and my mother."
He smirked. "Can't tell you how relieved she was when I told
her we were through."

Ouch. "I wasn't aware your mom felt that way."

"Oh, yeah." He laughed. Not being subtle at all, apparently.
"Just as well it didn't work out, huh?"

"Just as well," I agreed.

Lars frowned some more, but said nothing.

Aaron missed his next shot and handed the cue to Lars.
Now here was something worth watching. Lars bending over
a pool table. The way the denim molded to his thick thighs
and behind. How the muscles in his arms flexed as he lined
up his shot. I could watch this man do things all day. Or for
at least the next few minutes while I finished this drink.

Lars sank the first ball and moved on to the next.

When Aaron saw my ogling, his expression turned to one
of complete and utter contempt.

I drank some more cider.

"Too bad Hannah couldn't come tonight," he said. "I think
you two would get along."

"Oh?"

Lars's gaze jumped to me to gauge my reaction before re-
turning to the pool table.

"She messes around a lot on social media like you," Aaron
continued. "Has all these fans from her modeling days."

"Okay," I said.

"But she's much happier working as a systems analyst and

using her degree. Already got an offer for a position at a big company here."

"Let me guess...your mother loves her."

"As a matter of fact, she does."

Lars straightened, rising to his full height. "What the fuck, man?"

"We're just making conversation," said Aaron defensively. His smirk disappeared and the nice-guy persona made an appearance. To think I used to fall for this nonsense. Shame on me.

"What's with all this petty bullshit?" asked Lars. "You raised every negative thing you could think of, told her your mother hated her, and then rubbed your fiancée in her face."

"Lars..."

"I told you she was important to me and this is how you treat her?"

Aaron shifted on his feet. "We have history."

"I don't care."

"Look, I'm sorry, okay? She brings out the worst in me."

"She barely opened her mouth, man."

"I've finished my drink," I said, setting the empty glass aside. "I'll see you later, Lars."

"Give me a minute and I'll walk you out."

This time my smile was real. I'd done it. I hadn't reacted to the taunting. Glory was mine. "Thank you, but not necessary."

Aaron grabbed at his arm, "Lars, hang on. Let's talk about..."

I wound my way through the Friday-night crowd. As soon as I stepped outside, I could breathe again. The cool night and the music falling quiet was a relief. What I deserved was a long bath with a good book. I'd done my time and made it through the drink. The rest of this night could still be salvaged. Where there's a will there's a way and all that.

I walked down the street away from the parking lot, then I pulled my phone out of my purse and opened the car ride app.

"Hey," called a deep familiar voice.

"Hey," I called back in surprise.

Lars strode down the sidewalk toward me. I opened my mouth, but couldn't find the words. What did you say to someone who just discovered their best friend was a little bitch?

And how awesome that he'd come after me. That he'd chosen me this time. To be honest, I was sort of stunned.

In the light from the street lamp, the lines of his face seemed starker. A light breeze ruffled his golden Viking mane and all the while he strode toward me, big and solid and strong. Like I could crash up against him as much as I liked. He made me want to write bad poetry. That was the truth.

I was still searching for something to say when he walked straight up to me and kissed me stupid. This was nothing like last time. His tongue slipped into my mouth and stroked against mine. There was no easing in. No messing around. The man was passion unleashed. His hand slid beneath my hair to grab the back of my neck and hold me in place as his mouth claimed mine. And he had skills. It was hot and wet and oh so good. All lips and tongue and teeth. His other hand slid around my waist to the small of my back, pulling me against him. I clutched at his shirt as my head spun in dizzy circles. The sounds of need he made deep in his throat... I'd never heard the like. Every inch of my body was wide-awake and wanting.

We startled apart at the sound of the car horn beside us. How rude.

"My, um, my ride is here," I said, stating the obvious. Since when was standing, breathing, and thinking at the same time such a struggle?

In an apparently similar state, he just stared at my lips.

"Any chance you've made up your mind about us having sex?"

He paused. "Not yet."

"Okay."

Just over his shoulder, I could see Aaron standing outside the bar watching us. He was not happy.

"C'mon," said Lars.

He ushered me to the car and opened the door for me. As soon as I was settled safely inside, he nodded and closed the door. Then he took a step back and waited, watching me. The car pulled away from the curb and we drove off. I did not turn around and stare at him until he was out of sight. I was not quite that desperate and all up in my feelings. Not yet, at least. But I was dangerously close to getting there.

Ten

Lars: Working all of this weekend on a rush job. Catch up with you next week.

Me: Ok.

Lars: I'm not ignoring you.

Me: Ok.

Lars: Are you sure you're ok?

Me: Yes. Positive.

Lars: Last night was unexpected.

Me: Was it really?

Me: Do you regret it?

Lars: No.

Me: I'm glad.

With the divorce certificate in hand, I stood outside the legal offices of Johnson and Cavanagh on Monday afternoon. They were the lawyers mentioned on the decree. Though on the document they were Johnson, Cavanagh, and Yeoh. It was just your regular glass-and-concrete commercial building. Nothing special. But at the same time, it was all so very bizarre. Lars and I hadn't even slept together. However, years from now, this was where I'd apparently come to end our marriage. I checked the address on the certificate for the hundredth time. Still the same.

The internet confirmed the place existed, but I needed to see it for myself. And there it was. As with everything to do with the document, there were no answers, just more questions. I wondered what my frame of mind would be when I walked through those doors in ten years' time. How broken would I be, heart and soul?

Insert sigh here.

I hadn't told Lars about my plans. This was something I wanted to do on my own. Every morning I stared at the certificate. Made sure it still existed and remained this cryptic weird ass mystery. That I would, one day, feel so much for someone that it would overcome my abhorrence of marriage. And that my hopes and dreams would be rewarded in the worst damn way. Love sucked.

It was helpful of fate to put a hipster bar next door to the legal offices. No doubt, many sought solace there and I decided to do the same. The inside of the place was cool with a neon sign saying Ballard. Just in case you got so drunk you forgot where you were. The lunch rush was over when I took a seat at the bar next to a woman in a pink blouse, and ordered the bread with goat's cheese and honey. Along with a glass of sauvignon blanc, for medicinal reasons.

It was hard to think of the divorce certificate without feeling down. In the beginning it had been a mystery. Something sort of thrilling. But now...were we truly doomed before we even began?

"You look so sad," said the girl behind the bar when she passed me the glass of wine. She had a shaved head and the best eyebrows I'd ever seen. "Next drink is on the house."

"Thank you." I smiled and folded up the certificate. "That's kind. But I'm okay."

"Divorce, huh?"

I just winced.

The woman beside me was eating a wedge salad. She dabbed her lips with a napkin. "Better things ahead."

"Right. Yes."

"Any regrets?" asked the bartender with a suddenly serious gaze.

Apparently I was in the mood to pour my heart out to strangers because I said, "My feelings for him are...complicated."

This was quickly turning into one of those random personal conversations with strangers that tended to happen in bars. They usually took place in the bathroom late at night under the influence of alcohol, but whatever. Such conversations were enduring proof of the sisterhood.

"Charlotte here is a divorce lawyer," said the bartender, nodding at the woman in pink.

"Oh," I said. "Do you work in those offices next door?"

Charlotte smiled. "That's right."

"You must get sick of talking about this sort of thing."

She gave an elegant shrug.

To think, I could be sitting next to my future legal representation. I didn't know what the rules of time travel were, but the certificate didn't disappear or anything due to Charlotte and the document being in the same place. Guess that was as good a sign as any that I wasn't breaking the space-time continuum.

The bartender leaned in and rested her elbows on the bar. "When I need relationship advice, I go to Charlotte. She's seen it all. Knows exactly how to get to the heart of any problem. And she's not bitter."

"I wouldn't have thought it was a job you could do without becoming cynical," I said.

Charlotte shrugged. "I'm a romantic. But I'm also a realist."

"How does that work?"

"She has a healthy-relationship list," inserted the bartender.

"I do indeed," confirmed the lawyer.

"Can I hear it?" I asked.

"Sure." Charlotte took another bite of her salad, chewed, and swallowed. "You cannot change them. Assume anything you don't like is here to stay. The same goes for their friends and family." She ticked off the items one by one on her fingers. And her French manicure was immaculate.

"Ugh."

"That's not a good sign," she said. "But I'll continue. They might be hot stuff now, but do you have other things in common to help sustain the relationship? Sex and intimacy matter, but it's only one part of the whole. How good are you at communicating with one another?"

"I think we're okay. We're getting better at least."

"Do you feel comfortable discussing potentially toxic situations or behaviors with them before they escalate?" she asked. "Can you problem solve together?"

"Sort of. Sometimes."

"Are you both willing to work on the relationship? Are they putting an effort in that is at least equal to yours?"

"Good question. I'm going to have to think about it."

"Then you move on to having the unsexy discussions about finances and children—if you're going to have them and how you plan to raise them." She was running out of fingers at this point. "If you do get remarried, you're going to need insurance. Have a prenup, an escape plan, and know how marriage affects you legally. Then be prepared to choose each other and keep choosing each other. Every day, week, month, and year for the rest of your life. It's just that simple and that hard."

"Wow," I said. "You've really thought all of this through."

"I see a lot of sad and angry people." She lifted her cup of water and tapped it against my glass of wine. "Best of luck to you."

"Thank you," I said. "Can I show you something quickly?"

"You need to make an appointment if you're after my professional opinion."

I flattened the certificate out on the bar. "Just take a look. Please."

With a frown, she cast her eyes over it. "Is this a joke?"

"You're not the first person that's asked me that. But no, it's not. This was found recently during renovations on my house. It was in the cavity of a wall."

"Oh, really." She wrinkled her nose. "You seriously expect me to believe that?"

"As weird as it is, it's the truth. I swear."

"How much did Colin pay you?"

"I don't know anyone called Colin."

She laughed. "Him and his jokes. They're going to get him in trouble one of these days. The legalities of making something like this... He certainly did a good job. If it wasn't for the date and so on, I'd have thought it was real."

"So you believed it was—"

"You can tell my brother that I'm delighted he's so certain I'll make partner in the next ten years."

"Hold on," I said. "Are you...? You're Charlotte Yeoh? As in, Johnson, Cavanagh, and Yeoh?"

"Got it in one." She shook her head with a smile and hopped down off her barstool. "Have a nice day."

Lars was sitting on the front steps with the cat butting her head against his leg when I got home. He was in jeans, a black tee, and sneakers. No hint of the dust and dirt on him from a day's work. And it felt right, finding him there. A self-help book I'd been reading talked about how it's the human condition to struggle for something better. To ignore the moment and want more. This right here, however, was great. My day went from a two to a ten at the sight of him. I don't know what we were, exactly. But I refused to believe we were doomed. Our friendship at least would persevere. As long as we didn't get carried away and take it too far.

"I didn't know you were waiting," I said, my heart beating harder than it should.

"Figured you'd turn up sooner or later."

I sat down beside him. It was midafternoon and the street was quiet. The air was thick with the promise of dark clouds gathering overhead. Soon it would storm. But not just yet.

"How long have you been here?" I asked.

"An hour or so."

"Why didn't you text me? I would have hurried."

He scratched at his stubble. "Honestly...wasn't sure what I wanted to say."

"How did the job go?" I asked when he said no more.

"It was fine. Overtime is always useful," he said. "How was your weekend?"

"I joined an edible garden tour on Saturday and worked most of yesterday. Donated some time to helping a local climate change action group with their online presence." I smoothed the skirt of my black cotton fit and flare dress over my thighs. Not anxious, just nervous. Because there was totally a difference. "Today I went on a walk through the locks and botanical gardens. Took some selfies and made a couple of videos."

"I saw."

The man could stalk me on social media all he liked. It made me smile. Though my happiness didn't last for long, as I recalled what I did next. "Then I walked a few blocks east to the legal offices mentioned on the divorce certificate."

"Really?" His brows descended. "How was that?"

"The place definitely exists. Though it's currently just Johnson and Cavanagh. I needed to see it for myself, but... I don't know. Mostly, it just made me feel sad."

"Did you show them the certificate?"

"Yes. Turns out the lawyer I met was Charlotte Yeoh. The third name in the law office's title on our mystery divorce certificate. She thought I was pranking her. But she did say that if it wasn't for the date and the name change, she'd have thought it was real."

His brows drew together.

"Make of that what you will."

For a long moment he said nothing. "I would have gone with you if you'd told me."

"Thanks, but I wasn't sure how I felt about it. Thought it was best I went on my own."

"Okay," he said. "Guess if a professional authenticator couldn't tell if it was a forgery then a lawyer probably wouldn't say anything differently."

"I guess so. Do you really still think someone's playing a trick on us?"

He sighed. "Be rational. What else could it be?"

"But neither of the official people I showed it to could explain it."

"There's got to be another answer. I refuse to believe in magical documents appearing from the future."

I just shrugged.

"Hear anything from Austin?"

"He called yesterday. Said his friend at the guitar shop gave it a clean and a service and it was all good. Thank God." My fingers toyed with the hem of my skirt. "There's a small chance I don't always react well to stressful situations. Thank you for talking me down. And for asking Tore to help."

"You're fine," he said. "Did Austin ask you out again?"

"Yes. I said no."

Lars said nothing. He rested his elbows on his thighs, his head turned to watch me. But a careful distance remained between us. The cat used it to saunter back and forth, rubbing herself against his body.

"Look at her, she's all over you," I said, amused. "Acting like she's been treated badly. I gave her steak cut up into tiny bite-size pieces yesterday. There is nothing wrong with this feline's life. Even the vet said she's in excellent health considering."

He stretched out his fingers and gave her a scratch. "When are you going to name her?"

"If I pick something she'll probably just ignore me."

"You want me to do it?"

"Go for it," I said.

"Hmm. That's a big responsibility."

"I believe in you."

He picked up the cat and held her in front of his face. Of course the little monster started purring real loud. "I'm going to name you Kat with a K. Kat the cat. It's in honor of the girl who lived across the street when I was a kid. She was a handful. Her name was Kate, but she'd only ever answer to Kat. Drove her mom wild."

"Kat with a *K*. That's ridiculous, but I'll allow it. Mind you, I'll sound like an idiot calling for her. The whole neighborhood will mock me."

"I'm sorry about Friday night at the bar," he said, tone sober. "Guess I didn't really understand before. I've known him a long time and he's only ever been a good friend to me."

"I know."

"I'm sorry I asked you to stay in a situation where you were the target of that bullshit. It won't happen again."

"Let's talk about something else." Thunder echoed in the distance and the first drops of rain fell. "Would you like to come in?"

"Sure."

As soon as the front door opened, Kat darted inside.

"What I'd like is to take you out to dinner," he said, wiping the soles of his shoes on the mat.

"Or I could cook something and we could hang out here," I counteroffered.

"Would that feel like less of a date to you?"

"Yes."

He laughed and followed me into the kitchen. "At least it's not just me you don't want to date," he said. "That does actually make me feel better."

"I'm here with you, aren't I?" I opened the fridge door and said, "Have you considered that maybe your friendship is so important to me that I don't want to risk it by dating?"

"But you'll risk it with sex?"

"I'm only mortal, Lars. I have needs. And I know you said

to be rational, but what if the divorce certificate is in fact the great beyond's way of saying not to push things between us?"

He just sighed.

"Now, we've got Seattle Strong Cold Brew or Reuben's Super Crush Hazy IPA. What are you in the mood for? Coffee or beer?"

Instead of answering, he stared at me. There was neither a smile nor a frown on his face. Just this quiet kind of thoughtfulness.

"Lars?"

"Yeah?"

"What are you thinking about?"

He neither blinked nor looked away. "I know what I want to say to you now."

"Okay." I closed the fridge door and tried not to be nervous. Which didn't work since I was soon tugging on my ponytail. "I'm listening."

"If you're using anyone for sex, it's going to be me."

It took me a moment to find my voice. "Huh."

Nothing from him.

"There's, um, a lot to unpack there," I said. "And we will, I just feel like right now we need to focus on more-immediate things."

"Such as?"

I stepped closer. The ever-careful distance between us served nothing at all. My hands skimmed up his arms and over his shoulders, meeting at last behind his neck. Then I rose up on tippy-toes and pressed my mouth to his. A sweet kiss. A question needing an answer. And immediately his mouth opened and he gave. Hands grabbed my hips, holding me against his solid body. I'd have climbed the man if I could. My desire to be as close to him as possible was absolute. What he did to me was more than evidenced by the state of my panties. And the thrill of feeling him harden against my stomach as we devoured each other. I'd never felt anything like it.

Then he performed the ultimate swoon move. Hoisting me up with both hands beneath my ass, the man lifted me right off the floor. I wrapped my legs around him tight, my breasts smooshed against his chest. Our faces were so close together. The tip of his nose just a hairsbreadth from mine. Being plastered all up against him with his hands on my ass was most definitely my natural habitat. Outside the storm raged, thunder crashing while the wind howled.

When we broke apart, my heart was hammering, my breath coming fast. I'd much rather we were making out, but that thing he'd said needed addressing. "Hey," I whispered, taking a breath. "I can go without sex, Lars. That's not what this is about."

A line appeared between his brows, but he said nothing. The man sure could say a lot with silence.

"If it was just sex I wanted, I could have gotten it from Austin, or just about anywhere."

He actually growled, his chest rumbling against me. Holy shit.

Staring into his eyes, I smiled. "It's about you."

"Is that so?"

"Yes."

He nodded contemplatively and gave me a long look. "Okay, Susie."

"Okay?"

"Yeah."

I've never been accused of being deep. My talents consisted of having great style and saying weird shit. If I'd hurt him, however, then I had to make it better. It was easy to mistake Lars as a bad-tempered beast. He frowned like it was his life calling. But there was so much more to the man.

"What does that mean?" I asked. *"Okay?"*

In answer, he groped at my ass.

"We also need to address your use of the word *using*. Because if the lusting isn't mutual—"

He gave me a half smile and kissed me. Guess that answered that.

Everything was perfect with his arms around me and his tongue in my mouth. My hands were in his hair and my legs around him tight. The ridge of his hard-on was right there and grinding against him was so good. Like a fever building. And we were moving. He brushed against the wall heading out of the kitchen, bumped into the entryway between the dining and living rooms, and kicked open my bedroom door. That's when my back met the mattress.

How he gazed down at me with such lust in his eyes. To be the single point of focus of all that was breathtaking. His fingers traced a path over the curve of my hip and down the length of my thigh. He didn't stop until he reached my sneaker, which he unlaced and tossed into the corner. As soon as that was done, he started in on the other. If my feet were sweaty and smelly I would die. But Lars had other things on his mind. Because he stuck his hands up my skirt and robbed me of my underwear in one smooth move. And I do mean robbed. He dangled my black cotton thong from a finger before slipping it into his back pocket.

"I'm not going to see that again, am I?"

"How do I get you out of that dress?" he asked in a voice as rough as the weather.

"There's a zip down the side that loosens the bodice and then you lift the skirt and sort of maneuver the whole thing up over my head."

He grunted. "Too complicated."

"I'm appalled that a man of your age and experience would be defeated by a frock."

But Lars had no time for my nonsense. He was far too busy burying his head beneath my skirt. With his hands on my thighs, holding them open, he got straight to business. Dragging the flat of his tongue up through my folds and finishing with a flourish. Each and every nerve in my clitoris was wide the fuck awake.

"Oh, God," I groaned.

The newly crowned deity under my dress didn't say a word. He just continued on with his ministrations. Sucking on my labia, first the left and then the right. Then he dragged his tongue through me again, this time with a zigzag motion that made my toes curl. Next his thumbs held me open as he French kissed my sex. All the while there was the occasional slight scratch of his stubble against the sensitive skin of my inner thighs turning me into gooseflesh. He went down on me with the same skill and single-mindedness that he did everything else. And it was wonderful.

I slapped a hand over my mouth to try and keep quiet. To let the man concentrate. But it was no use. He was just too talented. All of my blood rushed right to my pussy and the knot of tension between my hips pulled tighter. Every muscle in my legs and low in my stomach drew taut. When he settled into sucking on my clit, flicking his tongue over it back and forth, it was all over. My whole body tingled and my mind blanked. The orgasm shook the soul right of me. I gave a startled shriek and held on to the sheets for dear life. My thighs trembled and my pussy quaked. And I was high above the clouds, my body flooded with all of the good chemicals. All of my cares and worries fell away.

Meanwhile, Lars stood and grabbed the bottle of water off the bedside table. His jaw was set. His cock straining the front of his jeans. As he grabbed the back of his shirt and pulled it off over his head, it occurred to me that there was every chance I'd taken on more than I could handle.

My laughter was weak. "Sex noises, huh?"

"I made you scream. I'm good with that."

"Would we call it a scream, exactly?"

"Yes," he said without hesitation.

"O-okay." My head...it wouldn't stop spinning. "You went down on me without having to be asked."

He cocked his head. "That's unusual?"

"Among the men I've dated? Yes."

"Idiots."

He toed off his shoes and tore off his socks. Dragged down his zipper and pushed down his pants. Until all he was wearing was a pair of dark gray boxer briefs. Sweet baby Jesus, they outlined everything. Then they were gone too. More golden skin and muscles than I'd ever seen. And his dick was long, thick, and potent as all hell. I'd looked at him before. But this time I got to touch. And the warm hug of it all was the realization that he wasn't going to change his mind. That he'd chosen me and we were really going to do this. It made me strangely humble. Grateful, even.

"Oh no. I don't have any condoms," I said. "I was going to buy some but then I didn't because it might jinx us."

From the pocket of his jeans he withdrew a condom and rolled it on. Pausing to give his dick a firm squeeze once it was sheathed. All of this was performed with expert precision. Making me wonder if there was anything he did badly. Thank goodness the man came prepared with prophylactics. Never have I felt such relief.

My dress was hiked up around my hips and he glared at the thing as if it were his nemesis. The neckline in particular. His teeth sunk into his bottom lip as he stared at my covered breasts, as if he were a child being denied Christmas. I couldn't do it. Even if it was his own damn fault for being impatient.

"Wait," I said, sitting up and struggling with the zip. "It'll only take me a minute."

I wriggled and twisted while he grabbed the hem and carefully tugged. I was free. Then, in a practiced move, he unhooked my bra and slid the straps down my arms. The man knew his way around a woman. His eyes widened appreciatively at the sight of my breasts. He took their weight in his hands, thumbs stroking over my skin.

"Better?" I asked, pulling my hair tie free.

He nodded, then said, "Are you okay?"

"Yes."

He cradled the back of my head with his hand, feeding me hot wet kisses. It was just like a drug going straight to my head. The slide of his tongue and bite of his teeth. And all the while, he eased onto the bed and climbed on top of me. The warmth and weight of him was exquisite. His cock slid against my sex and oh yeah. That was nice. Shivers straight up my spine. His hand shifted from my breast to my butt and back again. Like he couldn't quite decide. Nice that my abundance of tits and ass seemed to please him.

I buried my face in the side of his neck. The feel of his smooth skin and the faint scent of sweat. Salt and the woodsy cologne thing and him. Heavenly. As for Lars, he took his weight on one arm while grabbing a breast with his free hand. Guess we were both fascinated with each other. He gasped when I nibbled on his earlobe and my breath caught when he pinched my nipple. For every action came a perfect reaction. And all the while the heavy width of his cock pressed against me. Any small movement was ecstasy making my empty pussy clench.

The man was torturing us both.

When his mouth found my nipple, my hips shifted against the mattress. He sucked and licked and enjoyed himself thoroughly. I didn't mind it either. Then he kissed his way up to my jaw. His gaze intensified as he notched the blunt crown of his cock against me. He pushed in slowly. Not stopping until there was no room left. Until he had everything. And all the while he watched me. I had to be a glazed-eyed slack-jawed mess. However, there was nothing but desire and determination on his face.

The kiss he gave me was gentle. Like a benediction. A thank-you for letting him into my body. Which was quite nice and polite. Though it didn't stay that way for long. Tender turned into hunger in no time. My hands pawed at his shoulders and one of his slid into my hair. And the grip he took on those strands was firm. When I didn't complain, he pulled just a little, lighting me up from head to toe. Then he pulled harder. The grin on his face contained an edge of mean and damn that was hot.

At long last, he moved, drawing his hard length out of me. Then thrusting back in with a snap of the hips. Pulling out slow and pushing back in fast. That was how he did it. His cock dragging over the sweet spots inside of me. His pelvis angled to grind against my clit. When he threw in a swivel of his hips I moaned wantonly. He knew exactly how to use that big strong body of his. Because each move he made was designed and perfected to bring me pleasure. His past lovers and girlfriends deserved thank-you notes. And cupcakes, maybe?

His control fell away slowly and then all at once. It was thrilling to see. Our mouths melded as our bodies slickened with sweat. His careful pace deteriorated until it was him fucking me into the mattress. My nails left lines across his back. His teeth left a bruise on my neck. We had to stop kissing/biting before someone broke a tooth. The storm raged outside, but I had lightning in my veins like my body was on fire. Thunder was the sound of blood beating behind my ears.

The heat radiating off his body and the heady scent of sex filled the room. I clutched and clawed at him while he kept my hair in a tight fist. All the while, he hammered that great cock into me. When he hit the perfect place inside of me, my back arched off the bed. But he didn't stop. Hell no. He hadn't lost his finesse at all. Because he kept right at me until I was whining his name. The pressure inside me was coiling higher and tighter as a tsunami broke over me. Pleasure and pain. I'd never come so hard in my life. A couple of tears streamed down my cheek, the release was so damn intense.

Lars swore and bucked against me. Burying his face in my neck as he came too. The way his cock throbbed inside of me and the harsh panting against my neck seemed like the only things that were real. Like he was my tether. Like without his body to weigh me down, I might float away. We both groaned when he eased his cock out of me. Then he fell onto the bed at my side.

It took a while for anyone to speak. And then of course it was me. "Was it okay for you?"

He opened one eyelid, stared at me, and said nothing.

"I'm not sure what to do with that," I said.

A small smile curled his lips. Phew.

I rolled onto my side to face him. The masculine beauty of the man. His hair should always be disheveled by my hands. And the peace in his expression. The smoothness of his brow and how his gaze had softened…maybe my pussy was magic after all. My heart beat hard and heavy; the pulse echoed between my legs. Again. Already. "How many condoms did you bring with you?"

"I only carry one around, sorry."

To be charmed that he'd had no expectations coming here

or annoyed that he hadn't planned ahead? It was a tough call.
What was for certain was that any hidden hopes I had regarding Lars and I being able to fuck this fascination out of our
system were a bust. Like having sex with him once would resolve any and all feelings and we could just be friends. Nope.
Nada. Not a chance.

Then he reached out and caught a tear off my cheek.
"What's wrong?"

"Nothing. It was just…a lot of pent-up sexual energy, I
guess."

He nodded.

"Okay," I said, moving right along. "Here's the plan. We
hit up the pharmacy for prophylactics then the Korean place
for dinner. I'll get the rib eye, you get the fish, and we'll
swap halfway through. We can share the kimchi fries. What
do you say?"

He didn't say anything.

Which was when it hit me. "Unless you have plans, of
course. There might be somewhere you need to be or something."

"Susie," he said. "Dinner and bed sounds good."

The smile owned my face. "Great."

Eleven

"I'm out of my mind."

"No," I said. "You're not."

Cleo stood in the middle of the living room of her condo with boxes at her feet. "I met him less than a month ago and now he's moving in. I've already been through one divorce. What am I doing?"

"You're the smartest person I know. If you're moving him in with you then it's for a damn good reason," I said. "But if you tell me you've changed your mind, or that you have doubts you want to act on, I'll help you haul all of his shit straight back out of here."

She pressed a hand to her heart. "Love at first sight is the worst. I never even used to believe it existed. Now look at me acting the fool!"

"You really love him, huh?"

"Yes, and it's terrifying. I don't want to get hurt again."

That fear I could understand all too well. I basically had

cuddle time with it each and every night. Weaknesses were the worst.

Tore walked in carrying another box followed by Lars. It had been six days since the night of sexing. He'd been working more overtime and I'd been busy too. Because we were grown adults with our own lives. My bed, however, had been an especially sad and lonely place this week. It turned out that if you renounced your celibacy and got some good dick it was hard to wait for more. Hard. Heh.

They added their boxes to the humongous pile. Since when did dudes own so much stuff? With all his tennis shoes and graphic novels and smoking pipes collection, we'd been lugging Tore's belongings in here for hours. Tore set down the box and dusted off his hands. "That's the last of it. Now to unpack."

Cleo attempted a smile. And failed.

"Babe," he said, putting his arms around her. "Hey."

"It's okay. Just having a moment."

"Have as many moments as you like."

She cupped his face and kissed him soundly. "I love you."

"I love you too."

Lars and I exchanged glances. As you do when you're caught in a personal moment. One that's not of your own making.

"The last man I lived with was my ex-husband and we all know how that worked out. I haven't even met your parents, Tore," said Cleo. "We're doing it all out of order."

"You can meet them as soon as they get back from visiting my sister and her family in San Diego. Come with me to pick them up from the airport next weekend if you like."

"Are we doing the right thing?" asked Cleo.

Tore shrugged. "We want to be together, don't we?"

"But it's all happening so fast."

"Why don't we put all these boxes aside for now and just see how things go?" he suggested. "Take it in baby steps."

"I do want you here. I'm just…"

"It's okay."

"I don't want this to go wrong."

"Then it won't," said Tore. "We'll be careful and work things out together."

She gave him a much more believable smile. "That sounds good. We could try what Susie's been doing over at her place and unpack one box a day. Less overwhelming that way."

I smiled. "That's true."

Tore turned to his brother. "Lars, let's stack them against the wall. I'll sort out what I need later."

Cleo pushed her shoulders back. "I'll get us some drinks."

As for me, I sat my weary ass on the couch. All the better to watch Lars. He tossed his head to flick back his ridiculously photogenic hair and oh man. My hormones were at his mercy. That was the truth of the matter.

"What was that?" asked Tore. Though *accused* would be closer.

Cleo wandered out of the kitchen with cans of cider. "What was what?"

This time he even went so far as to point at me. "The way Susie was just staring at Lars."

"Was I looking at him like he's a good friend that I appreciate very much?" I asked, downing some of my drink.

"No. You were not."

"Thank you," said Lars, accepting his drink from Cleo. He seemed calm, considering Tore's questioning. "Leave her be, man."

Tore narrowed his gaze on us. One at a time.

"Honey," said Cleo, passing her beloved his drink. "Don't worry about it."

"What is this *it* you speak of?" Tore stood with a hand on

his hip. Guess he wasn't going to leave it be. Dammit. "That's what I need to know."

Lars crossed his arms. "You're imagining things."

"Thou doth protest too much, brother."

Lars shook his head and sat in an armchair. "At least I don't sound like an idiot."

"You two have always been dubious. There's always been something there. But that expression on Susie's face just now? All dreamy and carnal?"

"I was, um, thinking about the laundry I have to do when I get home," I said. "It's been piling up all week. It's going to be really good to get it done. Satisfying, you know?"

"Liar. Unless all that talk about getting your laundry done was coded dirty talk. In which case you're still a liar, but well played."

I laughed. "Tore, honestly, I don't know what you're talking about."

"An Oscar-worthy performance," Tore mumbled. "I'll give her that."

Cleo snorted. "Oh, please," she said. "It was obvious the minute you showed up here. Did you really think you were going to be able to keep it a secret?"

My face was on fire. The best option was to shut up. And I would, right after I stated for the record, "We're not dating. This is all very early days and the situation is complicated and I'd rather not go into it and... I'm going to stop talking now."

Tore clicked his tongue. "Well, well, well."

Meanwhile, Lars just sat there, placid as can be. He obviously didn't care what they knew. Nor did he come to my rescue when I started to blather. Jerk.

"Are you telling me that Lars doesn't have an actual official girlfriend?" asked his brother in disbelief.

Cleo cocked her head. "That's a big deal?"

"Hell yeah," said Tore. "He's basically been in one relationship after another since first discovering catch-and-kiss in the playground. It's right up there on his list. Decent job. Check. Working toward owning own business. Check. Be a good son. Check. Spend quality time with friends. Check. Have a girlfriend. Check."

Lars took another swig of his drink. He didn't seem as happy now.

Tore didn't seem to care. "Those are just the boxes to be checked for now. Others will appear as he nears forty. He and I will have established our house-flipping business. This will be followed by him acquiring a wife. Someone high-achieving, yet grounded. The type who would never dream of wearing white after Labor Day. Their offspring will follow shortly thereafter."

Lars started grinding his teeth.

"Sounds organized," said Cleo.

"You mean anal," corrected Tore.

Cleo frowned. "This plan definitely doesn't allow for the existence of the mysterious divorce certificate. Which makes sense. I mean, it can't be real. Susie has sworn never to get married. It's the one thing she never changes her mind about. Her parents ruined her for life on that front. Get her anywhere near a white dress and she makes the sign of the cross. And none of your brother's planning sounds the least bit like her either. She's much more of a fly-by-the-seat-of-her-pants kind of girl."

It was like Lars and I weren't even there. Holy shit.

"I heard about the antimarriage stance," said Tore. "I just hope these two messing around doesn't make things awkward for us in the future."

"I'm so glad we took time out of our busy weekends to help your brother and my friend," I mumbled.

Lars glowered.

"What about you?" asked Cleo. "Do you have a list?"

Tore shook his head. "Not anymore. I am at your disposal."

"Good answer." She bit back a smile. "I wonder if that's an older-child trait, being so structured. Only children like me are kind of all over the place."

"Youngest are the best," said Tore. "Creative, problem solving, we've got it all. Right, Susie?"

"Oh, yeah." Grateful for the change of subject, I turned to Lars and asked, "How are you going to be, living on your own?"

Tore smiled. "You're worried about my thirty-five-year-old big brother being by his lonesome?"

"Between you and me," said Lars. "I'm kind of looking forward to it. Especially after the last few minutes."

I nodded. "Fair enough."

"Are you kidding?" asked Tore. "Late-night beer and nachos after a long day? And I watched *Mythbusters* all the way through with you. They made a ridiculous number of seasons of that show. How about having a jogging partner? Huh? That was handy. Not to mention, if it weren't for me, none of your socks would match. I'm a rock star at sorting laundry."

"That's what you bring to the relationship, huh?" Cleo grinned. "Good to know."

"Along with my baked salmon. Babe, you've never tasted better."

"You only make one dish?" I asked.

Tore slung an arm around Cleo's shoulders and fit her against his side. "When you make it as well as I do, you don't need another."

"He made it so well most of the ladies never returned for another," said Lars with smile.

Tore's brows descended. "That's not true."

"Isn't it?"

"Are you staying in the condo?" I asked, before the siblings could start brawling.

Lars turned back to me. "Actually we had a good offer on it so we're selling. Contract goes through in two weeks. The owners next door want to expand."

"It's one of the reasons I asked Tore to move in." Cleo slipped her arms around his waist. They fit together perfectly. "He's been here every night anyway."

"She can't get rid of me," said Tore.

The way they gazed at each other—I'd never had anything like that. Such devotion. A veritable outpouring of love and affection. There was a solid chance I hadn't put enough thought into previous relationships. You meet a guy and sparks fly, he looks nice and he seems okay, so you give it a go. It seemed straightforward. And yet this simple process had bitten me on the ass more times than I cared to admit. There had to be a sweet spot between wearing your heart on your sleeve and encasing said organ in steel. Surely.

"Time for us to go," said Lars, getting to his feet.

Cleo and Tore had started making out and they showed no signs of stopping.

I set my drink aside and made for the door, rubbing my lower back with the heel of my hand. "This was fun. Let's not do it again anytime soon."

Lars followed. "I told you to leave the heavier stuff for me."

"I was more referring to the part where they dissected us in front of us."

He just grunted.

Tore waved a hand in our general direction. Cleo broke away from his mouth with a chuckle. It did my heart good to see her so happy. Before she could wish us adieu or whatever, Tore was kissing her again. New couples. What can you do?

Lars shut the door behind us. He followed me down the stairs. No point waiting for the elevator, though my calf muscles disagreed. A long hot bath with a good book was what I needed. Of course, it tended to be the best answer eleven times out of ten.

"Are we still on for tonight?" I asked.

He nodded.

"What do you feel like doing?"

"Whatever you want," he said, casting a look back over his shoulder. Not that there was anything to see.

"Why don't I make you dinner?"

"Okay. What can I bring?"

"A bottle of red would be great," I said. "Like a cabernet. Does seven o'clock work?"

"Sure." He took a step closer, gaze filling with warmth. "We can eat first and then see what mood we're in, sound good?"

"Very good."

For a moment, he just stared at me. "You are very unexpected, Susie."

"I thought I was inevitable."

"That too. And one day, you're going to agree to go on a date with me."

My smile disappeared. "Lars, you do know me not wanting to date isn't an indictment of you, right? I mean, have you seen yourself? And don't get me wrong. I think you're clever and capable along with being handsome. I'm just not ready."

"It's not me, it's you?"

"Yes."

He looked at me for a moment then reached past and opened the front door to the building. "I honestly didn't mean to pressure you. Let's talk about something else."

"All right. When was the last time you lived on your own?" I asked.

"Guess it's been four or five years."

"That's a while. It'll be an adjustment. Having the space to yourself can be great. But not having anyone to talk to can get a little lonely."

"I'll be fine, Susie." He gave me a half smile. It wasn't very convincing. "I'm thinking of buying a houseboat at the marina. Someone I know through work is moving to Colorado and needs to sell."

I raised a hand to shield my face from the afternoon sun. "A houseboat? Cool."

"Yeah." But he still didn't seem exactly happy. He gripped the back of his neck. "It's good that Tore and Cleo are moving in together. I hope it works out for them."

I just smiled and waited. And it worked.

"You're right, I'll miss my brother, but...life goes on."

"This is true. And it's not like he'll be far away."

"Exactly."

"You'll be fine."

"Yes," he said. "I will be fine. Can we stop talking about feelings now?"

"Yes." I grinned. "Thank you for sharing, Lars."

By ten o'clock, I was pacing in my black knee-length sleeveless body con dress. My wedges made a satisfying sound against the wood, a nice, angry smacking noise that soothed my soul. Because there'd been no sign of the man. No call, no text. I tried phoning and got his voice mail. I did not leave a message. My emotions had run the gamut from fury to fear and back again. Where the hell was he?

I'd snuffed out the candles when they started to burn down and the risotto I'd made for dinner had probably dried out. I hope he had a good excuse. No. He would have. Lars wasn't the type to just let me down. Though it was hard to convince myself of that after three hours of waiting and thirty years' worth of bad experiences. This was exactly why I didn't want to date. Hurt made you take a step back from the world for your own protection. But there was nil distance between me and my burgeoning feelings for this man now. Dammit.

Maybe he changed his mind about our friends-with-benefits situation. Maybe he had car trouble. And his cell broke so of course he couldn't call. Oh, no. Maybe he was sick. Though he'd been the picture of good health today. Whatever. I would trust in our friendship. There was bound to be a perfectly rational explanation. Fingers crossed.

The woman I'd like to be would have kicked off her heels, poured herself a glass of wine, and settled down in front of a good movie. Bid adieu to anxiety and made the night enjoyable all on her own. She didn't need no man. She didn't need anyone. That girl could slay dragons (emotional and otherwise) all on her own. Meanwhile, I kept pacing.

Kat bravely hid under the couch twitching her tail. All of my clomping back and forth did not please her.

My phone buzzed in my hand and I jumped. "Hello?"

"Susie," Cleo said. "Don't freak, but there's been an accident."

The emergency ward on Saturday night was bedlam. Machines beeping, people talking too loudly, a drunkard yelling, and people moaning in pain. And beneath it all was the sound of his voice behind a curtained-off bed in the corner. Thank God. Perhaps now my heart could calm the fuck down. It had been on the edge of either an attack or a break for the past half hour. The drive from home had been one of the longest of my life. My hands had gripped the wheel so tight my fingers started cramping.

The overwhelming scent of disinfectant didn't help. Last time I'd been in one of these places I'd been identifying Aunt Susan's body. An experience both horrible and horrifying. But Lars wasn't going to die. There would be no sudden second phone call to tell me he'd taken a turn for the worse. Everything was fine. Cleo had said she and Tore could handle it, but I needed to see him. To know that he was okay. And him asking for me just reinforced my need to be there.

"Hey," Cleo greeted me behind the curtain with a wan smile. "Breathe."

"I'm breathing." Though hyperventilating would be a better description. "How is he?"

"Not bad considering he got hit by a car."

On the bed, a shirtless Lars lay among the white sheets. Jeans covered his bottom half. He looked paler than normal. There was a brace around his neck, a cast on his left wrist, a freshly stitched cut a couple of inches long on his cheek, and bruises and grazes everywhere. The dark marks on his torso were horrific. Holy shit.

"This is the princess I was telling you about," said Lars with all due seriousness.

"She's very pretty," the doctor tending to him said and gave me a smile. As if to say she'd seen and heard it all before. The tag on her white coat read *Dr. Kelly Lopez*.

"Don't tell her I call her Princess, though. It's just in my head."

"Got it."

Tore leaned closer. "They gave him the good stuff."

Lars shuffled on the bed and winced. He might be high as a kite, but he was still feeling some pain. "We're going to get married, but then we'll get divorced."

"That's a pity," said Dr. Lopez.

"Yeah." He sighed. "Fourth of December. Damn shame."

Dr. Lopez's brows went up. "You've picked a date?"

"Lars loves a plan." I laid my hand on his arm. Doing my best to avoid any damage. "Hey there."

His smile was blissful, his gaze glued to the region of my chest. "Susie. Hey. Great dress. It's really tight."

"Thanks."

"Sorry I missed our sex date."

Tore made a choking noise.

"Oh, sorry," Lars said. "Not supposed to call it a date."

"That's okay." I smiled. "What happened?"

"I was buying you that bottle of wine and some fucker ran a red light." His words were slurred. "Sent me flying. Can you believe that shit?"

"This happened when you were buying the wine?"

"Not your fault, Susie," said Tore.

Lars frowned. Which made him wince again. "Of course it's not her fault. Fuck's sake, Tore. Why would you say that, man?"

"Sorry. My bad," said Tore, keeping a straight face. "Susie, I apologize."

"Do you forgive him?" asked Lars in a grave voice. "You don't have to. It's okay."

"Um. Yes. I forgive him."

Tore gave me a wink.

"You're not going to cry, are you?" asked Lars.

"I'm fine. I promise. You just gave me a scare." I sniffed and smiled. "What's the damage?"

Dr. Lopez slipped her hands into the pockets of her lab coat. "Can I just clarify your relationship to Lars?"

"She's my sig...my signif... She's my other." Lars nodded. "I, ah, I love...her and yeah."

I held my breath and waited, but he said no more. Which was for the best. Lars was on a lot of drugs and didn't know what he was saying. Obviously. But on the off chance I did suffer from sudden heart failure brought on by his words, I was in the right place.

Dr. Lopez just nodded. "Hairline fracture in the wrist, rib contusion, and neck strain. No sign of a concussion, but it was a hard knock. I'd like you to keep an eye on him for the next couple of days. Just to be safe."

"Of course. He's getting discharged tonight?"

"Yes. Bed rest and pain relief for the next seventy-two hours with gentle movement. It's important you get up and walk around, just take it easy. We'll make a follow-up appointment for the cast in a couple of weeks."

Lars stared bemusedly at the light above his bed. Blissfully unaware.

"I can move back into the condo with him," said Tore. "Sleep on the floor or something. Buy one of those air mattresses from Walmart."

"You only just moved in with Cleo." I frowned. "And he'd be alone during the day. I work from home. Why doesn't he just stay with me?"

"It's not a bad idea," said Tore. "But I'm not sure he'll go for it."

"Only one way to find out." I turned to the wounded one. "Lars, you're coming home with me."

"But, Princess," said Lars, tuning back into the conversation, "I don't want to be like a... Shit. What's that word?"

"A hassle?" suggested Tore. Then he said more quietly, "Wish they'd give me some of whatever he's on."

Cleo elbowed him in ribs.

Lars thought it over. It took a while. "Yeah. That's it. A hassle."

"You're not a hassle," I said.

"But you don't have a spare bed."

"Are you worried if you sleep in my bed you'll catch girl germs?"

Lars laughed and answered loudly, "No!"

"Then what's the big deal?"

"I'm just not sure it's a good idea," he mumbled.

I gave him my best, most reassuring smile. "Why don't we try it for a few days and see? I mean, how bad can it be?"

Twelve

"Are you all right?"

Slowly and carefully, Lars turned around to face me. The fridge door sat open behind him. His face was pale and lined with pain. In one hand he held the leftovers from my dinner last night. In the other he held a fork. "Got hungry. This was all I could find."

"I'm due a grocery shop."

He filled the fork and shoveled it into his mouth. Eating straight out of the casserole dish. Which was fine, I guess. "Want me to get you a plate?"

A grunt in the negative.

"The good drugs wore off, huh?"

Another grunt, as he shuffled past me over to the dining table. There he sat in the same slow and careful manner. With lots of scowling. "I didn't realize how good they were until they stopped working. Honestly, who takes someone off morphine to give them Tylenol? I'm amazed they can even say it with a straight face, without laughing their asses off."

"Did you sleep okay?"

He shrugged.

"I actually slept really well. Sharing a bed with you works, apparently," I said.

I filled a glass with water and set it beside him. Then I started making my morning coffee. Because caffeine. I'd sneaked into the bathroom upon waking and brushed my teeth and my hair. Then washed my face and applied concealer, mascara and a tinted lip balm—going for the epitome of natural woke-up-this-way beauty. Wanting to impress a man was hard work. I'd even worn my best pajamas: black cotton with white piping. Much nicer than my usual old tee and panties. Not that he was in any condition to notice.

But having him in my space in any condition made me nervous, apparently.

"The only time I've cohabitated with a male was when I went on trips with a boyfriend," I said. Just making conversation. "Beside my father and brother when I was little, of course. Have you ever lived with someone? Not that it's what we're doing. You know what I mean."

"No." His voice was gruffer than normal. "Things never got that serious."

I gave him a half smile. "You mean you didn't let them get that serious."

"Guess not."

"So just vacations?"

"Yeah."

"This'll be a learning experience for both of us," I said. "I've put out fresh towels in the bathroom if you want to take a shower."

"Thanks. Feels like I'm still covered in grit and dirt from the road."

"I'll change the sheets so those are fresh for you too. The waterproof cover for your cast is in the bathroom. Do you want any help in the shower with bandages or anything?"

"No," he said quietly and kept eating.

I sipped my coffee and watched Kat butt her head against his leg. He reached down in slow motion and gave her a scratch. Seeing him in pain was horrible. He was normally so big and strong and sturdy. Why, a mountain couldn't take the man down. And some asshole behind a wheel had almost succeeded. A terrifying thought.

"Have you taken your meds or do you want me to grab them?"

"I've taken them," he said. "Think it might be best if I go home."

I paused. "Why?"

Nothing from him.

"The doctor said you should have someone keep an eye on you."

"I'll be fine."

"You got hit by a car," I said. "Give yourself a minute. Please."

"I don't know." He glared at the chicken and rice. "This feels off being here like this. I don't want to be in your way."

"You're not in my way. I know this is different than what we're used to, but it's okay to need a little help right now. And, Lars, I would like to help you."

His free hand curled into a fist. This was not normal Lars. This was in-pain-and-pissed-off Lars. A very different creature. "Because you think it's your fault I was crossing that fucking street."

"Because I care about you and want to help."

"Susie, the shit I said at the hospital last night..."

"You remember that?"

A line appeared between his brows. "Some."

"You were high as a kite. People say all sorts of things when they're under the influence."

"Yeah," he said finally. "About me staying here. We don't have the sort of relationship where—"

"You mean like friends?"

For a long moment, he said nothing. Then he looked up with his usual frown and took in the still cluttered dining table. I had been too worried about him after getting back from the hospital to deal with it all. Sitting in the darkened bedroom watching him sleep instead. What that said about my feelings for the man was best ignored. The napkins, candles, and silverware were still laid out. He blinked and stared as if he couldn't make sense of the scene. "You did all of this for last night?"

"It's not a big deal." I shrugged. "I wanted to do something nice for you with Tore moving out. I know you said you were fine with it, but..."

He just stared at me.

I took another mouthful of brew.

"From what I remember at the hospital, you were dressed up pretty fancy for a night in, too."

"I like to dress up. I mean... I like to look nice for you too. That's allowed, isn't it?"

"Sure."

No way did I hide behind my mug. Such behavior would be childish and cowardly.

"Okay," he said as if he'd reached some decision. Then his shoulders eased and he relaxed back into the chair. "Can I have coffee?"

I straightened. "You're staying?"

"Yes, Susie. I'm staying."

★ ★ ★

Tore arrived midmorning. "Hello, fellow kids!"

"About time," grumbled Lars.

He took in his brother sitting in the armchair in my short black silk robe and grinned. "I like that look for you."

"Go fuck yourself."

"Why would I? That is a job my girlfriend does far better than I ever could."

"Tore, hush," ordered Cleo.

Despite encouraging Lars to return to bed, he insisted otherwise. Throw cushions were stuffed behind and beside him and an adoring cat sat on his lap. A baseball game played silently on the TV and kept him occupied. The side table was within easy reach with a variety of drinks and snacks, all of his medications, and the TV and AC remote controls. When his grunting turned into growling, I stopped fussing and left him alone. After enjoying the view of his muscular hairy legs beneath the short robe, of course. It was the little things that made life worthwhile.

Tore deposited the overnight bag full of Lars's belongings beside the bedroom door. "I grabbed an assortment of stuff. Let me know if you want me to pick up anything else."

"Thanks," said Lars.

"How are you feeling?" asked Cleo with a disposable coffee cup in hand.

"Like I got hit by a car."

"Funny thing." Tore sat in the armchair. "We almost lost you last night."

"It'll take more than a hatchback to end me."

"That's very manly of you," said Cleo.

Tore nodded. "Personally, I insist on getting taken out by nothing less than a Humvee."

"Don't even joke about it." Cleo leveled a finger on him. "I mean it, Tore."

"Sorry," he said, chastened.

I sat at the dining table with my laptop open in front of me. Nothing like dealing with my clients' trolls on a Sunday morning. After taking screen shots of the nasty comments for the business owner, I blocked their asses. Yay for job satisfaction.

Tore shook his head. "You look a damn mess."

"I think the new scar on your face is very sexy, pirate." I smiled. "Just in case you're after my opinion."

"I agree," said Cleo. "The whole look says hot wounded buccaneer to me."

Lars's lips twitched.

Tore just sniffed. "What happened with the police?"

"Couldn't give them much. I honestly didn't see a damn thing," said Lars. "Too busy trying to remember what kind of wine you'd asked me to pick up. I was about to pull out my phone and text you when it happened. But I had the right of way and there was a camera installed at that intersection so they should get whoever hit me."

"Good."

I shook my head. "You should have seen what was left of the shirt. It's a wonder you're still in one piece."

Lars grunted and shifted in the chair. I jumped to my feet to help, but his cranky face stopped me. Big yikes. He slowly rose and made his way across the room. As soon as he attempted to reach down for his bag and lift it, his hand clutched at his side. The gasping wheeze noise that came out of him was horrible.

"Would you just ask for help for once?" Tore got to his feet, grabbed the bag, and followed after him. "Stubborn asshole."

The brothers disappeared into the bedroom and closed the door. Guess Lars was over the black silk and needed some assistance getting dressed. Fair enough.

"Is it just me or does he wear that robe really well?" asked Cleo.

"Oh, yeah." I nodded. "Half of his clothes went in the trash and the other half in the wash. It was the only thing I owned that would fit him."

"Has he been in that mood all morning?"

"You mean like sunshine?"

"Yes," she said. "Except the opposite."

"Mmm."

She sipped her drink. "Do you need to be at the shoot with the coffee trucks on Wednesday?"

"Yeah. There's some things I need to go over with the owner and I was planning on making some behind the scenes videos. But Lars should be fine to be on his own for a while by then. He hasn't had any dizziness or anything else to suggest a traumatic brain injury. The ribs, wrist, and hip seem to have taken the brunt of the impact."

"How are you?"

"Good. He woke up once in pain during the night and I got him his meds and helped him to the bathroom. Other than that I slept well. Though the dude does take up a lot of room."

She gazed at me over the rim of her coffee cup. "Tore called his parents last night. He told them Lars was okay, but they're coming back today on an earlier flight. His mom is pretty upset, apparently."

"Understandably."

"They should be here around five."

My eyes opened wide. "Here as in *here*?"

"That's right. They've already got someone picking them up from the airport and we've got dinner with my folks so…"

"Parents. Wow."

"I'm sure they're good people. Tore has a lot of respect for them." Her smile gentled. "Relax, Susie. They're going to love you."

"Sure. Right. It'll be fine."

★ ★ ★

I answered the door late in the afternoon to a slender woman with a long gray bob. Behind her stood a handsome man with a short gray beard. Lars and Tore took after their father. But they had their mother's blue eyes.

"You must be Susie," said Lars's mother with a tight worried smile. "I'm Deborah and this is my husband, Henning."

"Nice to meet you." I stepped back. "Come in. Please."

And behind Lars's parents stood Aaron. Because they were all that damn close, apparently. Awesome. He nodded stiffly. "Susie."

I said nothing.

Deborah and Henning went straight to their son. Lars was propped up in the chair watching a sports channel. There might be people out there who were worse at being sick. But it was doubtful. The man refused to stay in bed. It was only his pain tolerance that kept him in the armchair instead of being up and about. While they gave him the good stuff at the hospital, the pain relief they sent him home with was far less effective.

Deborah carefully kissed the unhurt side of his face. "I've been so worried."

"Son," said Henning, with a frown. They had the same frown. For some reason, this was charming.

"What happened?" asked his mom.

"I was crossing the street and some asshole ran a red light." Lars gave his best friend a nod. Though what the actual status on their friendship was these days, I had no idea. He didn't, however, seem surprised to see Aaron here. Guess they'd been friends for so long he was treated like family. His parents did live next door to Lars's. The ties between them all obviously ran deep.

"You look like a mess," said Aaron.

Lars tried to smile and winced. "Yeah."

"As soon as we found out, I booked us flights home," said Deborah.

"Your mom called to ask if I'd been to the hospital." Aaron hovered near the door. He should be unsure of his unwelcome. "If I'd spoken to your doctor."

Deborah shook her head in amazement. "He hadn't even heard about the accident."

"It all happened pretty fast," said Lars. "They've had me on strong painkillers."

Aaron gave a brief flicker of a smile. "I offered to pick Deborah and Henning up from the airport and drive them here. Thought it'd give me a chance to confirm that you're still alive with my own eyes."

Lars gave him a wan smile.

"It's so good of your friend to let you stay here." Deborah crouched by the armchair and placed her hand on her son's. A real live loving mother. It was a beautiful thing to see.

Henning nodded. "Thank you, Susie."

I smiled.

"You'll come home with us now, though, won't you?" asked Deborah. "I know you prefer to do everything for yourself. You always have. But obviously this is a case where you need some help. My craft things are in your old room. But you can stay in the guest room while you recuperate. Then I'll be able to look after you."

"Mom—"

"That would be best, I think."

"My mom said to say she's glad you're okay," reported Aaron. "She's making her chicken noodle soup for you. I told her you'd probably prefer brownies."

"And if I have to pop out and your dad is busy she said she'd come over and sit with you," said Deborah. "We have it all worked out. Around-the-clock care."

Lars's gaze jumped to where I was standing off to the side. He seemed to be trying to communicate something to me. But I wasn't sure what exactly.

"We should go soon. Get you settled in at home so you can rest." Deborah stood and surveyed the wreck of my house. Because of course the grocery delivery had arrived five minutes before them. Bags and bottles were everywhere. And my work was spread out across the dining room table so I could keep an eye on Lars. His mom's smile was understanding. "Get out of Susie's way."

I smiled back at her. Then I turned to her son. "Whatever you want is fine with me. You know that."

Lars kept right on staring at me.

"That's very kind of you, Susie," said Deborah. "I understand you used to date—"

"Yes," I said.

Aaron jangled his car key fob.

Deborah smiled softly. "How wonderful that you've all been able to remain friends."

Aaron's smile was not the least bit convincing. Schmuck.

"We'll have to have you over, Susie," said Deborah. "Thank you for taking such good care of our son."

"I'd like that."

She gave Lars's shoulder a pat. "Though I was a little surprised you weren't at Amie's."

"That ended," said Lars.

"What a shame. She was such a lovely accomplished young woman. What happened?"

"He'll tell us if and when he wants to," said Henning, giving his son a wink.

"Of course." Deborah's hands fluttered. "You know me, I'm not one to pry."

"You know Lars isn't ready to settle down." Aaron gave her an affectionate smile. "He has big plans."

Deborah laughed. "Forgive a mother for hoping. I just thought that with you getting engaged and Tore meeting someone, that my eldest might also make the leap."

The alarm on my cell chimed. "Lars, it's time for your pills."

He grunted and reached for the little box on the side table.

Immediately, his mom sprang into action. "Have you got them there? Let me get you some fresh water. Or would you rather iced tea or juice? Maybe Susie has something. Are you supposed to take them with food? I have half a cookie from a café at the airport in my purse. That reminds me, Tore said they gave you a neck brace. Shouldn't you be wearing that?"

Lars popped the pill on his tongue and dry swallowed. "I'm fine."

"But—"

"I'm fine, Mom."

"You will be once we get you home and put you to bed. Some rest and good home-cooked food and you'll be back on your feet again." Deborah nodded, pleased at the thought.

The furrows on Lars's forehead were out in full force now. "I need to talk to you."

"Me?" I asked.

He nodded and began the laborious process of hauling himself out of the armchair. His mom grabbed his arm while his dad stepped closer just in case he was needed. "Mom, just... I'm okay," said Lars. "Please let me do it myself."

Deborah's lips turned down. But she did as asked.

Lars shuffled into the bedroom and I followed. He shut the door and turned on me with a serious face. "I need you."

"You what?"

"You heard me."

"Yeah. But I still want to hear you say it again."

He sighed. "I need you."

"That's lovely. Okay. Now explain what you mean."

He shuffled forward and I took a step back and we didn't stop until my spine touched the wall. Then he got all up in my personal space. Not stopping until I was looking up at him and he was looking down at me, and our noses were a bare handbreadth apart. The long line of stitches on his cheek made my stomach roll over. Same went for the dark bruise that had blossomed beneath his golden stubble. The thought of him being hurt was the worst.

And he was still frowning. Though that was kind of his normal setting. "I hate being in pain. Can't stand being injured. It's frustrating and infuriating and it pisses me off. So when I tell you I'm sorry for being a grumpy asshole today I mean it, okay?"

"Thank you for the apology."

He nodded.

"Was there something else you wanted to talk about?"

He rested his cast on the wall above my head and leaned even closer. Close enough to brush his mouth against mine. The heat and scent of him were all welcome, as per the usual. Just having him close was a delight.

"I needed that." I happy-sighed. Then I stopped smiling. "You smell like my shampoo. Why didn't you ask me to help you wash your hair?"

"Remember how we discussed me being a cranky asshole?"

"Right."

"And you were busy working and doing your grocery shopping on the laptop and I didn't want to disturb you."

"Okay."

He kissed me again. With a bit more fervency this time. Sucking on my top lip and biting on the bottom. He didn't open his jaw too wide because that would hurt. But it was slow and lovely. Weird, however, given his parents and best friend were waiting in the next room. He traced his nose against mine and stayed nice and close. I hadn't realized how much I needed this. After the scare last night and those days of waiting to see him again. I was starved for the man. And I was pretty damn sure he knew it. We kissed until he flinched and touched the side of his mouth. "Shit."

"Are you saying goodbye or sweetening me up for something?" I asked. "Not that I mind. Just curious."

"I like how your eyes go all lusty when I kiss you. But I can't even breathe without it hurting right now." He took a breath and let it out slowly and carefully. "Susie?"

"Yes, Lars?"

"Please don't make me go home with my mother."

I tried not to smile.

"She'll smother me. She means well, but I can't handle it." He rested his forehead against mine with a sigh. "And if I try to go back to my place on my own she'll follow and it'll be the same deal only with her trying to tidy up and getting all into my things."

"Oh, dear."

He just nodded.

"I see now that your big strong exterior hides the heart of a little boy who is secretly afraid of his mommy."

"I'm not afraid of her." He scowled. "I just can't fucking handle being babied. There's a difference. Stop laughing at me."

"Sorry."

"Please, Princess?"

I gasped. "You said the *P* word. That endearment was only meant to be used inside your head."

"The secret's out." His face remained paler than usual and his gaze dulled with pain. Like there was anything I wouldn't do for the behemoth. "Can I stay here with you? Please?"

"What lovely manners you have. Of course you can."

He smiled in victory and shuffled back toward the door. Without even stopping to give me another kiss. How rude. Then he was back out in the living room announcing, "Thanks, Mom. But I'm going to stay here."

"But, sweetie…"

Nice and slowly, he lowered himself back into the armchair. His mom immediately placed all of the cushions around him with care. "Susie asked me if I wouldn't mind staying."

Every pair of eyes in the room turned my way. He'd thrown me in the deep end. The dick.

"Why is that?" asked Deborah.

My mouth opened, but all I had was, "Um."

"She just feels better when I'm here," said Lars.

That was me. Codependent, apparently. For fuck's sake.

Aaron looked from Lars to me and back again. Then he looked to heaven and jangled his car key fob harder.

"She sleeps better when I'm here," said Lars. "Don't you, Susie?"

"I see," said Deborah. "How long have you two been together?"

Lars gave me a wary glance. So he should. Then he licked his lips and said, "It's early days. Look, I would just feel better staying here with her. That's the truth."

Deborah shook her head in wonder. "You two met when Susie used to date… Well. Isn't it funny how things work out?"

Aaron didn't find it funny, however. His expression was about as far from laughter as possible. He glared at me like I'd stolen his bestie. Then he turned to Lars and said, "I was thinking of taking tomorrow off to keep you company."

"Maybe another time," said Lars.

"Right." Aaron clutched the key fob in a white-knuckled grip. "I'll go wait in the car."

"Did he not know about you and Susie?" asked Deborah, thanks to Aaron's dramatic exit.

"He knew." Lars carefully stretched his neck. "It's complicated, Mom."

Deborah turned her questioning gaze to me.

I'd never been good at dealing with other people's parents. Mine tended to have as little to do with me as possible so the relationship dynamics remained an unknown quantity for me. Given how precarious this situation was, I should have kept my mouth shut. But wanting people to like you is a bitch. "Our breakup was…it was messy. A lot of hurt feelings. I would just be more comfortable if…"

"You don't have to explain yourself," said Lars.

"Are you saying he isn't welcome here?" Deborah sighed as if she bore the world's burdens. "But Lars is staying here, apparently. Aaron and Lars have been friends for so long. Why, they're just like brothers."

"We just want you to be happy, son," said Henning.

Lars's mother blinked wide eyes. "Well, of course we do, but—"

"Time for us to go," Henning announced.

But Deborah wasn't finished. "I really think we need to call him back in here and talk this out. Just sit down together and—"

"It was nice to meet you, Susie." Henning ushered his wife out the door with a hand to the small of her back. She was not happy. That much was certain.

I tried to smile. But the whole situation was beyond awkward. "Nice to meet you both."

Then they were gone.

"So," I said, taking a seat. "That happened."

"Sorry I told them about us."

"No, you're not."

"No, I'm not," he agreed. "They were bound to find out sooner or later."

"You just didn't want to go home and have your mother fuss over you so you used me as a shield."

He gazed at me for a moment. "You're right. But, Susie, we are in a relationship. Have you noticed how we both keep choosing each other?"

"It's *inevitable*."

"That's right. And I'm going to ignore your sarcastic tone for now because I feel like shit."

"You still owe me and your mother now hates me. She thinks I'm breaking up you and your bestie." I slumped back in the chair. "How do you handle having your parents all up in your business? Mine barely remember my birthday. But yours..."

"I'll deal with my mother."

"Does she expect to be told and to share her opinion about everything in your life?"

He lifted one shoulder in a small shrug and grimaced. "In all honesty, when she gets like that, I just tune her out. I love my mom. But I make my own choices."

"Even Aunt Susan gave me space. Maybe that's why we get divorced," I said. "Because your mother and I never get along."

"Not really something I can see myself getting a divorce over. But I've been thinking. Maybe we should just forget about the certificate."

"Forget about it?"

"Yeah."

"You've given up on being able to explain it."

He winced. "Yeah."

"We wouldn't have gotten to know one another if it wasn't for that thing. It's like an Ouroboros." I made a circle with my fingers. "A snake biting its own tail. Fate in an infinite loop. I don't think it's something we can just ignore."

"Thought you said fate was changeable."

"But we already found the certificate and ever so reluctantly grew feelings for one another. Those events are now established," I said. "Though by that thinking there's no avoiding us getting married and divorced. Because both of those events are also established by the certificate's existence. Which is sad. And a little confusing."

He rested his head against the back of the seat. "You just admitted you have feelings for me."

"You already knew that."

"No. I suspected. You were fine with friendship and sex. But when you didn't want to date, it made me wonder."

I sighed. "Feelings, huh?"

He just grunted.

"What we really need is a physicist to explain holes in time. How the certificate could have come to be in the wall." I thought it over. "Do you think I should get a priest to bless the house? Or a mystic, maybe?"

"I love how science, religion, and magic all kind of happily coexist for you."

"Got to keep an open mind. Though I've never really given any of them that much thought. I was always more of a creative type than a deep thinker."

"And what am I?" he asked.

"You build and fix and plan. You're smart and good with your hands. Very good." I smiled back at him. "What can I do to help with the pain, Lars?"

He stared solemnly at my chest region. "Can't think of any sex position that wouldn't hurt, unfortunately."

"I love that your thoughts went straight to my crotch. But I was thinking more like running you a bath or finding you a heat pack or something along those lines."

"Oh." His face fell. "No, thanks."

"Let me know if you change your mind."

"Will do. And my mom will love you when she gets to know you."

I looked away. "Yeah."

Thirteen

"What are you doing?"

Lars looked down at me from his lofty height halfway up the ladder. "Drilling holes for the picture hooks you wanted. This was where you wanted the first one, right?"

It was Wednesday. Four days postaccident. And apparently he was done with taking it easy. I set the grocery bags on the floor. This was so not the day for him to pull this shit.

"Lars, get down, please. Slowly."

With a heavy ass sigh, he did as asked. "Smoothed off some of the plaster work in the bedroom too. Wasn't quite happy with it. I'll repaint later."

"You've been busy."

"I'm sick of watching TV," he grumped.

"Then read a book."

"I don't own any."

His bruises were starting to fade. Lots of yellow with splotches of purple. The stitches in his cheek should start dissolving in a couple of days though the cast would remain on his wrist for another week. The grazes up his arm and on his chest were healing well. All of which were on view since he'd taken to only wearing a pair of athletic shorts around the house. A decision I could only applaud. Still, treating himself with some caution, however, would have been the sensible thing to do. Because the idea of him hurting himself more freaked me right the fuck out.

"Read one of my books."

"They're all Romances."

"So?"

"All right." He groaned. "I'll read one of your books."

"Great. Enjoy."

"You're in a mood," he said, giving me a wary glance. "How'd the shoot go?"

"The business owner brought his new partner with him. He's a visual person and very active online so he had lots of helpful hints for Cleo and me. Because we both love having our jobs mansplained to us. Made the shoot take twice as long as it should have."

"Damn."

"Then some charming asshole followed me around the grocery store asking for my number and refused to take no for an answer."

His brows descended. "What the fuck?"

"Indeed. Then I come home to find you performing daring physical feats. Dr. Wong said gentle movement. Do you honestly believe climbing ladders falls under that purview?"

He set the drill on the coffee table. "You've had a bad day."

"Yeah. I really have."

"How can I make it better?"

"Keep your feet on solid ground, please."

"Got it."

"Thank you." Which was when I saw it. A black shoe box with silver writing sitting on the dining table. "What's that?"

"Take a look."

The logo that adorned the lid… My heart was stuck in my throat. "You bought me Pradas?"

"I didn't know what you wanted. So if they're the wrong size or style or whatever just send them back." He scratched at his head. "It's my way of saying thank you."

I opened the box with all due ceremony. Within layers of tissue paper sat a pair of black block heel sandals. Such strappy retro gorgeousness. "Oh my God."

"Is that good or bad?"

"They're beautiful." I would not cry. It had just been a hell of a day and his thoughtfulness had caught me off guard. My father hadn't remembered my birthday for over a decade and Aaron had been too busy with work to celebrate my thirtieth last year. But Lars bought me these beauties just because. It kind of blew my mind. "Can I kiss you?"

"Yeah." And the heat in his gaze lit an answering fire in me.

His good hand slipped beneath my ponytail and cupped the back of my neck. The feel of his warm breath on my lips gave me life. How he pressed his body against mine and took ownership of my mouth. With his cast pressing into my back, he kissed me all hot and demanding. The feel of his mouth on mine and his tongue slipping inside. A lot of thought had clearly gone into this moment. Because we hit fevered in well under a minute. With his grip on my neck, and all of the delicious heat and wetness of his mouth, my day improved at an alarming rate—rocketing from shitty to shiny.

"I don't know where to touch you that won't hurt you," I said, breathing heavily.

"Guess you'll have to keep your hands to yourself and let me be in charge." And there was something in his tone of voice. Something raw and needy, with a touch of demanding thrown in for good measure. His gaze lingered over the hard nipples pressing into my dress. Then he studied my face. "That works for you, huh?"

I was the very picture of horny innocence. "What do you mean?"

The man had no time for my nonsense, diving right back in, kissing me until my head spun. And all the while his dick hardened against my belly. His tongue stroked against mine, making me moan. I let out a low growl of frustration because he was eminently gropeable and I wanted to touch too. That's when he said, "Lose the clothes."

"Are you sure?"

"Yes."

"But what about your—"

"Susie," he said, looming over me. "Here's what's going to happen. I'm going to lay on my back on the bed and you're going to be a good girl and ride me."

"I'm going to be a good girl, huh?"

"Yes. My good girl." His smile was all sorts of suggestive and so damn confident. "Strip, Princess."

My knees went weak. It was the truth. There was approximately one male I trusted to take control and there he stood. My fingers fumbled over the buttons on my short-sleeve black shirt dress. I kicked off my sandals and let the dress float to the floor, leaving me in my underwear, a black lace balconette bra and matching hipster briefs.

"Fuck." His voice was guttural. "Turn around. Show me."

I turned slowly.

"Beautiful. Next time we fuck you'll be wearing the designer heels for me. But for now, get on your knees."

"Are you sure you're up for this?"

"Trust me, getting it up is not a problem."

"That's obvious," I said to his tented short fronts. "But I meant muscle strain and bruised-ribs-wise."

"I'm good. And I think we both need this." He held out his good hand. "Yes or no, Susie?"

No need for words when actions would convey. I took his hand and lowered myself slowly to my knees. Guess I'd forgotten quite how impressive his dick was. Or it just looked bigger at this angle.

With all due care, I dragged his shorts and boxer briefs down his legs to the floor. He stepped out of them and kicked them aside. And all the while he stared down at me with that dark gaze. My nipples were so hard they hurt. The man could wind me up so tight with only a kiss and some words. While it was awesome, it wasn't fair.

I took his cock in my hand, wrapping my fingers around it tightly and nuzzling him. The musky scent of him went straight to my head. My tongue traced the path of a vein. All the way back to the swollen head. Such soft skin over stone. I guided the crown into my mouth, licking and sucking. His hand slid over my head, taking my ponytail in a tight hold. With one hand I fondled his balls, while the other held firm to his length.

I teased the opening with the tip of my tongue before taking him as deep as I could. The noise he made when I sucked hard on the bulbous head was almost as good as when I dug my tongue into the dip of his frenulum. He tugged on my hair and swore up a storm. It was nice to be appreciated. It felt wondrous to make him feel good. And the way the muscles in his thighs flexed was nothing less than thrilling. The salty taste of his pre-cum…

"Stop," he ordered. "Stand up."

I gave his cock a parting kiss and did as asked. He cradled my face with his good hand and kissed me on the lips. What my day had been before this, no longer mattered. There was only here and now. And this moment was spectacular.

"That was very good, Susie."

"I'm glad."

"Now lose the lingerie."

I undid the bra and dropped it to the floor and wiggled out of my panties. He pressed his body full length against my back. With the cast firmly against my stomach, he slid his other hand between my legs and cupped me.

"You're wet," he murmured.

"Can't imagine how that happened."

"Widen your stance."

I did as told.

His teeth pressed into my shoulder as his fingertip trailed along the seam of my labia. Back and forth. A tremble worked its way through me. When he stuck two fingers and his thumb into his mouth and wet them…holy shit, that was hot. Men had done intimate things with me before. Though with Lars it was different. How tight he held me. The bite on my shoulder. His general intensity, I don't know. And then he slid those fingers deep inside me and pressed on my clit with the pad of his thumb. He finger fucked me like a pro.

And then he stopped.

"Wait," I whined. "Lars."

"You come on me this time." And he was so damn calm about it. Like denial was ever okay when it came to me and orgasms. But he just turned his back, walked into the bedroom, and lay down on the mattress. If it wasn't for the hard-on pointing at the ceiling you would think he was about to take a nap. "Hurry up."

"Bossy bastard."

"What was that?"

"Nothing."

"Grab a condom," he ordered.

With one hand tucked behind his head and his cast resting on his chest, he watched me. My skin turned to gooseflesh at the lust in his gaze. And I needed to remember to ask the man for nudes one of these days. Because even when battered he was beautiful. I grabbed the correct-sized condom out of the bedside drawer and carefully straddled his hips. The bruise on his side was still huge. I needed to be careful and keep my knees to myself. Once the wrapper was opened, I tossed it aside, and rolled the prophylactic down him with care.

Being on top was one of my favorite positions. What's not to like? You get a great view and complete control, even if you do have to do all the work.

I took his cock in my hand and lined it up with my opening, sinking down on him nice and slowly. The feel of him filling me was wonderful. My pussy clenched and he hissed. The man was lucky I had strong thighs. Because I couldn't place my hands on him for leverage. And he was so damn tall I couldn't quite reach the bedhead. This would definitely count as a workout for my core.

Then he winced and I froze. "What's wrong? Lars?"

"Nothing. Ride me."

I exhaled and rocked on him gently. When he didn't show any obvious signs of discomfort or agony, I rocked on him harder. Rising and falling just a little. Squeezing him again with my internal muscles. All the while, he watched me with a mix of tenderness and possession in his gaze. My face and breasts and belly. My thighs and cunt. Strong hands gripped my thighs, giving them a squeeze, testing the flesh with his fingers. Then he raised his upper half a little and smacked me on the ass, making me squeak.

"Fuck, you're gorgeous. Getting to be around you has been

the only good thing about this week." The man winced and smiled. "Harder."

"I don't want to hurt you."

"If you're hurting me, I'll tell you," he said. "Now do as you're told and ride me harder. You know you want to."

He was right. I really did. The feel of him so solid inside of me. How he dragged over all my good places as I rose. Then the sweet shock of impaling myself on that thick length. Over and over again. Harder and faster. Nothing could be better than losing myself with him. His jaw shifted and his nostrils flared. The tension low in my belly spread throughout me. Like a light working its way through me. I was all heat and motion, reaching for that thrill, until it got so bright I was blinded. I came with a gasp and he gripped my thigh, pulling me down on him and holding me there. Like there was anywhere else I wanted to be. His cock surged inside of me, pumping out his cum as he groaned. This was it. This was what I needed. The world far away and just him being near.

I think I died a little. It is called *the little death* in French. It made sense.

Beneath me, he made a wheezing sound. "Susie."

"Shit." I carefully climbed off and sat on the mattress at his side. He was in no condition for a well-fucked woman to collapse on top of him. Seriously. "Oh, God. I'm so sorry, Lars. Are you okay?"

"Yeah. I'm fine now." He smiled and dealt with the condom. Wrapping it in a Kleenex and depositing it on the bedside table. "You're on my good side. Lie down. Put your head on my shoulder."

"Are you sure?"

He just waited.

After-sex cuddles were weird. With some partners, once the deed was done, you just wanted them gone. Wanted to get your space back. But with others, wasting a couple of hours on room service and a hot tub would be divine. Lars was of the latter variety. He smelled good and felt good and I was happy. There'd been no cuddling of late due to his injuries, but cuddling with Lars felt a lot like Christmas. And there were all those feelings again, making my heart feel too big for my ribs. Like with all of this his sweet words and great sex, the organ might break out of its bone cage.

"Thanks for letting me stay with you," he said in a low voice.

"You're very welcome. I think all in all this impromptu living-together situation has been a success."

"Yeah."

I smiled.

"Though I've been meaning to ask you," he said, staring at the ceiling. "Would you mind putting some of your skin care and makeup away? There's no room on the bathroom counter for my shaving stuff."

Huh. "I'll take a look."

"Thanks."

"Anything else been bothering you?"

He made a noise in his throat. "Not really."

I raised myself up on one elbow. "*Not really* doesn't mean no."

"It sort of does."

"Come on. You've been living here for four days now. What else?"

He smiled. Lars after sex was chill. "I'm very grateful that you let me stay and take such good care of me without getting all up in my face. Even if you did yell at me as soon as you walked through the door today."

"You were being an idiot."

"I knew what I was doing."

"Let's agree to disagree," I said. "It's funny the things you learn about someone when you live with them. I was surprised to find how much of a morning person you weren't. Considering your chosen profession requires early starts. You kind of bumble around like a big sleepy bear for the first hour or so. Half the time I wonder if you're going to walk into a wall or something."

He grunted.

"Though I appreciate your lack of interest in wearing shirts. Because ogling you is a favorite pastime of mine."

He smiled and smoothed a hand over my head, stroking my hair.

"Though the stubble in the bathroom sink I could do without."

"We're giving each other feedback?"

"Sure."

"Okay," he said. "I love watching you get dressed. The way you make yourself look all perfect. I'm scared to touch you because I don't want to rumple you. But then I get sad because you're wearing clothes and I really like it when you're naked."

I smiled. "That's nice. Now what about the things that annoy you?"

"Is this a trap?" he asked. "'Cause it feels like a trap."

"I swear it is not a trap. I'm just curious."

He sighed. "Well, you leave coffee mugs and water glasses everywhere. You never remember to turn off lights and your shoes are always scattered all over the damn house."

"But I have really great shoes. Don't you think they deserve to be on display?"

"Almost tripped on some the other day."

"Sorry."

"What about me?" he asked. "What do I do that annoys you apart from the stubble?"

"Nothing. You're perfect."

He just snorted.

"Though you did murder the toothpaste by squeezing it from the middle. And you didn't just squeeze it, you throttled it." I made the coordinating hand motions. "I don't know where all of that anger came from, but it was seriously misplaced. That toothpaste never did anything to you. Then you left an empty toilet roll on the holder when there's a trash pail and a basket full of toilet paper right there. And what's with the kitchen cabinets and drawers being half-open all the time? Do you have commitment issues about fully closing them, or something?"

He just looked at me.

"You also ate all of the good snacks and left me none. But I'm going to let that slide because you were bored and in pain."

"Thank you," he said drily. "That's big of you, Susie."

"You're welcome."

He went back to staring at the ceiling, then said, "Of course, the weirdest thing you do is sniff me when you think I'm asleep."

I choked on a laugh. "Never would I ever."

"Then you gently press your face into my arm and just stay that way for a minute or two." He gave me side eyes. "Want to explain that to me?"

"I like being close to you. What do you want me to say?"

He grunted.

My face felt a little hot, but oh well. There were worse things to be busted doing than searching for intimacy with someone. "Does it bother you?"

"No."

"So you tolerate my weirdness?"

"I like your weirdness," he said. "You think maybe you divorced me because I kept eating all of the snacks? Or do you think it had more to do with me mangling the toothpaste?"

"I thought you wanted to ignore the divorce certificate."

"You're probably right that it's not something we can ignore."

"Relationships are hard." I squished my cheek back against his bicep. "One thing I know, I'm going to miss you when you move back home."

He pressed a kiss to the top of my head.

"Thank you for the designer shoes and the orgasm. You made my day much better."

"You're welcome."

"Are you sure about this?"

"Yes." Lars pulled himself out of my car in slow motion. Being careful not to do himself any damage. Easier said than done, since I drove a Mini Cooper. It was one of the larger four-door models, but still. The dude was tall. It was a week since the accident and he was doing much better. But still. You could tell by the way that he moved that he was in pain. "My parents want to thank you for looking after me and to get to know you better. Why are you so worried?"

I nodded and chewed at the inside of my cheek. "Well, I don't have a great track record with parents in general. But my top two reasons currently are your bestie took me to meet his mom and she apparently hated me with a passion. And last weekend you told your parents I'm so clingy you had to stay with me. Pretty sure that didn't endear me to anyone."

He pressed a kiss to my forehead. "Everything is going to be fine."

"Hmm."

It was Saturday night and I was standing on the lawn in front of his childhood home with a charcuterie board in hand.

How I'd agonized over the placement of the olives and pro-sciutto. Not to mention the selection of cheeses. Their home was a sprawling two-story on a hill in Lakewood. Next door sat the house owned by the Ex's parents. And surprising no one, it was the biggest on the street. I spotted one of the up-stairs curtains moving. We were being watched. Not sure if Aaron's mother was sticking pins in a voodoo doll of me, but I could feel a headache coming on.

"Hey," he said, leading me down the garden path. "You look beautiful."

While it was true that my black linen shorts, silk camisole top, and new platform sandals were splendid, I still had serious reservations about attending this small family BBQ. Deborah hadn't visited again while he was recuperating at my house. Instead, she texted and called her darling son. Given the level of concern she initially displayed, it was hard not to read things into this. Or maybe I was just paranoid. Could be either.

"You even wore a strapless bra for me." He stopped to kiss me on the neck. A move that never failed to make me shiver. "Thank you, Princess."

"You're welcome."

He opened the front door and shouted, "We're here."

"Back deck," called out Henning.

It was a beautiful evening with a warm breeze, the scent of fir trees, and a killer view of Lake Washington. Clouds in the distance threatened wet weather later. But not for hours yet. Their house was nice, tasteful and homey. Lots of dis-tressed wood, cream accents, and family pictures. Terra-cotta pots full of flowers in bloom decorated the back deck. Maybe Deborah could give me some tips on how to keep my tomato plants alive. Jazz played over the sound system and Henning stood at the grill. He waved his tongs at us in greeting. The same way Tore did at the pool party. Family likenesses fascinated me. How Henning and his sons had the same smile, for instance. My closest relations had little in common with me. Although I had Mom's dark hair and Dad's stubborn chin. That was about all.

"Hello, Susie." Deborah gave me a cool smile and her son a kiss on the cheek. "How have you been, sweetie?"

"On the mend," Lars said then took a seat at the table. When she went to grab his arm to help, he gently shook her off. "I'm fine, Mom."

"Of course, you are."

"I wasn't sure what to bring," I said, setting the charcuterie board on the table beside the salads and bread rolls. "Hope this is okay."

"A cheeseboard." Deborah smiled. "Unfortunately, I'm lactose intolerant and Henning is watching his cholesterol."

My return smile was weak as water.

"What would you both like to drink?" she asked. "We have beer, wine, soda…"

"Beer would be great, thank you," I said.

Lars threw a stuffed habanero into his mouth. "Same."

As soon as Deborah was gone, I hissed, "Your mom is lactose intolerant?"

"Sorry. Forgot." He rested his free hand high on my leg. "I'll eat your charcuterie board, Susie. And that's not a euphemism."

"Yeah, but you already like me. I was trying to suck up to your mother."

He gave my thigh a squeeze. "I appreciate the effort."

"I'm not sure I'm supposed to interact with families. It's not my natural environment."

"Such a pity Tore and his new girlfriend couldn't come," said Deborah, handing out the bottles of beer. And there was a distinctly judgmental tone to her voice. Oh this night would be awesome.

"They had tickets to a show. You weren't supposed to be home until tomorrow," Lars reminded her. "You can hardly blame them."

"Of course I'm not blaming them, Lars. Don't be silly."

If I drank every time his mother made a passive-aggressive comment, there was a good chance Lars would have to carry me out at the end of the night. And Lars was in no condition to carry me anywhere. It was a damn shame I hadn't put an edible in my purse. Just a nibble would have made everything better.

"So what have you been up to?" asked Deborah. "Watching a lot of TV?"

Lars finished chewing some cheese. "Actually, I read a couple of books Susie recommended. Romance novels."

"Romance?" Deborah raised a brow. "Goodness."

Henning's gaze turned curious. "What did you think?"

"They were...interesting," said Lars. "Instructional."

I just smiled. Any day I converted a reader to romance was a good day.

"Hear you're heading back to work on Monday," said Henning.

"Mostly in a supervisory capacity." Lars waved his cast in the air. "Not good for much until this comes off."

"I imagine you'll be glad to move back home," said Deborah. "You were always so keen on having your own space."

He shrugged. "Lived with Tore for years."

"But never with a girlfriend," said Deborah. "We were surprised you chose to stay at Susie's. And I'm sure she's eager to have her house to herself again."

I kept my mouth shut. This seemed like another situation where the less I said the better.

Lars hadn't volunteered any information regarding plans to move back to his condo and I hadn't asked. I liked him just fine where he was. Not that I was ready to invite him to stay long-term, or anything. And as for being labeled his girl-friend...hmm. Interesting. No alarm bells were ringing inside my head. Despite my fear of dating, I guess I didn't mind. After some sexing and almost a week of living together I was willing to admit we were something. I just wasn't sure what, exactly.

"This isn't the first time he's been injured," said Henning. "Tell Susie about all of the times Lars hurt himself when he was little."

"Oh, goodness." Deborah smiled broadly. "He always was a handful. Bucked off a pony he wasn't supposed to be on at a petting zoo at the age of five. That was two broken fingers. Hit by a falling potted plant at a friend's house when he was eight. Seven stitches on the top of his head. I still have no idea how that even happened. Ran into a log at the park when he was eleven. They had this play fort and...well. Five stitches to his forehead. The scar disappeared into his hairline as he grew, fortunately. Then he fell off his bike when he was fourteen. No stitches or broken bones, but lots of nasty little cuts on his back and a sprained ankle. Those were all of the major incidents."

"Holy shit," I said. Then I winced. "Sorry. I mean *gosh*."

Deborah actually laughed. "You should have heard some of the language I used when they were growing up."

"You'd think Tore would be the problem child," said Lars. "But strangely not."

"You always had to go first." His mother waggled a finger at him. "Lars led the way. Undisputed leader of the pack. That's what we used to say."

"It was either that or let Tore crack his skull open attempting something stupid." Lars smiled. "Though it meant I always got in trouble for everything, too."

Henning chuckled. "You did a good job keeping your siblings out of trouble. Even if it did come at a cost."

"Your sister rolled off a top bunk in her sleep one time and broke her arm," continued Deborah. "Tore really only ever had his tonsils and wisdom teeth out."

"Show Susie the photo albums of Lars when he was little," said Henning, placing a dish of grilled chicken and vegetables on the table.

"Do not bring out the baby photos," said Lars, handing me a plate.

"Why not?" asked his father. "A big healthy naked baby lying on a sheepskin rug. What's there to be ashamed of?"

Lars frowned.

"I need to see that photo and possibly take a copy." I bit back a smile. "Please."

"No," said Lars. "What about you? Any childhood injuries?"

"Um, I broke my foot skateboarding when I was ten or so. Mom made Aunt Susan get rid of the board after that."

"You could have been one of the greats."

"I definitely could not have been one of the greats." I laughed. "But thank you for your vote of confidence."

Deborah suddenly stiffened, her head turned toward the neighboring property where Aaron's mother was now tending to the plants on her back deck with much serenity and grace. I'd been willing to ignore his claim of her hating me as another attempt to get under my skin. Given Deborah had returned to giving me guarded looks, however, I guess it was true. Who knows what they'd been saying about me?

While other people's opinion of me was none of my business, this bullshit I could do without.

"Hey," said Lars. "Come here."

"Yeah?"

He grabbed me by the back of my neck like a Neanderthal and kissed me. Which was kind of great. Clearly, he was on my side.

"Hannah left," announced Deborah apropos of nothing.

Lars frowned. "What?"

"Just boarded a plane to London this morning and left. No explanation. No nothing. Put her engagement ring on the kitchen counter and walked out." Deborah sighed. "Aaron's taking it very hard, as you'd imagine."

Lars said nothing.

"I thought he might have reached out to you." She cleared her throat. "I don't know what happened between you and him, Susie. But what I do know, Lars, is that he's been a good friend to you for a long time. It's a pity that you feel you have to choose between him and your new girlfriend."

"I'll give him a call," said Lars.

"I'd hope so."

Time to prove I could support Lars while still hating on his bestie. "Why don't you drop me off at home after this and go check on him? My car is probably easier to drive in your delicate condition than your big truck."

Lars's smile was everything good and right in the world. "Thanks."

The BBQ didn't really pick up again after that. Guess meeting families just wasn't my thing. So Lars was going to visit the Ex. It was fine. Everything was fine. And I refused to believe differently.

Fourteen

Cleo burst into my house a couple of hours later with a bottle of wine in each hand. She toed off her wet shoes and announced, "You're not going to believe what Tore said when I told him I was coming to see you."

"Tell me," I said, setting out the glasses on the coffee table.

"Don't you think we should sort out our problems without involving your best friend?" Cleo repeated in a low and cranky voice. "If he'd been open to listening to me and resolving the issue like an adult in the first place, I wouldn't have had to come see you to cool off."

"Did you kick him out of your condo?"

"Hell no," she said. "I want to know exactly where he is when I'm ready to yell at him some more."

"That makes sense." I nodded and poured the wine. We sat on cushions on the floor with our backs against the sofa. It was our way. Something about getting down and disheveled in times of trouble worked for us.

"He cracked jokes through the whole damn show," she said, taking a sip of white wine before wiping drops of rain off her face. "There I am, trying to enjoy myself watching something I've been waiting months to see, and the man would not shut up."

"Rude."

"What did Lars do to put that sad expression on your face?"

"We went to his parents' house for dinner and his mom broke the news that Aaron's fiancée dumped him and ran," I said, grabbing my cardigan off the sofa. The temperature had cooled off care of the wet. "She also threw in a wee guilt trip for fun."

"As you do."

"As soon as we got home, he called the asshole and is now over there consoling him. Which is fine. I just...ugh."

"So the new girl ran, huh?" Cleo raised a brow. "Good for her."

I downed a mouthful. "Yeah."

"You still have issues with Lars being friends with him?"

"I'm trying not to. It has nothing to do with me, really."

Cleo tapped her nails against her knee. "Hmm."

"I take it you asked Tore to stop complaining and he didn't?"

"Twice. Just because he didn't like the show, he didn't have to ruin it for me." She shook her head. "He behaved like a damn child. Then when he finally realized I was pissed at him, he got all defensive!"

"Idiot." I downed a mouthful of vino. "I know Lars and Aaron have been friends a long time and there's a bond there. But he was just such a shit to me. I don't know how to reconcile it, but I don't want it to be a thing between us."

"You're serious about him," said Cleo.

I scowled and nodded. "I tried to keep things casual be-

tween us, but it feels like I'm fighting a losing battle. If this
doesn't work out I'm joining a nunnery."

"Sounds reasonable. How much of you is angry at Lars for
being Aaron's friend, versus you being mad at yourself for
staying with the asshole for so long and making excuses for
his behavior?"

"Good question. Gah. Stop being so insightful."

"Relationships." She sighed. "The thing is, Tore didn't
have to like the stupid show. I just needed him to shut up and
sit there so I could enjoy it. Now I know not to take him to
a play, especially if it's a tragedy, because it fries his little-boy
brain and makes him act out."

"Have you considered a ball gag?"

"I'd rather go on my own than run the risk of him yelling
You can do better, honey to Ophelia."

I snorted. "Hamlet is a total fuck-boy. I'm with him there."

"Oh, I'm not debating that. It's the appropriateness of interacting uninvited with actors during a live performance that's
the issue," she said. "This is the problem with new relationships. Working through what you can and cannot tolerate.
What you can do together and what you should absolutely do
apart. And after all of that if the sex is good, deciding whether
there's enough common ground left to warrant still having
anything to do with each other."

"Yeah," I said glumly. "I have the worst feeling Lars and I
are in a relationship."

Cleo cocked her head. "Has that honestly only just occurred to you?"

"The idea may have dawned on me a few days ago."

"Well done. Your dramatic run through the hospital ward
last weekend kind of gave it away."

I scoffed. "I run for no man."

"Hauled ass like your pants were on fire."

"Actually, that reminds me," I said. "A local athletic wear brand might be giving you a call. They reached out regarding one of our combined projects and I told them you were the genius behind the camera lens."

"Okay. Are you working with them?"

"They have their own in-house social media manager. But they were shook by your shots."

"Nice. I'll keep an eye out." She smiled. "How else did dinner with the folks go?"

I downed some more wine. "Eh. I don't know..."

"Talk to me, Susie," she said. "Tell me everything."

Everything ok?

"If I wind up getting possessed I will be so pissed at you," said Cleo several hours later. During which time Lars had not answered my text. Not a good sign.

"We're not going to become possessed. And I promise to find you a hot priest on the off chance your head starts spinning around."

"Oh, good."

We were lying on the living room rug, attempting a séance. On the coffee table sat the divorce certificate, a bunch of candles, and a number of empty bottles. There was an ever-so-small chance we were wine drunk. But hey, it happened to the best of us now and then. Especially if you drank a lot of wine. That really increased the chances.

"It's not easy being your bestie," she said. "You know that, right?"

"I do."

"Hmm."

"Would anything like to communicate with us?" I asked the darkened room. Shadows from the flickering candles danced on the ceiling. But otherwise the spirit world was still. "Unless you're evil, in which case, bye."

"Nice save."

"Thanks."

"Specifically we would like to talk to Aunt Susan," added Cleo. "We have questions."

Nothing happened. Then Kat the cat dashed into the room with her tail all fluffed like a toilet brush and, seeing nothing in need of the immediate attention of her claws, she jumped onto the sofa and settled down to give herself a bath. In all likelihood, she was waiting on Lars's return. She was far more his feline than mine. When he finally got around to moving back to his condo, Kat would be heartbroken. And she would not be alone. Dammit.

"Aren't you supposed to cast a circle of protection or something?" asked Cleo, rising up on her elbow to down some more wine. She was drinking out of a glass. How pretentious. I'd been chugging chardonnay straight from the bottle like a basic bitch for the last hour, at least.

"How would I know? I'm not a witch and it's been years since I watched *Supernatural*. I'm not even convinced ghosts are real."

"And you think I am?" Cleo shook her head. "Talk about your aunt. Maybe that'll stir the interest of something on the other side."

"Okay." I cleared my throat. "Aunt Susan died of stroke a little over six months ago. I talked to her the night before and she said she was fine, just a little tired. She invited me over for breakfast the next morning. But she never woke up. I hope that means it was painless. That she was gone before she ever even knew what was happening. Her face looked peaceful, but… I don't know. Her hand was cold to the touch. She must have been dead for hours when I found her. At any rate,

I loved her very much. Mostly I'm bummed that I never got to say goodbye to her. To hear her last words of wisdom."

"I bet she would have had something good to say."

"Yeah," I said. "She would definitely have advice for handling the current drama happening in my life. I know she always said to ask if Oprah would approve of the choices I'm making. But that's not much use when I can't decide what to do about him. And I have no idea what Dolly Parton would do about any of my relationship woes. Apart from write a song maybe."

"It would make for a really cool song, too."

"Oh, it would be great. In Dolly's hands, finding the divorce certificate would seem all poetical. You know, symbolical of stuff." I sighed as the ceiling drifted in lazy drunken circles above my head. "That's about it. Did you want to add anything?"

"No. I'm fine."

"Okay."

A soft tapping came from the back of the house. We both gasped and turned in its direction, but nada, nothing. No floating specter. Not even one of those little orbs of light. Kat gave us a disgruntled look before going back to sleep.

Cleo swallowed. "Probably just the wind blowing a branch against the side of the house or...you know. It's an old building. It could be anything."

"Maybe what we need is the right equipment," I said, picking up my cell.

"What are you doing?"

"Checking Etsy for ghost-hunting stuff."

"Because that makes sense."

"When in doubt, accessorize."

Cleo snorted.

"Well, we've already tried a psychic, psychometry reading,

and tarot cards. There's obviously something we're missing. Because weird shit has happened in this house. As evidenced by the divorce certificate."

"Has it ever occurred to you that maybe *the certificate was* meant to be your aunt's last words?"

I thought it over. Not that my brain was particularly functioning well, soaked in alcohol. "Wouldn't that be something?"

"Aunt Susan sending you hints about your future from the other side."

We both pondered the idea for a moment. Then Cleo said, "You should also tell them what your current issues are. Just to be clear."

"Them being the ghosts? You think there's more than one listening?"

She shrugged. "I'm not convinced any are. But we should at least attempt to be thorough."

"Right. Okay." I took a deep breath. "My problem is Lars."

The room sat in silence.

"Yes, but what about him exactly is a problem?" asked Cleo, eventually.

"Well...he exists."

"You're ridiculous." Cleo laughed. "I mean, you've always been dubious about love. We have that in common. But never to this degree."

"You see how you feel when the universe tells you not only who you should marry, but that the marriage is going to be a bust. Making you question why you would ever even go there in the first damn place."

She sighed. "Spirits, if you have any advice for my love-lorn friend here, please speak or moan or whatever. We're listening."

Nothing.

A car drove by.

More nothing.

Followed by a banging on the front door. Cleo and I both screeched.

Which was when Tore wandered in all calm-like. "Why are you sprawled drunkenly on the floor?"

"Holy shit," I muttered, pressing a hand to my galloping heart. "*Sprawled* sounds ungainly."

Lars followed his brother in and gave me a chin tip. Such a dude thing to do.

"We're classier than that," added Cleo. "More refined."

"What word would you use then?" asked Tore. "And why were you screaming?"

Cleo sniffed. "I haven't even decided if I'm ready to talk to you yet. Let alone if I'm prepared to explain my current inebriated behavior."

Tore frowned. "I said I was sorry."

"Susie, dismiss the spirits, please," said Cleo.

Lars's brows went up, but he said nothing.

"Thank you for your time, spirits and anything spirit adjacent. You can go now. And you should. Please. Bye."

Cleo turned her attention back to her boyfriend. "Come here, you."

Tore smiled and lay down beside her. They started talking in whispers. Soon her arm was slung over his shoulders, fingers toying with his hair.

"You left me on Read," I said in an unhappy tone.

Lars scratched at his stubble. "There was a lot going on. I didn't have time to text you back, sorry."

"Was everything okay with your bestie?"

"He'd drunk half a bottle of bourbon by the time I got there. I put him to bed in the recovery position with some water, ibuprofen, and a bucket in case he pukes."

I nodded.

Cleo and Tore had progressed to making out. Guess their fight was over.

Lars offered me his hand. Despite the gallantry, I did most of the lifting of my drunken ass off the floor. His body was still healing.

"Are you mad at me?" he asked, pulling me toward the bedroom for some privacy. Both for us, and the couple on the floor. Kat followed, winding herself around his legs.

I sighed. "No."

"Miss Lillian called," he said. "I talked to her the night of your party about her place down the street and she finally got back to me. Decided she wants to sell. That's where Tore and I have been for the last couple of hours, checking it out and settling on a price."

"Wow. She always was a night owl. But shouldn't you have waited for daylight to check out the house?"

"It was fine. We saw what we needed to. The place is going to be a lot of work, but it's like this one. In a great location with a ton of potential." He smiled. "She wants to close as soon as possible. Apparently she's decided she belongs in the desert, better for her arthritis. She's already got her eye on a place down in Arizona. I'll call my boss and talk things over in the morning. The plan is I'll move into Miss Lillian's house in a week when the condo closes and get started straight away doing what I can. It's not like I'm good for anything at work with this cast on my wrist. Hopefully my boss will agree."

"That's a shame that Miss Lillian is leaving. But you're really doing it?" My eyebrows reached for the sky. "You and Tore are starting your business?"

This time his smile was much larger. "Yeah."

"That's fantastic, Lars."

"Thank you. The time is right. Feels like everything is finally coming together." He shuffled his feet. "This is big. I'm still trying to wrap my head around it."

"It's huge."

"Mateo will hopefully come work for us on the next flip if Lillian's sells for what we're hoping. Tore will stay on at his job for a little longer to ensure there's definitely still cash coming in. But otherwise we're all set. This is what we've been planning and saving toward all these years."

"I'm so happy for you. You're going to do great."

"That damn car could have killed me last week."

"I know," I said quietly. "I can see why that would push you to put the plan into motion sooner rather than later."

He nodded. "There's a hell of a lot I still want to do in life. Things I want to achieve."

"Yeah."

Then he raised a finger to boop my nose, making me giggle. Either he was a comedy god, or I was drunk off my ass. It honestly could have been either.

"Any luck talking to ghosts?" he asked.

"No. Nothing."

"And you actually sound surprised by that."

"Hope springs eternal." I smiled. "Wonder if you'll find anything in the walls of Miss Lillian's house."

"I fucking hope not. Things are complicated enough." He turned away. "I'm going to head back over to the condo tomorrow. Pack everything up."

My face fell. "Oh."

He narrowed his eyes at me. "What does that look mean, Susie?"

"Nothing."

"You sure about that?"

"Well, I mean, are you going to do that and then come back

for the next week?" I asked. "Or are you like leaving now on a more permanent basis?"

"I'm getting out of your hair for the time being," he clarified. "But I'll be around."

"Right. That's...that's good."

"That's good?" His gaze roamed over my face. As if I were in any condition to be examined. It was past time for me to get my ass into bed. He took a step back and leaned against the wall. Was it just my imagination or was he putting distance between us?

"Yes." I frowned. But that wasn't the right face. So I smiled instead. "Everything is working out so well for you, Lars. Your whole life plan is coming together."

"Yeah."

"Yeah," I repeated softly. "I, um... Can we maybe talk some more about this in the morning?"

He nodded. "Okay."

The best cure for a hangover has long been debated. Some swear by hair of the dog. While others are big on electrolytes. One college friend of mine simply refused to rise until any and all symptoms had passed. Which might have been why she had a tendency to fail any subjects scheduled for Monday morning. My own personal cure-all involved caffeine, grease, and painkillers. Since it was summer, I went with an ice-cold can of Coke. This was served with eggs, bacon, and toast, with two Tylenol on the side. A combination that soon worked wonders on my headache and queasy stomach.

Not waking until after ten meant Lars was long gone. But he'd left me a note. He'd be back tonight for our talk. What the hell was I going to say to the man? That was the question. Feelings frightened me. The house was strangely quiet without him. For someone who'd loved having a place to herself just a few short months ago, this was a not-so-welcome reaction to his absence. Was I willing to sacrifice some of my independence for his companionship? He might not even want to take this thing between us further. Or at least, not so fast. His reactions last night had been confusing. Though that might have been the booze.

With no immediate answer to these questions, I buried myself in work, liaising with influencers regarding the recent launch of the period panties. Their online presence on a Sunday was normal. Social media could be a 24-7 thing. Although I tried to find a life/work balance, it didn't always happen. Though being my own boss more than made up for it on most occasions. That I'd been forced to don a pair of the panties that morning made the work even more relevant. Little wonder I was in a weird emotional state with my hormones raging and blood flowing. Having your period was so bleh.

Then I switched my phone to silent for a couple of hours and took flowers to Aunt Susan's grave. It gave me a chance to fill her in on everything that had been happening. Whether she was any more present at the cemetery than she had been in the house, I had no idea. But it made me feel better just the same. The cemetery was peaceful and green and reasonably close to home. I think it's what Aunt Susan would have chosen. And the bouquet of wildflowers I bought would have delighted her. She loved bright colorful things.

Life had changed a lot since the day I helped carry her coffin out to the hearse. It had been raining, the sky a dark, sea gray. While I'd given up on having a relationship with my father years before, I'd held out hope for some sort of friendship with my brother. But he'd put that dream to rest at the funeral. Aunt Susan raised me to be resilient. Self-reliant. Somewhere along the line, I'd set those lessons aside and started chasing crappy relationships with men who reminded me of my father. Of all the obvious damn mistakes to make. Lars at least was nothing like him. Not even a little.

It was odd how much had changed in the half a year since I'd lost Aunt Susan. How I saw myself and the world. My grief seemed to be settling into more of an ongoing ache. Less sharp-edged than it had been. But then grief was weird, the way it played with your mind. The last time I thought I was doing okay, I wound up crying in the candy aisle at a grocery store. Seeing her favorite brand of chocolate had set me off for some reason. It sucked that in life you only had some people with you for a short time. Guess it was why we needed to live and love with conviction. Like she'd done. To be colorful and wild and free of spirit. To stop being so fucking afraid.

On the way home, I picked up some soft tacos liberally topped with cilantro. Lars hated cilantro. But it didn't matter what he liked because he wasn't there and they were just for me. And I didn't put my shoes away when I got back to the house either. Grown ass women could leave their stuff where they liked in their own homes. I was the queen of this castle. Which made it time for a *Gilmore Girls* binge. Lars would have hated it. He liked shows full of action and adventure where characters most definitely did not discuss their emotions or what book they were currently reading. Though he had recently become a Romance reader so who knows. I also took up all of the space on the sofa. Just me. So there.

I didn't need a man in my life. That was the God's honest truth. But did I want one?

When the show failed to hold my interest, I wandered from room to room. In search of something. I don't know what. Kat was not impressed with my restlessness. All of the kitchen cupboards and drawers were firmly closed. My snack stash was low, but oh well. It's not like I was hungry after all the tacos. I retrieved the mysterious divorce certificate and laid it out on the bed. No further messages had appeared. Not from the past or the future. In the bathroom, I attempted to smooth out the strangled tube of toothpaste. Easier said than done. Next I strewed my skincare and makeup back across the entirety of the bathroom counter. Spread that stuff around like it was my job. Then I stood back and stared at the mess. It was an apt metaphor. This was my life. My normal state of being.

"Hey," said Lars, appearing at the bathroom door. There was a smudge of dirt on his forehead and a general air of tired and sweaty to him. He took in the disaster atop the bathroom counter and smiled. "Hope you don't mind I let myself in. How's your day been?"

"Fine. Did you get the condo sorted out?"

"Everything I don't need is in storage and the rest is either here or easy enough to pack up at the end of the week."

"I would have helped, you know."

"You deserved to sleep in," he said. "Did you know you snore when you're drunk?"

"You're awful lucky you're so pretty. It makes up for the petty lies you tell."

"They're not loud snores, but still." His smile was there and gone in a moment. "I went and checked on Aaron."

"How is he?"

"Over the worst of it, I think."

"It's never easy getting dumped."

"I wouldn't know." Lars stretched his neck. "It's never happened to me."

"Seriously?" My brows rose. "You say that like it's a good thing. Thirty-five years old and you've always been the first to give up."

"Not necessarily. Sometimes it was a mutual decision."

"Hmm. Ask yourself this, have you ever actually been invested in a single romantic relationship you've been a part of? I mean *really*?"

He opened his mouth and shut it again. Then he turned his gaze back to the bathroom counter. "After today you'll have all of your space back again."

"No more stubble in the sink," I agreed, letting him change the topic of conversation.

"I'm going to miss your bed. You have a really good mattress."

"Is that all you're going to miss?"

"No," he said, his expression grave. "It's not."

I sighed. This man...what the hell was I going to do with him?

"You said you wanted to talk last night. What's on your mind, Susie?"

I perched on the edge of the old claw-foot tub and thought deep thoughts. The same ones that had been spinning around inside my head all day. "I, um, I..."

"Yeah?"

"You're planning on starting work on Lillian's place this week, right?"

"That's right. There's still a lot of prep stuff I can get done while we sign contracts and wait for the sale to finalize."

"Right." Then I opened my mouth and blurted out, "You should stay."

He blinked. "What?"

"I mean, when you think about it, it would be stupid for you to move back to the condo. If you were here you'd be much closer. And it's only for a little while longer."

"You want me to stay with you for another week?"

"Yes."

"That wouldn't be a hassle?" He cocked his head. "You're not asking to be polite or anything, are you? I don't want to be in your way. You've been more than kind enough letting me be here for the last week already. And I'm doing okay now with all of the sore neck and meds and everything."

"No hassle. You'd be very welcome."

"Okay." He smiled, but it was restrained. "All right. Thanks, Susie."

I'd solved the problem of me and this man for another week. The truth was, it was still early days for Lars and me. For whatever we were doing together. He didn't feel like a bad choice, though. In fact, having him close felt incredibly good. Which was scary in its own way. One day soon I was going to need to pull up my big-girl panties and make some serious decisions regarding the man. But not just yet. I had rushed in with Aaron and I was determined not to make that mistake again.

"Sure, Lars. Not a problem."

Fifteen

Week two of living with Lars had a distinctly different vibe. With his injuries on the mend, he was less cranky and more motivated. And while he still took up the bulk of the bed, he now did so in the big spoon position. For the last couple of days, I'd woken with my back pressed to his chest and his arm thrown over my hips. He was a cuddler, apparently. The new positioning did not disturb my sleep in the least. Though his morning wood had a tendency to rouse me before my alarm. The man was fortunate I was fond of his private parts.

Monday and Tuesday he spent doing light work around Lillian's house. Measuring and planning, ordering and cleaning. He'd push my first cup of caffeine into my hands then disappear for the day. Tore joined him for his lunch breaks at the property. He also came back in the evening to do any of the heavier or more difficult work. Lars and I fell into a routine of eating dinner together, sometimes in front of the TV and sometimes at the table. Living with him felt easy. Just having him there being a daily part of my life. But it also felt horribly temporary. I thought keeping things casual was what I wanted, but I was wrong. I needed to ask him to stay. The fear of him shrugging me off, though…what if he thought it was too soon? As his mom had pointed out, the man had never actually lived with a girlfriend before.

Once the sun set and the heat had dissipated, we would go for a walk. While he wasn't up for jogging, Lars could stroll just fine. Heading away from Salmon Bay, we'd lap the playground and pass by a local pizza place. Despite not holding hands, it seemed a distinctly couple-type thing to do. Way more than a friends-with-benefits or amorous-roommates or whatever-we-were-these-days type of activity. Though that might have been because of my chosen topic of conversation on this particular occasion.

"You want to know what I'm looking for in a relationship?" asked Lars in a surprised voice. "Ah, man…honestly, I don't know. Companionship, compatibility, things like that."

"Okay. What's your idea of a perfect date? And don't say April 25th."

He gave me a blank look.

"You've never seen *Miss Congeniality*?"

"No," he said. "And I usually take dates out to dinner."

"Your loss and that's a highly unimaginative answer. Moving right along. What's one thing about yourself that no one else knows?"

"I don't know. Probably that I let you harass me."

"You're not taking this seriously," I said. "The article I read said these questions are supposed to provide us with valuable insights into each other. To help share hidden facets of our personality. All the better to build our union of souls upon solid unshakeable ground."

"Our union of souls?" His tone was more derision than wonder. "Did you seriously just say that?"

"It's like you don't care about working on our friendship-slash-burgeoning relationship at all."

"Is that what we're doing, huh?"

"It's as good a description as any." I smiled serenely and let my gaze wander. It was a big ask not to ogle him when he was wearing cut-off sweatpants. My respect for soft cotton was at an all-time high. Healing from the accident had slowed our sex life right down and my hormones were not pleased. Given how sore his muscles had been the day after the one time we'd done it, I refused to open my legs to the man for his own safety. And he hadn't pushed, making me think the pain was far worse than he admitted. My knees, however, were getting awfully weak of will and my thick thighs were all but crying out for his touch. Waking up pressed against him was a special sort of torment. Lars was walking around with my libido in his back pocket and I'm not even sure he was aware of the fact.

"What are you looking at?" he asked, voice curious.

"You."

The smile he gave me was all sorts of satisfied mixed with male pride. Swoon.

"What are you thinking about?" I asked.

"How you taste."

"Huh." My throat was a dry and barren desert. All of the moisture in me was heading south. "I have nothing clever to say to that."

"Amazing. There's a first time for everything." He smiled. "I've been meaning to ask, do you have the third book in Naima Simone's *Rose Bend* series?"

"No, but I can order it for you."

"That's all right. I'll buy it. Here's another question," he said. "What do you think it means that you get such enjoyment out of driving me crazy asking me all of this shit?"

"I'm just trying to help. Do you want to get divorced? Is that what you want, Lars?"

"Wish it didn't always come back to that damn certificate."

"Yeah." The less said about it the better. "Okay. No more first-date icebreaker questions. Though the point remains that your favorite song should be something from this century."

"Led Zeppelin is classic," he grumbled.

"As for your superpower being invisibility?" I screwed up my nose. "Ew. Pervert."

"I didn't mean it like that." So much man pain in his groan. "I'm changing my answer to super strength."

"Too late."

"What? You changed your answer like five times. You went from flight, to speed, to… I don't even know what."

I smiled. "We've moved on. You're too late. Deal with it."

"This is rigged."

"And how can you not even know what makes you happy? I will never understand why you menfolk are so repressed. Get in touch with your feelings, dude."

"You're in touch with your feelings?" he asked with a dubious glance.

"Sure. Mostly. Sort of."

He grunted.

"Come on, Lars, what makes you happy?"

"Well, I thought being with you made me happy," he said. "But then you kept asking me all these damn questions."

"Aw. You say the sweetest things."

He hooked an arm around my neck and drew me closer. "Susie, were you always this much trouble?"

"You mean did I give my other special male friends this much grief?" I thought it over. "No. Just you."

"Interesting. Why do you think that is?"

"You want honesty?"

"Always."

Insert big sigh here. "I don't know that I felt safe enough to really be myself with them."

"You didn't feel safe?"

"No. I guess not."

He stared at me for a moment. Then he stared past me at the front steps of the house. At the well-dressed man standing with his hand raised to knock on my door.

"Andrew?" I said, surprised.

"Your brother?" asked Lars in a low voice.

I nodded.

Lars's hand slipped down my spine, resting in the small of my back. While I was grateful for the support, I could handle this on my own. "Andrew, why are you here?"

He frowned at Lars before turning to me and saying, "Just thought I'd stop by and say hello. It's been a while."

"Okay," I said cautiously. "Hi."

"I've been busy starting my own business."

"Dad mentioned."

He peered around him. "The old place is looking good. You've had some work done."

"Yes."

"Have you gotten an updated appraisal on what it's worth?"

"For insurance purposes, yes."

Andrew nodded. Then he shuffled his feet. He'd run out of conversation, apparently. "So...aren't you going to invite me in? I'd love to see what you've done."

"No, Andrew. You're not coming into my home until you apologize for the way you behaved at Aunt Susan's funeral. For the shitty way you talked to me. It was over six months ago now. I think you've delayed long enough."

His brows snapped into place. "What?"

"You heard me."

"Susan blatantly favored you. It was unfair," he bitched. "I didn't say anything that wasn't true."

"I *loved* her. You barely tolerated her. She owed you nothing and neither do I."

"We're family."

"Family is about more than just finding people useful occasionally. Or so I'm told."

Lars's hand covered mine, holding it against his chest. Anchoring me. As much as I was used to handling my family, it was nice to have the support.

"Is that what you came here for?" I continued. "To see if I'd softened on the idea of selling my home and giving you half?"

Andrew drew himself up. "It would be the right thing to do."

"No, it wouldn't. Not that I expect you to understand." I smiled sadly. "Go away, please."

He blinked in disbelief. Though it'd been years since I'd fallen for his particular brand of bullshit, it still stunned him. "Susie—"

"She asked you to leave," Lars ground out. "And she did it a hell of a lot nicer than I will if you're still here in a minute."

"Fuck you," said Andrew. "I don't even know who you are."

"I'm the man who has your sister's back. Now get the fuck out of here."

Despite asking Lars to stay out of it, I had to admit, that was a pretty great line. No one of the male persuasion had ever been willing to put themselves between me and my problems before. And what a big handsome barricade he made. Though I could have handled it on my own. However, if I had, I'd have missed the sight of Lars drawn up to his full height with his jaw set and hands curled into fists.

"You should go, Andrew," I repeated.

"Susie—"

"You are not going to wear me down with your self-entitled

bullshit. I should not have to buy your supposed brotherly love. Now leave."

Andrew ground his teeth together, then stomped down the steps and over to the shiny new sedan parked across the street. Odds were he and his business would be just fine. Mom or Dad would give him the rest of the money. There was a solid history of them bailing the golden boy out of all sorts of trouble. The same kind of situations that earned me a lecture and an admonition to do better. Groan.

That was why Andrew never learned to do for himself. Was I jealous he got more love than I did? Maybe I used to be. But not anymore. With a rev of the engine he tore off down the street. Odd how my sibling had lost the ability to upset me. Guess you had to be emotionally invested in someone for that to happen. We'd never been close. Now I knew we never would be. Not after that scene at Aunt Susan's funeral. Sure as hell, not after tonight.

"There goeth the mediocre white man," I said in a dry tone.

Lars grunted.

"Thanks for having my back."

"Anytime," he said gently. It kind of killed me when he used that tone of voice. Like I was precious.

"Look at us, consciously coupling," I joked. At least, it was sort of a joke.

He cocked his head. "Are we seriously a couple?"

"I don't know." I took a deep breath and let it out slowly. "You tell me."

"Well, you've admitted to having feelings for me."

"I even accept that there's some sort of romantic relationship between you and me. Just in case all of the first-date icebreaker questions didn't give it away."

"That's a big step," he said, voice thoughtful. "You were pretty adamant about not wanting to date."

"My refusal really stung you, huh?"

"Yeah. It did," he said, with all due seriousness. "But I guess you trust me now. At least a little. Despite my taste in friends and the mystery divorce certificate."

My mouth opened and nothing came out. Awkward as heck. Our issues did give me cause for concern. That much was true.

Kat appeared, winding herself around Lars's ankles. When he picked her up, she happily flopped boneless over his shoulder baby style. Long firm strokes down her back soon had her purring loudly.

Lars's return smile was wry. "It's okay, Susie. You don't have to say it."

"I do trust you." The words hardly stuck in my throat at all. "But, Lars, what exactly do you want from me here? I guess that's the question I was ever so slowly working my way toward with all of the icebreaker nonsense."

The smile faded and his expression turned somber. "You're ready to get serious and talk this out?"

"Yeah."

"Okay," he said in a soft voice. "Tell me what you're thinking."

"I mean, do you still want to just date?" My shoulders were approximately up around my ears. "Because you've got your business happening and that's great. But is there room for me in your life or are we...? I don't know. I feel like I don't fit into your plan."

The man set the cat down gently, looked me straight in the eye, and said, "Fuck the plan."

Wow.

"You need me to repeat that?"

"Ah, no. Heard you loud and clear."

"Good. We're together, right?" he asked. "It feels like we're together. I'm staying with you for a few more days, at least."

"Right." I looked away. "Or you could stay longer."

A gentle hand to my chin directed my gaze back to his face. "You want me to stay longer?"

"If you want to."

"How much longer?"

"Um."

He said nothing, but his fingers stayed put. Warm and firm and just there for me. Like I wanted him to be. Like all of the others hadn't been.

"We could make it an ongoing-for-the-foreseeable-future kind of thing. Or not if that's moving too fast." My heart would be bruised black and blue from all of the crashing it was doing against my ribs. "I know you've never lived with a girlfriend before and when you think about it, we haven't actually been together for long, but—"

"Yes," he said with nil hesitation. "I want to live with you."

The way my mind started scrambling. Ugh. "Right. Okay. I mean, it is convenient, staying with me. The house is just down the—"

The emotion in his eyes was pure thunder. "Don't."

"Don't?"

The fingers on my chin tightened ever so slightly. "You're right. I'm new to this. The relationships I've been in… I don't normally let them get this far. But can we agree that if I'm living with you, it's because I want to be with you. Because we're together. Not because it's convenient or some other bullshit excuse, okay?"

"O-okay."

"Thank you."

"You're welcome."

A car parked down the street and a television boomed from the house opposite us before being silenced. Otherwise the night was peaceful. The suburbs were at rest.

"We're really doing this," I said, more than a little amazed.

"Yeah, we are."

I nodded slowly. "I'm afraid, but you're worth the risk."

"You don't have to be afraid."

"Lars, you like things organized and neat and making sense. That's not always me."

"Princess." He leaned in closer. "Do you honestly believe I don't know that by now?"

His slow smile was breathtaking and the truth of his words sent warmth spreading through my chest. The sense of rightness. He and I here in this moment—it was all as it should be. An urge to get poetic sat on the tip of my tongue. To liken him to a summer's day and maybe even throw the L-word out there for the very first time. Though he had said it in the hospital, he was under the influence of some heavy-duty painkillers. So that didn't count. He was high as a kite. There weren't many people in my life that I loved. I could count them on one hand. What I felt for this man was a lot and it made me so...hopeful. Even with the existence of the divorce certificate. Maybe this might work. Stranger things had happened. But would it be astonishing or scary if Lars said he loved me? Both, was the answer. Maybe I could annoy him into loving me. It was worth a try.

Whatever the expression on my face was, it made him smile. "Neither of us planned on getting together. I'm going to fuck up now and then and so are you. We just have to keep trying, okay?"

"Okay."

His phone buzzed in his back pocket and he pulled it out and looked at the screen. "It's Aaron. I can catch up with him later."

"No," I said. "It's okay. Answer it. I know you've been worried about him with the breakup and everything."

His forehead creased. "Are you sure?"

I nodded and smiled magnanimously. We were together. Everything was great. I refused to allow my Ex to be a point of contention between us. So there.

Sixteen

Lars strode along the hiking trail all primordial male let loose upon nature. A conquering Viking. Nothing could stand in his way. Though he did stop to rub his sore ribs now and then. I, meanwhile, was not doing as well on our first-ever couples hike. The wildflowers and old-growth forest were beautiful. Same with the bridges crossing the creek. I got some great shots and video for social media. Then the hiking began. It turned out that strolling around the neighborhood was quite different from scaling the side of a fucking mountain. I'd scared off an array of local wildlife with all of my panting and groaning. My new boyfriend better have a penchant for sweaty women with red faces. Otherwise he was in serious trouble.

"Are you sure this is supposed to be an easy trail?" I asked and slapped at my arm. "The damn bug spray is not working."

He stopped and looked me over. Taking in my low-slung ponytail, black racer-back ribbed cotton tank, and matching shorts with embroidery. And the look in his eye…talk about judgy. "I told you those shoes weren't a good idea."

"My black leather platform booties are great."

"No one wears platform booties to hike."

"It's a very small platform, Lars. Like an inch and a half at most. It's not like they've got a high heel or something. And they're one of the most comfortable pairs of shoes I own."

"You don't have a pair of sneakers?"

"Yes. But they're suede and it might have been muddy. These are easier to clean."

His stare was one of wonder. Just not the good kind. Which kind of summed up our day so far. Ever since he'd returned from having a drink with his bestie last night he had been in a mood.

"I feel sad for you that you don't understand my reasoning," I said.

He pressed his lips tightly together and said nothing. A whole lot of it.

"What?"

"I think it's great that you live up to your name, Princess. Also, I take it back," he said. "Our first couples outing should have been me acting as your pack mule, following you around the mall. I see now that you would have enjoyed that a lot more. Because yes, this is the easiest trail they have here."

"If you say so." I sniffed. "Do you normally take girlfriends hiking?"

"Not really. But you seemed keen on the idea."

"I thought by *commune with nature* you meant like a gentle walk on the beach, or hanging out in a beer garden or something. There's a very valid reason why I avoid the gym rats on Tinder."

He hung his head and grabbed at the back of his neck. "Maybe we should think of other things we can do together."

"While I appreciate you wanting to share this experience with me, I'm fine with you saving your hiking trips for your friends Brandon and River. That can be part of your me time."

He nodded.

"But following me around while I shop is neither going to bring us closer nor fill your heart with joy. The answer for our couples hobby lies elsewhere."

"Yeah."

"Maybe we should have put this whole idea off for another time. You had a big week. How are you feeling?"

In response, he grunted and stared at the path. Men. Such delicate emotional creatures.

"Want to talk about why you were staring at the divorce certificate this morning?"

He shoved an agitated hand through his hair. "I don't fucking know."

"Okay."

"Susie…shit."

I just waited.

"I'm sorry."

"You don't have to be happy all the time," I said. "No one is. But I'm here if you decide you want to talk about whatever's bothering you."

Nothing from him.

Time for less talking and more walking.

"Wait," he said. Then he did some more hanging of the head. Never had a man been treated so badly. Finally he said, "Normally this is the point where I'd leave. Go get some space. Or just end things entirely because it's too damn hard and messing with my head."

My heart lodged hard in my throat. "Right."

"But I don't want to do that with you."

"What do you want to do?"

"I told Aaron about the certificate last night."

My eyes were as wide as dinner plates. "You did?"

"He asked me how we got together and I didn't want to lie."

"That's understandable. He's your oldest friend."

"He had a lot of questions." Lars grabbed the back of his neck. "Same sort of things we've been thinking."

"How long did it take him to suggest that I had set this up as a way to get back at him?"

"That's not what he said. Not exactly."

"Right," I scoffed.

"Susie, he knows what you mean to me. He's just looking out for me, is all."

I crossed my arms.

"He asked all of the same things we did at the start too."

"What you tell him is your choice. But I think it's best if we leave off discussing your bestie the bulk of the time," I said. "I believe in you, Lars. But when it comes to him and his honesty and reliability, we're just going to have to agree to disagree."

"How about the way it's making things awkward with my mother?"

"You told your *mom* about the certificate?"

"No," he said. "I mean...this beef between you and Aaron makes her resistant to getting to know you."

"She's your mom, Lars. What do you want me to say?" I shrugged. "Deborah can love me or hate me. I'd prefer that we get along, but in the end, it doesn't really matter. I'm not here for her. I'm here for you. But I'm not going to change my mind about your friend anytime soon."

"I know. I'm not asking you to." He stepped closer, setting his hands on my hips. "I hate that these problems are coming from my side."

"That's understandable. Fixing things is sort of your mission in life," I said. "But, it's not like I don't have trust issues and other neuroses. We both have stuff to work through. Neither of us are perfect."

Furrows wrinkled his brow. "I know, but I can't help worrying that..."

My smile was not a particularly happy one. "That one of your problems will be what causes the divorce?"

"Yeah."

"I worry about that too. That I'm the one that wrecks us. Especially since I was the one who filed for divorce. But here's the thing about your best friend," I said. "Sooner or later, he's going show himself to be the utter and complete dick I know him to be. He's not smart enough to hide it from you forever. And he's too entitled to think he even has to. Then, at that time, you'll be able to embrace what you'll find you've really known deep down all along."

"And what's that?" asked Lars with a hint of a smile.

"That I'm always right."

"Come here." His hands slid around and down to my butt. And the warmth in his gaze turned me to mush.

I looped my arms around his neck, pressing the length of my body against his. Being this close to him could never get old. It was heavenly.

His fingers kneaded my ass cheeks in a demanding fashion. The way he pressed me against the growing bulge in his pants...it was nice to be wanted. I'd been a little worried after his lack of interest after he got home last night. But it was the gentle kiss he pressed to my forehead that made my heart roll over and offer itself up to him. There were no more walls or defenses to keep him out. He owned me body and soul. That was the truth.

He rested his cheek against the top of my head. "I'm sorry for being a grumpy asshole. Again."

"Thank you. That's very nice to hear."

"Is it?"

"Yes. I appreciate you staying and talking it out with me."

"Whatever makes you happy, Princess."

"Did we just have our first official couples fight?" I asked. "Though it might have been more stern words than an actual fight. Still. What a milestone!"

"Must mean it's time for makeup sex." He pushed his muscular thigh between my legs, urging me via the grip of my ass to press against him. My stomach tightened and my nipples hardened. That thick thigh of his flexed against me, making me clench. What a talented man. And he was all mine. He nuzzled my neck, teeth nipping and tongue licking. "Fuck, you're beautiful. You have no idea how much I've missed being inside you this last week and a half. Living with you and not being able to touch you has been torture."

"It's a pity we didn't have this fight where there's a mattress handy."

"Just occurred to me that sex is something we could do together that we both enjoy."

I laughed. "The article that I read about being a successful couple did specify that finding common interests was integral to maintaining a healthy relationship. Though I tend to think they already assumed we were doing it."

"Oh, that reminds me," he said, coming up for air. "You good with me putting some shelves in the bathroom?"

"What exactly about dry humping on a hiking trail made you think of that?" I asked, perplexed. "I have to know."

He just smiled. "They'll be recessed so they're neat and tidy and complement the style of the house. Then you'll have more room for all of your stuff where you can see it. I know you like having it all on display."

"You want to build shelves for my makeup and skincare?"

"Yeah. Reading the books made me think. Building and fixing things is my love language. Therefore, your home should be as perfect for you as I can make it."

I pursed my lips and blew out a breath. "You are so getting lucky when we get home."

"Why wait?" His hands slipped lower, lifting me off my feet. I wrapped my legs around him and tightened my grip on his neck. Which put the hardening ridge of his cock right where I needed it, thank you very much. Then he wandered off the track, through some bushes, and into the wilderness. "There's bound to be a nice tree back here somewhere."

"This is not gentle movement."

"Relax, Princess. The doctor cleared me for all sorts of things."

"Please do not drop my ass in any poison ivy."

"Have some trust." He snorted. "Such a city girl."

"Like you didn't already know that."

With a narrowed gaze, he assessed our surrounds. "That should be far enough from the track. I'm thinking the alder over there will be best. Their bark isn't as scaly as others."

"Do you have a tree kink? Just curious."

He laughed.

"We could go back to the car."

Leaves and sticks and other assorted natural debris crunched beneath his heavy ass hiking boots. "No. We're communing with nature."

"Lars, are we seriously going to fuck in the forest like animals?"

"Absolutely. Call it a late birthday present."

With my back against a large tree trunk, he covered my mouth with his. His tongue slipped into my mouth and that was all it took. I was down with doing it in the great outdoors. We could have been anywhere as long as his hands stayed on me. The press of his lips on mine. The heat and wetness of his hungry kiss. It was all so good. Apparently, I was fine with frolicking in a forest after all. I simply needed the man that badly. One of his hands stayed curved around my ass while the other skated up my side, under my shirt. Not stopping until he had his palm curved over my breast. And all the while, he grew harder against me.

Clever fingers toyed with my nipple and I gasped. Sensation zapped through me. From my breasts to my core and back again. This was going to be fast and hard if it was happening. And it had to happen.

"Put me down," I ordered.

He did as told and I immediately started dealing with the buttons on my shorts. Trying to toe off one of my boots at the same time had me almost tripping over. But Lars steadied me, thankfully. Then he grabbed his wallet out of his back pocket and the condom waiting within. Love a man who came prepared. With my shorts and panties hanging off one leg, I was ready. It was just a matter of waiting for Lars to push down his pants and boxer briefs and get sheathed. His dick was long and hard and ready. Strong hands lifted me back into his arms, positioned himself against me, and pushed in with one hard thrust. Forcing the air from my lungs and filling me up to perfection.

It all happened in under a minute. We'd score well if it ever became an Olympic sport. Fast-start fornicating for our great country. Go, team.

The sound of his groan against my ear as he sunk in deep was divine. "Fuck. Susie."

"Mmm."

With my back to the tree once more, he worked his hips, pumping in and out of me. The feel of his heavy cock drawing out of me before pushing back inside. How it lit up my nerve endings and made everything low in me draw tight and tingle. The friction was divine. I don't know how else to describe it. Being surrounded by the scent of him, held tight in his muscular arms. Like nothing could harm me. Only good things happened here between us. And I wanted to stay here forever.

But the fact remained that we were out in public. Even if we were hidden from the trail. He fucked me fast and furious. Shoving the thick length of his dick deep inside of me over and over again. Rubbing his pelvis against the top of my sex, stimulating my clit. My blood pumped harder and hotter and I hung on for dear life. Head to toe, I was electric. Blinded by the light when I came with a gasp. Who needed to see the Northern Lights? Lars lit me up with just his own sweet self. My whole body was wrapped around him, inner muscles clenched tight around his cock. I bit down where his neck met his shoulder to keep from making more noise. But the way he roared as his whole body shook and he pumped out his seed deep inside of me, anyone within fifty miles had to have heard. Bears would have run for cover he was so damn loud. Sheesh.

When all was quiet, I said, "I'm thinking you love the great outdoors."

Nothing from Lars.

"Ouch. Slap my ass. Quick."

"What's wrong?" he asked.

"A bug just bit me on the butt."

He set me down and we sorted out our clothing. The condom was dealt with, and when everyone was decent, we walked hand in hand back toward the trail. Arriving just in time to see a family of three hike past. The looks the parents gave us…they'd definitely heard. Oops. Their small child, however, smiled and waved and skipped up the steep path that nearly broke my spirit.

"Show-off," I grumbled.

Lars plucked a leaf out of my hair and let it drift to the ground. "It's funny you should say that."

"What? About the kid?"

"No. About me loving the great outdoors." He gently cupped my cheek, leaned down and kissed me on the lips. Then he smiled. "Because I'd just been thinking that I love you."

"You love me?"

"Yes," he said, and headed back down the track toward the parking lot. "You coming?"

For a moment, all I could do was stare. As for breathing and thinking, I'd completely lost those abilities. Shock kept me immobile. It seemed the whole world stood still. Lars loved me. And with absolutely no nudging, he'd come right out and said as much. He didn't even ask if I felt the same way. He simply handed over his heart to me.

"Susie?"

"Um. Yeah. Coming."

"I think that's the second time I've made you too stunned to speak."

"You're keeping count?" I asked.

"Damn right I am."

And not another word was said until we got home. But the looks he gave me, the smiles…they were a lot.

Seventeen

To say I distrusted love would be an understatement. But I did trust Lars. Or I was actively learning how to trust him. If he was going to throw around the L-word, however, he needed to know exactly what he was getting into with me. And up until now, I'd been on my best behavior. Like when you had a house guest. You didn't use up all of the hot water and make the dash from the shower to your bedroom in ugly old underwear. You did your best to be hospitable. But if this was going to be his forever home with me, there would definitely be times when I would have neither the time, energy, nor inclination to play at being perfect. Lars needed to know the truth.

When we returned home from our failed hike, he retired for an afternoon nap. Further proof that he was still recovering from the accident. This was the perfect time for me to prepare for the demonstration. It actually didn't take long to unleash chaos. Aaron used to drop helpful hints if he felt my appearance wasn't up to scratch. It stung coming from him. But if

Lars ever did something similar, undermined me like that, it would devastate me. So it was best we sorted this out now.

"Hey," he mumbled on a yawn upon rising.

This was it, the great reveal. I turned slowly, letting him take it all in. The lopsided messy bun my tangled hair had been pulled back into, the algae-green skin-purifying mask I'd packed onto my face, the stretched and faded Arctic Monkeys tee, and holey denim cutoffs that were in all likelihood a size too small.

And his reaction was…nothing. The man just scratched at his short beard and asked, "Did you want to do something tonight?"

"I thought we should have a little chat after your surprising statement earlier."

"That came as a surprise?"

"Yes."

"But I said it to you at the hospital."

"When you were high."

"Mmm." He nodded. "High enough to let the truth slip out."

"Take a seat, Lars."

"Okay." He deposited himself in an armchair. "I'm listening."

"It occurred to me that you haven't seen me at my worst." I set my hands on my hips. "I dealt with you in the week after the accident when you were…what shall we call it…being especially special?"

He snorted. "I already apologized for that."

"I know. Moving on," I said. "The point is, I've been maintaining a certain image around you. Always with the perfect hair and makeup and the cute outfits."

At this, he frowned.

"While this—" I ran a hand up and down myself "—is

probably more me. Are you sure you want to live with and love this?"

He set his ankle on the opposite knee. "You mean the messy hair and face mask?"

"Yes. And the ugly old shirt."

"Don't you dare call that tee ugly. Not only are they a great band, but that shirt has been washed so many times and is so thin I can make out the shape of your breasts through it. That is an awesome shirt and you should definitely wear it around me more often."

I frowned. Which wasn't easy because the mask had set and tightened. "You're not taking me seriously."

"No?"

"I can be messy and bitchy and difficult," I said. "Are you sure you want to deal with all that on a daily basis? Is this really something you can love?"

"You, messy and bitchy? I had no idea. Where have you been hiding these behaviors?"

"Are you being sarcastic?"

He pressed his lips together and his eyes welled with tears. Wait. Those weren't tears. The fucker was laughing at me. And he wasn't even bothering to hide it. This was outrageous.

"I am trying to be honest with you," I said. "I don't want you to have unreasonable expectations that I can't live up to in the long term."

"Susie, you are worthy of being loved. You do know that, don't you?"

It took me a moment to answer. To wrinkle my nose and smile and say, "Of course. It's not about that."

"Then what is it about?"

"I would just prefer that if you're going to change your mind about being in love with me, because you discover something that is a deal breaker, that we get that out of the way sooner than later."

"Not going to happen," he said in a serious tone.

"But you don't know that for sure! There's no way you can!"

He sighed. "This is about the divorce certificate."

"Among other things," I admitted.

"Okay, Princess. Go ahead. Tell me how awful you are. Talk me out of loving you."

"Well..."

"I'm waiting," he said.

"This was supposed to be more of a visual presentation."

"Your legs look incredibly long in those tight little shorts," he said, head cocked to the side to take in the view.

"They give me a bit of a muffin top. Did you want to see?"

He just shrugged.

"Ooh. I know, I can be jealous at times. That's a pretty annoying habit."

"Yeah. You got upset about Jane. I got upset about Austin. Guess we both need to work through that, huh?" He yawned again and cracked his neck. The man was so not taking this seriously. "But if we both agree not to date other people it would probably take care of that issue."

"True."

"Next?"

"I don't know." My shoulders slumped. "I once worked with someone who mispronounced *chic* as *chick* and I disliked her so much I never corrected her."

He nodded. "That is petty. I'll give you that. What else have you got?"

"I see now that I should have taken the time to write a speech."

"Preparation is important." He smiled. "I feel it's only fair to tell you that I'm quite enjoying the cute dimples above your knees. If you're trying to turn me off, you're failing miserably."

"My bad hair and attitude would have scared off most of my exes."

"Idiots."

"Yeah."

"I knew telling you I loved you would get a reaction. But I have to admit, I did not see this coming," he said. "You know how I panicked and kissed you that time?"

I nodded.

"Do you think maybe this is you panicking?"

"Maybe."

"Princess, now that I'm back at work, I get up earlier than you. I give you your first coffee of the day. I see you every morning before you have a chance to do all of the makeup and everything. I consider it an honor to be the man who gets to see you half-asleep with your hair in your face and dried drool on your chin."

"I don't drool in my sleep," I said, outraged. "The rest, however, is valid."

"If you think I give a fuck that you want to put on something old and comfortable then you are sadly mistaken. And it's not as if you've ever made any real attempt to tone down the things you say around me." He crooked his finger in my direction. "Come here."

I climbed into his lap and he wrapped his arms around me, holding me to his chest.

"You're going to get algae face mask on you," I said.

"I don't care," he mumbled. "I know who you are and I am not going to change my mind. I am not some careless asshole who's going to mess with your heart."

"I know you're not, but…"

He pressed a kiss to my messy hair. "But?"

"This would probably be my neuroses making an appearance."

"Yeah," he agreed.

"Want to get Greek for dinner? You could get the gyro platter and I'll get the moussaka and then we'll swap."

He smiled. "Sounds good."

My cell vibrated on the coffee table. *Mom* flashed up on screen. "I should probably get that. I've been expecting this call."

In lieu of a response, he started rubbing my back. A suitable reaction to any contact with my family. The man was learning.

I picked up the phone and answered. "Hi, Mom. How are you?"

"Susie. We're good. How are you, sweetie?"

"I'm good."

"Great," she said. "Listen. Your brother called me having a meltdown. Do you know what that's about?"

This was a time-honored tactic of my mother's. To pretend to be unaware of any possible contention between Andrew and me in hopes of staying out of it. Not that it worked. Case in point.

"It was about money," I said. "Did he ask you to call me?"

"Oh, good Lord. He went on and on." Note her avoidance as my question remained unanswered. She sighed heavily. "I don't know what to tell him. Do you have any ideas?"

"No."

"Maybe you could give him a call."

"I'm not going to do that."

"Why ever not?" she asked. "He's your brother."

"Because he came over uninvited, stood on my front porch, and yelled at me. That's not behavior I'm going to encourage. And I don't owe him any money. You can tell him that if you like."

Silence.

"Just out of curiosity, Mom, did you give him money for his new business?"

Mom cleared her throat, gearing up for more avoidance. "Andrew said you had some lowlife man with you? That he threatened him?"

"That lowlife man would be my new partner, Lars," I said. "He just moved in with me and we're very happy together. I've been meaning to call and tell you about him. It'd be great if you could meet sometime."

"You're seeing someone? How exciting!" Mom enthused. "When are you going to bring him for a visit?"

"We're both pretty busy right now. But we'll definitely have to organize that sometime soon."

"Wonderful. Tell me all about him." Mom, having entirely sidestepped the nonsense with Andrew, happily interrogated me about Lars for the next ten minutes. She loved good gossip. I think it made us both feel close.

When we finally hung up, Lars gave me a smile. "Your brother's been busy, huh?"

"What's that saying about the squeaky wheel getting the grease?"

He grunted. "You done trying to talk me out of loving you?"

"Guess so. You didn't seem to be especially receptive to my demonstration."

"You have to admit," he said, "your demonstration was kind of ridiculous."

"With more time to prepare, I could—"

"Just try trusting me?"

"Right. That's exactly what I was going to say." I laid my head on his shoulder. "Did you know you're my favorite person in the whole wide world?"

"I do now." He pressed his cheek against the top of my head. "You going to wash that green stuff off your face some-time?"

I smiled. "Eventually."

Deborah and Henning's fortieth wedding anniversary was held the next weekend in a jazz bar and restaurant near their home. It was a cool space with a checkered floor and lots of wrought iron. A four-piece band was set up in the corner playing classics.

"You ready?" asked Lars.

I nodded and passed him my half-full plate of chicken en-chiladas with black beans and chopped salad. He passed me his half-eaten Cajun-spiced grilled catfish with rice and greens.

"They do this," Tore explained to his sister. "Weirdos."

Ella just nodded. "It makes more sense than me stealing my husband's food every time he orders something I want to try."

"Right?" I asked. "This way we both get to try two things."

Ella was tall and blonde like Lars. She was a radiographer in San Diego, where she lived with her husband and two small children. Since Henning and Deborah visited them a few weeks back, Emilio and the kids stayed home this trip. Which was fair enough. I don't think I'd want to wrangle two tod-dlers at a party either.

Cleo was at the bar chatting with Deborah. Because of course they got on like a house on fire. I was the only one who'd been besmirched by the Ex and his mom. But it was great that Deborah saw how wonderful my best friend was. How lucky Tore had been to catch Cleo.

"Everything okay?" asked Lars after taking a sip of his Co-rona.

"Yes. All good." And it wasn't totally a lie. My black crepe fit and flare dress with a plunging neckline was fire. It complemented my Prada heeled sandals to perfection. With my hair up and my new nude lip stain, I looked a treat. It just wasn't in me to be miserable while wearing a great outfit, eating good food, and listening to live music. I'd met some of my new partner's extended family and everything had been perfectly pleasant. Mostly.

Tore and Lars exchanged worried glances.

"What's going on?" asked Ella.

"The neighbors are causing issues for Susie," reported Tore, who possibly had the biggest mouth on anyone I'd ever met.

"I wondered why he was seated over with his mom instead of hanging out with us." Ella took a sip of her margarita. "Not that I mind the distance."

Lars frowned. "Didn't know you had something against him."

"Of course not. You can kind of have tunnel vision, sometimes." She smiled. "His niceness just always felt fake to me, you know?"

"The whole family is like that," said Tore. "Did I ever tell you about the time I heard his mom talking smack about our mom?"

Lars's brows rose. "What?"

"Yeah." Tore nodded. "And they're supposed to be besties. It was some small-minded judgmental mean-girl shit about our new couch coming from a cheap store. She was wandering around her yard and talking on the phone at the top of her lungs. Not the brightest move."

"You never told Mom?" asked Lars.

"No." Tore shook his head. "It only would have hurt her."

"Plus you told a lot of stories back then," said Ella.

"That's true. I had a vivid imagination. But I sure as hell didn't imagine that."

"I believe you. The way she'd look down on us when we

played at her house," said Ella. "As if we were going to steal the family silver. But she was always nice as pie to Mom's face. Why does it not surprise me that that woman raised such a spoiled brat?"

Tore chuckled.

"I knew you two weren't his biggest fans, but I didn't know you felt like this," said Lars with dismay.

Tore shrugged. "You didn't want to know."

"Loyalty can be an issue for you, big brother," said Ella.

As for me, I said a whole lot of nothing. And I sat with my back to the Ex and his mother. All the better to enjoy my evening. A waiter came to clear the table and I passed them my plate. The conversation was turning me off to food, though I'd recover in time to try the coconut flan. I was a stoic like that.

"Let's talk about something else." Ella sighed. "Susie, did you know when we were children and it was my turn to pick the game, I would always choose to play royal wedding. I'd seen one on TV in some documentary on England and was obsessed."

Lars groaned.

"And Lars was always the groom. Weren't you, brother?"

"Wouldn't that be illegal?" I asked. "Not only that you were underage but family-relations-wise?"

"Oh, no," said Ella. "Kat from across the road played the part of the blushing bride."

"Kat?"

"You've heard of her?" Ella laughed, delighted. "She was fun. I wonder what she's up to these days."

"I can't believe you named my cat after a girl you exchanged vows with. Repeatedly." I gave Lars a look of displeasure. "The betrayal, Lars. It hurts."

Lars just sighed.

"She kissed him one time, too," said Ella.

"And then promptly ran away and hid in her tree house. Though I suspect the vows they exchanged weren't actually legally binding," added Tore. "Seeing as how I played the part of the priest and was like six and not ordained at the time."

"Are you ordained now?" asked Ella.

"No." Tore rubbed at his chin. "But I have been thinking of getting a hobby. Why not choose the church?"

"Cleo, your boyfriend is considering becoming a priest," reported Ella.

"Is that so?" Cleo sat down beside her not-so-holy partner with a glass of ice water in her hand. "I don't even know what to say to that."

"It'll be great." Tore grinned. "Rest assured, I'll be available to hear your sins anytime."

Cleo just smiled.

"What role did you play in the wedding, Ella?" I asked.

"Flower girl," she answered. "We'd raid the neighbor's gardens for bouquets. Made us pretty unpopular."

Tore's grin turned wistful. "I forgot how much Lars loved being the groom. He'd stand in front of the mailbox proud as can be."

"The mailbox was our stand-in altar," supplied Ella. "His Ninja Turtle also married my Barbie on numerous occasions."

"How curious that getting married was your childhood dream." I took hold of his hand.

He leaned in for a kiss. "That's a bit of an overstatement."

"Hmm. Back in a minute," I said, rising and heading for the bathroom.

Deborah and Henning took to the dance floor with much applause as the jazz quartet started playing "Mad about the Boy." A song that had been on one of the albums I found by Ernestine Anderson. There was something about live music and party lights that made everything lovely, the atmosphere they created. Wedding photos had been set up on a side table. Deborah dressed in a big white '80s-style wedding dress. High hair with lots of lace and puffed sleeves. Her bouquet was pink carnations surrounded by a circle of the tiny white baby's breath flowers. Henning looked dapper in his suit despite the overly large shoulder pads. Both of their smiles were wide as could be.

I'd never seen my own parents' wedding photos. Mom made a bonfire out of them long before I could think to ask. It was hard to imagine documented evidence of Mom and Dad standing side by side and actually looking happy.

Forty years was a long time. Longer than I'd been alive. And there Henning and Deborah were on the dance floor, grinning and gazing into each other's eyes. Of course Lars wanted that. The pictures and the parties and the presents and the anniversaries year after year. The happy family they'd made together. And if there were times when things weren't exactly smooth—that was life. But they stuck together. They loved each other enough to do that and their children witnessed it all.

When I came out of the bathroom, Aaron was waiting for me. Leaning against the wall with his arms crossed. When I tried to walk right past him, he stepped into my path. "Hey, Susie. I think it's time we talked."

Eighteen

"You win," said Aaron, checking out my cleavage with a leer. To think I once took that behavior as a compliment. Never again. Not from him. "Didn't think you'd take it this far, but I've got to say, it's kind of impressive."

I gave him a look loaded with wtf.

When I continued to hold my tongue, he said, "Aren't you going to say something?"

"Well." I chose my words with care. "At first, I didn't speak because I didn't have a clue what you were talking about. But then I realized, I also don't care what you're talking about. Nothing you have to say interests me. Just get out of my way. Now."

"Susie," he said with a harsh laugh. "Enough already. I'm telling you, you've won."

"What have I won exactly?"

"Me."

"You?" I asked, incredulous. "I don't want you."

He flicked back his hair with a smirk. "Of course you do. It's why you've been fucking around with Lars. Putting the divorce certificate in your wall and everything. That really could have backfired. But kudos to you for using it to reel him in."

"I...what?"

"You've been chasing my best friend to make me jealous," he said, as if it was obvious. How had I ever thought this asshat man-child was a sensible choice for a life partner? He was the worst. "It worked. I think we should get back together. I mean, I don't want Lars getting hurt so that needs to stop. The way he's been simping over you is ridiculous. But it's not like we didn't used to have fun. What I'm saying is, I'm willing to give you another try."

"Wow." My eyes were wide the heck open. "That's so incredibly giving of you. I must have been born under a lucky star."

So much smirking. It was a wonder his lips didn't fall off from overuse.

"You actually believe all that shit you just spouted, don't you?"

He frowned. "It's the truth."

"You honestly believe I would do that to Lars? Lie and manipulate him? Treat him like his feelings mean nothing?" I said. "But you also believe that I have so little self-respect that I would actually give your narcissistic, immature, shallow, useless, tedious ass another chance?"

His face twisted into a sneer. "For fuck's sake. How long are you going to deny it? Come on. You can't seriously expect me to believe in a divorce certificate sent back from the future. Only you would come up with something so wild."

"I don't care what you believe."

"Look, Susie, I forgive you, okay?"

"You are... I don't... No. Just no."

"Don't be fucking stupid," Aaron said, and grabbed my face to kiss me.

It only took me a moment to react. But that was long enough to have his gross wet lips make contact with mine. I was definitely going to have to wash my mouth out with soap when all of this was over. Bathing with bleach wasn't out of the question. I tried to push him away, but he didn't budge. Instead, his hold on me tightened to the point of being painful, and his tongue tried to worm its way into my mouth. Which was stomach turning on a whole new level. Both the violence and sense of entitlement made me nauseous. Bile rose in the back of my throat. It was time to get serious. Thank goodness I hadn't worn a dress with a tight skirt. With my hands gripping his shoulders tight, I kneed him in the groin. The man crumpled. There was no other word for it. A mangled groan escaped him as he hit the ground.

"Never touch a woman without her permission."

Aaron curled up into a ball, all the better to protect himself. Like I'd kick him when he was down. I'd already made my point.

"You utter asshole."

He just lay there. But I was on the move. Back out through the party and to our table. I would not be the one to make a scene at Deborah and Henning's party. There would be no pinning this mess on me. Not this time.

"Susie?" asked Cleo. "Are you okay?"

"Yeah, I, um…"

When Lars saw my face, his smile faded. "What's wrong?"

"Nothing. Really I'm fine." My smile was all teeth and my hands were shaking. Too much adrenaline. "But I'm going to go. You stay. I'll see you at home."

"Wait. Wh—"

"It would be best if we talked about this later. Please just trust me."

Lars got to his feet. "Hang on. What happened?"

"That bitch attacked me," announced a loud, familiar, and much-hated voice on the other side of the room. All conversation ceased as the band stopped playing. The space between us cleared and there stood Aaron. The not-so-innocent man cradling his poor sore junk with his hands. And oh the venom in his eyes. Not only had I rejected him, but I'd laid him low. Me. His ego couldn't comprehend the situation.

Meanwhile, his mother, Vivian, started making these high-pitched sounds of rage and distress that really should have broken glass. Just shattered every wineglass and window in the room. Guess she took the sanctity of the family jewels deathly serious. Though I was pretty sure the world could do without more of this particular family.

Deborah and Henning looked between me and Aaron in horror. Talk about trashing their party.

"It's true," I said to Lars, keeping my voice down and pressing my fists against my stomach. My spirits sank through the floor. "He said I was only with you to make him jealous. Then he tried to kiss me. So I fed him his balls with my knee. The end."

Lars's forehead filled with furrows. All the furrows in all the land. He was confused.

"Whatever shit she's saying to you, man, she's lying." Aaron pushed his way through the crowd, heading toward us. And Lars's parents followed. The way Aaron walked was…awkward. He was most definitely in pain. As much as he deserved it, I so did not want to be responsible for an ugly scene. Though I doubted there was any way to prevent it now.

Fuck. "I'm sorry—"

"She just fucking attacked me out of nowhere," continued

Aaron. He was the picture of disarray with his suit creased, face red, and hair a mess. I'd never seen him so unkempt. Or in such a rage.

The daggers Vivian were glaring at me were razor-sharp. Ouch.

Lars started rolling up his sleeves. In another time and place, I would have enjoyed the sight. The revelation of his muscular forearms and the way the white cotton of his button-down framed the bulge of his biceps. Due to my life imploding, however, I didn't have time to gawk.

"*I* attacked *you*, out of nowhere?" I asked with much scorn. "Me? Outside the women's bathroom just now? Are you sure about those facts?"

"What on earth happened?" asked Deborah. "What did you do?"

Though her gaze took in the both of us, Aaron froze. To be fair, he never had been great in high-stress situations. And after he'd had a couple of drinks, he was worse. It was how we broke up in the first place. He couldn't keep his mouth shut about what a duplicitous shit he was, and how he planned to cheat on me when he got to London. But back to the here and now. With much jabbing of his finger in my direction, Aaron said, "Susie came onto me and of course I turned her down. Told her I'd be telling Lars what she was about. That's when she lost it and attacked me."

Someone gasped. Another person snickered. I don't know who. Each and every one of the seventy-odd guests was watching. This debacle had their full attention. Even the band was hanging on our every word. What a disaster this was turning out to be. Here I was meeting Lars's extended family for the first time, and providing them with a floor show.

Cleo snorted. "What complete and utter bullshit."

I gave her a small grateful smile.

Henning slipped a supportive arm around his wife's waist.

"Oh, really? This doesn't surprise me at all. It's just more of the same. She's always behaved this way," said Vivian with an evil glint in her eye. "I told you. I said you could do better than some grasping sl—"

"That's enough," said Tore. And the man was not happy.

Wish I knew what I'd done to the woman to earn such enmity. Just dared to date her precious son, I guess. But she didn't matter. Neither did her asshole of a child. The only person who mattered was Lars.

"You were saying something?" Lars took a step closer, his gaze questioning. "You said you were sorry. What are you sorry for, Susie?"

Oh, no. That didn't sound good. Not at all.

Accusing gazes locked on to me from all around, and fear grabbed hold. The intense expression on his face. This was it, the moment of truth. Lars didn't believe me and he certainly wouldn't love me anymore. Not after this. He was going to take the word of his oldest friend. My luck with men always had been shit. Why should this be any different?

I would not cry or yell or any of that nonsense. No. I'd carry out the messy public breakup of my relationship with the utmost dignity—even if the break was going to be so much worse than any that came before. I knew it without a doubt. Because the man standing in front of me...he was my heart. No idea when it had happened. But there could be no denying it. His beloved face and strong hands and the way that, even now, he listened. He gave me his full attention. A small but important thing.

I swallowed hard. "I...um."

"Hey," he said, slipping his hand around the back of my neck. Giving me a comforting squeeze before letting go again. "Take a breath and tell me, Susie. What are you sorry for?"

"For wrecking your parents' party."

He nodded.

"I didn't mean for that to happen. I'm so sorry."

"You said he grabbed you and tried to kiss you," said Lars, voice loud enough to be clear to all. "Is that right?"

"Yes."

Aaron spluttered while his mom made indignant noises.

"Excuse me," said Deborah, raising her voice. "You had your chance. It's Susie's turn to talk now."

Henning gave them a stern nod of warning.

"I wanted him off me and he wouldn't let go so I kneed him in the balls," I said.

Lars nodded. "That's everything?"

"Yes. Basically. He spouted all sorts of bullshit about me leading you on to make him jealous, but those were the main points," I said. "If I'd known I was going to disrupt the party and embarrass you this way...well, I don't actually know that I would have done anything differently. Given the situation and all. But I am sorry it happened, Lars."

His serious gaze took me. He had the most beautiful blue eyes I'd ever seen. "I know you are," he said. "But it's not your fault. You didn't start any of this, did you?"

"No," I agreed.

"No," repeated Lars. "Of course you didn't. No more than you'd lead me on or any of that other shit."

And oh my God the relief. He believed me. He was on my side. My smile was shaky as all hell, but he returned it without hesitation. It was me and him against the world. Without reservation, this was something I could trust.

Then Aaron aggressively grabbed at my arm, yelling, "You lying little bi—"

Boom. That's as far as he got. Lars's fist shot out and connected with Aaron's face. Aaron rebounded with a whimper

as blood gushed from his nose. His mother went into apo-
plexy. That's the order it happened in. And the party pretty
much ended there.

While Aaron held ice wrapped in a kitchen towel to his
face, Vivian ranted on. And on. And on some more. If only
people had mute buttons. That would be so useful. When she
turned my way, I just rolled my eyes. It only encouraged her
to condemn me all the more, but I couldn't help it. Deborah
had asked them to wait until she'd seen off her guests. Promised that they'd straighten things out then. Whatever.

Santa better bring me some more fucks this Christmas.
Because I was officially out of them. This had to have been
the longest year in creation. At least with Lars at my side, it
would eventually end on a high. Because I now believed we
had a strong chance of making this work. We had to. Any
other thought was...just, no.

Deborah and Henning had been hugging people and shaking hands and generally clearing the room of all their guests
while the wait staff cleared the tables and the band packed
away their instruments. It had been quite the night.

"He should press charges," hollered the evil witch. Though
that was being too mean to witches. Even the ones that were
evil. Like I'm sure they had their reasons.

"And explain to the police how he assaulted Susie not once,
but twice?" asked Cleo. "I'd very much like to hear that."

She seemed to swell with rage, though her gaze turned
wary. "My boy didn't assault anyone."

"We all saw him grab her. Try again."

"Well, if he did it was only to make her apologize for all
of those terrible lies!"

"Mom," hissed Aaron. "That's enough. You're making it
worse."

The expression of affront Vivian displayed was quite good. I'd have given it a solid eight out of ten. But it was the stunned and beleaguered look of victimhood which followed that really won the day. The woman could overact. It sucked that the anniversary party had been ruined. I'd be sending Deborah flowers for sure.

We sat to the side of the room, Lars's hand in my lap. I don't think he really needed the bag of ice that I held to his knuckles. He'd repeatedly told me it was fine. But it gave me something to do. Nervous energy was running rife through me, though the worst of it was over. Too much adrenaline or something.

What mattered was that he'd chosen me. I should have known he would. However, shaking off thirty years of self-doubt took a little time.

"Not your fault," said Lars. Again.

"I know, I know."

"It's time for us all to have a little talk." Deborah, having sent off the last of the guests, stood between the two parties of contention. Henning stood beside her.

"We demand an apology," said Vivian. "It's the very least that we deserve."

"That's odd." Deborah looked down her nose at her neighbor. "I was thinking the same thing. Only, I was hoping your son would come to his senses and realize how appalling his behavior has been tonight."

"You're taking that horrible girl's side against ours?"

"Be careful what you say," said Deborah. "You're talking about a member of my family."

Evil mom was aghast at this announcement. Her lips a perfect O of astonishment. "We've known each other for over twenty-five years. Our children grew up together. We're close friends."

"And I've excused and overlooked a lot in that time. But

it ends now." Deborah pushed back her shoulders. "Will you be apologizing to Susie or not?"

Before Aaron could answer, Vivian started talking for him. Which surprised approximately nobody. "Not. Most definitely not. He has done nothing to apologize for."

"Then it's time for you to leave." And while Deborah's voice was calm and measured, you could tell she meant every word.

"What?"

"Get out."

"With pleasure," sneered Vivian.

"This is just like a scene on a Turkish soap opera I saw once." Tore sat with his arm slung around Cleo's shoulders. If anything, he seemed pleased by the night's events. Or at least, how they'd worked out. "Only she was waving her arms about as she said, 'You'll regret this! Mark my words!' But in Turkish."

"Sounds very dramatic," said Cleo.

"Oh. It was."

"I didn't know you watched soap operas."

Tore grinned. "I aim to constantly surprise and delight."

Aaron slowly rose to his feet. "Lars, I..."

"Don't you dare apologize," interjected Vivian. Then she grabbed his arm and tried dragging him toward the door.

Lars shook his head.

Pain crossed Aaron's face. "You could at least let me explain."

"There is nothing you can say that I'd want to hear, man," said Lars. "My mom told you to get out."

Aaron hung his head in defeat. And I did not fist pump the sky. Yay for maturity.

"You don't come near either of us again," said Lars. "Understood?"

With a final nod, Aaron left, following his terror of a mother out the door. Phew. The silence in the dimly lit room was complete for a moment. All eyes on the door. But nothing else happened. They did not reappear. The night's drama seemed to be done. Thank goodness.

"Well," said Ella with a drawl. "That felt really awkward to me. Was that awkward for anyone else?"

"Stop trying to be the funny one in the family." Tore frowned. "There's only room for one and the title is already claimed."

Ella stuck out her tongue at him.

"Children," chided Henning. He passed out small glasses with a shot of clear liquid. When we all had one, he raised his glass in a toast. "To family. *Skol.*"

I smiled and took a sip. And promptly wanted to spit it out, but managed to choke it down. Then I whispered, "What was that?"

"Aquavit," said Lars.

"It tastes like licorice."

"Yeah."

"Susie," said Deborah, taking a seat nearby. "I owe you an apology. I didn't welcome you as I should have. I will do better in the future."

My smile felt lopsided. I didn't know what to say.

"You guys should throw another party," said Tore. "You deserve a do-over."

"After what this one cost?" asked Henning, incredulous. "Absolutely not."

"We could do it at home on the deck."

"It's an idea," said Deborah with a shrug. "Though it would be a lot of work."

Ella smiled. "We'll all help."

"Tore could do his baked salmon," suggested Cleo.

Henning screwed up his face. "Have you tasted my youngest son's cooking? No, thank you. I don't even trust him with the grill. Tore's gifts lie elsewhere."

"You're just jealous, old man," said Tore. "I'm a legend in the kitchen and you know it. Back me up, honey."

Cleo held up her hands with a grin. "I just don't feel it's right to come between you and your father."

"When I first met you," said Henning, "I thought, now there is a kind and compassionate woman. Too kind to tell you, Tore, how bad your cooking is."

Tore and Henning bickered while Cleo watched on, amused. She too set aside her glass of aquavit, so I wasn't the only one who hated anise. Ella and Deborah were busy chatting about something. All of the tension had left the room. Thank goodness for that.

Lars leaned closer. "You sure you're okay?"

"I'm fine." I smiled. "Nothing you can't fix at home with some kisses."

He pressed one to my forehead. "You got it, Princess. Whatever you want."

"I've been thinking. I'm going to burn the divorce certificate."

"You are?" he asked, surprised.

I nodded. "I trust you. I trust us. And that's good enough for me. We don't need any messages from the future or whatever the heck it is telling us we can't make it. We deserve a chance to be together without that black cloud hanging over our heads."

"Okay," he said. "Just do me a favor and take a couple of days to make sure this is what you really want. I don't want you to regret anything. Decide too late that there's some exorcist you want to get to look it over or something."

"Agreed."

Nineteen

I woke up the next morning in the middle of the bed. Alone. Dammit. But Lars wouldn't be far away. The sun rimmed the curtain edges in bright white light. Summer would be ending soon. The nights were getting cooler as proven by the extra blankets on our bed. It had been a heck of a year. It was my first summer as caretaker of this house, and I'd even managed not to kill many of Aunt Susan's plants.

Halloween needed to hurry up so I could get out her decorations. Talk about all-time favorite holiday. She had a plastic life-size skeleton nicknamed Stanley who hung from the front porch, along with a veritable army of ghosts that fluttered alongside him in the wind. Pumpkins and gourds would line the front steps. A tombstone sat in the bed of lavender by the sidewalk. One of my earliest memories was of Aunt Susan making a witch costume for me while I waited not so patiently. I'd worn the black dress and pointed hat for years until I burst the seams.

I'd be the person standing at the front door handing candy out to trick or treaters as she'd done every year...that would be bittersweet. But it was nice to be able to look forward to things. The grief seemed to shift a little more every day and her absence no longer made me feel quite so hollow inside. Memories didn't hurt in the way that they had. Instead there was an awareness of what a blessing it had been to have her in my life all of those years.

As for the mess of feelings that used to roil inside me at the thought of Aaron, those were long gone. Never to be seen again. And good riddance.

I rolled over and stared at the shadows on the ceiling. The world was quiet on this Sunday morning. Peaceful. Right up until a lawnmower roared to life nearby, and a bird started screeching in protest. Which might have been the universe telling me to get my butt out of bed and go find my boyfriend. Though *boyfriend* sounded middle school and *lover* was...no. *Partner* was fine. Or was it? Another thing to ponder.

Lars's request to wait a while before destroying the divorce certificate surprised me. Although, I guess he had a point. Once it was gone, it was gone for good. I got up and retrieved it from my underwear drawer and stared at the worn creases in the paper. At how the text had faded with age. The scent of dust and dirt from the wall lingered on it.

The same old feelings flooded back to me: Frustration over not knowing what caused the failure of our marriage. Wonder that I would agree to get wed in the first place...though I was beginning to see how that might have happened. My feelings for the man were big. Huge. And a mix of sadness and anger that our union might fall apart. That we wouldn't last.

Fuck that noise.

I was done with listening to it.

My fingers tightened on the piece of paper. The desire to

scrunch it up and throw it into the trash was tempting as all hell. To light the fucker on fire.

But a strong case could be made that Lars and I were only together because it existed. Only after its discovery did we take the time to really get to know one another. To grow close. Turns out sharing a secret, trying to unravel a mystery, is great for bringing people together. It might have happened anyway with him working on the house. But knowing me, I would have wanted to keep my distance from the Ex's best friend. That would have trumped everything—and to think of what I would have missed out on.

Maybe I should be grateful to it, after all.

Out in the back garden, Lars was hard at work sanding one of the old Adirondack chairs. Kat sat nearby keeping an eye on him, as she was wont to do. Her new rainbow collar was very cool. An empty coffee cup and the latest book from Tessa Bailey sat nearby. He hadn't been only working.

As always, the sun loved Lars. Both his hair and the faint sheen of sweat on his skin. I could happily stare at him for hours. I sat on the back steps in the shade with a cup of coffee in my hands, wearing only an old tee and panties. As nice as it was to dress up, you needed to be comfortable hanging out in your own home. To be comfortable in your own skin. Which included not caring whether the love of my life saw my cellulite and messy hair.

"Hey," he said with a warm smile. "Thought I'd give these a sanding down and a fresh coat of paint. They were pretty rough and I don't want you getting any splinters."

"Thank you," I said. "Every day I appreciate a little more how much it must have driven you up the wall to have to sit still and let yourself heal after the accident. You were really quite restrained."

"That your way of asking why I wasn't still in bed this morning?"

"I may have woken in a somewhat amorous mood."

He gazed up at me, squinting against the bright midmorning light. "Sorry I missed it. Make it up to you later?"

"Sure."

His smile...ugh. So beautiful.

"I cleared out some more space in the wardrobe for you."

His smile turned into a bigger grin. "You're giving up some of your wardrobe space for me? I'm beginning to think you really do like me."

"I'm not going to lie," I said. "It hurt. But then I remembered I have the whole closet in the spare room as well. Fair is fair. I figure you're entitled to a quarter of the clothing storage in the house. Just don't push for any more."

He laughed. "That's my girl. Such a giver."

"How's your hand this morning?"

A shadow crossed his face. There and gone in an instant. "It's fine. You okay?"

"There's a couple of small bruises. I took a picture of them just in case he tries anything."

"Fucker," he muttered

"Tucker who is now out of our lives." Which made it time to change the subject. "Are you hungry? What would you like for breakfast?"

"Yeah. I'm starving. How about pancakes?"

"You got it. I'll get started on them as soon as I finish this." I took another sip of coffee. Then I took a deep breath and said, "I do love you, you know?"

"I know," he replied, casual as can be.

Huh.

"Wait a minute, Han Solo. That was a rhetorical question. You're supposed to be shocked and stunned at such an admission." My brows descended, but my smile was wide. "How exactly do you know? Was it the wardrobe space that gave it away?"

"Something like that."

The happiness in his eyes made my toes curl and heart skip a beat. "Lars. Tell me. What gave it away?"

"Well, I've been pretty much all-in since the inevitable thing. Just wasn't sure of my ability to convince you."

"It's not like you to doubt yourself."

"Maybe it unnerved me...how much you mattered," he said. "But then you kept giving me signs. Like setting the table for a romantic dinner after saying you didn't want to date me. It made me hope that deep down you were all-in too. You just needed to feel safe enough to trust me and tell me. And that was going to take time."

"Okay."

"Come here, Susie."

I set aside the coffee cup and walked across the grass to him. His warm hand curled around one of my bare thighs as I leaned down to kiss him. The sweet press of our lips like a promise. In all honesty, I could see me happily kissing this man for a good long time to come. The rest of my life even. And what a beautiful life that would be.

For some reason, Kat the cat was watching us and purring. Guess she was a fan of love.

"You still going to burn the divorce certificate?" he asked.

"I think so."

"Okay," he murmured. "Say it again."

"I love you."

"Good," he said, and smacked me on the ass. "Go make me breakfast. Please."

"You got it. Though there was one thing I was going to ask you."

"Hmm?"

"Will you marry me?"

His whole body seemed to stop with a jolt. "What did you say?"

"You heard me."

"Susie…" Lars got to his feet. He stood staring down at me with a serious face. "Is this about the talk last night about playing those games when I was little? Because I can live without getting to be the groom in real life."

"I think it's about a variety of things, actually."

"Such as?" he asked. "Because you were pretty adamant about not getting married."

"I was. That's true. But then it occurred to me that maybe life isn't about always playing it safe."

His rough fingers rubbed comforting circles on the outside of my thigh.

"Marriage is important to you, Lars." He opened his mouth to speak but I put a finger to his lips. "Let me finish. You've always seen it as part of your great journey through life. And I want to give that to you. Because I trust you enough to take the risk."

His gaze remained worried.

"Listen to me. The truth is, I want to give this to you much more than I distrust the institution. Thus proving forever more that my love for you is greater than your love for me. Please say yes."

"This is a competition?"

"Absolutely."

"It saddens me how full of crap you are, Princess. Since it's obvious that I love you more."

"You're just saying that to make conversation. It doesn't mean a thing." I gave him a haughty look. "Why, your love is a grain of sand while mine is all of the beaches in all of the world."

Which was about when Lars ever so carefully and skillfully tackled me into the grass. I found myself subdued and on my back in no time. Clear blue sky overhead, and the weight of his body on me felt heavenly.

"What about the divorce certificate?" he asked.

"We prove it wrong."

"Is that why you want to do this?"

"Like I said, there are a lot of reasons why I want to do this. But my main priority is your happiness. And while I know you said you'd be fine without it, I want to give it to you. It's important to me." I smoothed the line between his brows with my fingers. "Make me an honest woman. Say yes, Lars."

"Wait a minute." He picked something out of my hair and carefully placed it on a nearby leaf. "You have a ladybug on you."

"Huh. Though I'm not wearing a white dress for the ceremony. You need to know and embrace that fact right now. But there's this black strapless Christian Siriano gown that would work a treat."

"You're serious about this."

"I have to mention fashion for you to believe me?"

"Just making sure you're all onboard and have thought this through."

I smiled. "I am and I have. You know, I keep thinking about what the divorce lawyer said that day. How we have to keep choosing each other. How building a relationship and keeping it intact is just that hard, and that simple. This is me choosing you."

"Are you in this for keeps?" he asked in a deep serious tone.

"Wouldn't have asked you to marry me if I wasn't. What about you?"

"I promise you, married or not, I'm not going anywhere." I nodded.

"Thank you for asking me to marry you."

"You're very welcome."

"Okay," he said, rising back onto his knees. Kat the cat appeared beside him and he picked her up and gave her a pat. "Good talk, Princess. Let me give it some thought and I'll get back to you. You want a hand with the pancakes?"

I sat up with a frown. "Wait. That's it?"

But the man was already gone. Back inside the house carrying his damn cat and his empty coffee cup. Despite all of my deep thinking and rehearsing my lines, I'd seriously lost control of the conversation. Though to be honest, I wasn't entirely sure I'd ever been in control.

"The man likes screwing with you," said Cleo.

"Oh, yeah," I agreed. "While it's good that he's taking his time and thinking it through. I wouldn't have minded if he said yes right away."

A light rain had started falling, filling the air with petrichor. Wet pine needles and mulch and rain was the scent of Seattle. Along with barley from the microbreweries, fresh bread from the bakeries, and a dash of mildew for good measure. The scent of home sweet home.

In the five days since my proposal, nothing had been resolved. Nothing much had even been said. Whenever I raised the topic, Lars was suddenly busy or required elsewhere. But every day he would ask, "Still want to marry me?" And I would say, "Yes." He'd tip his chin and go about his business. Even though I never planned on getting married, this delay was annoying as all hell.

In the meantime, I decided to make an event out of destroying the divorce certificate. While I planned to make use of the fire bowl in the back garden, the weather forced us indoors. Wood was laid in the fireplace in preparation, and Cleo and Tore were invited over to witness the momentous occasion.

"How's the couples hobby hunt going?" asked Cleo.

"Chess, Scrabble and salsa have been scrapped. He kept winning at chess, I kept winning at Scrabble, and we both lost at salsa," I said. "Not a trace of dance talent to be found between us."

"What's up next?"

"I'm thinking a couples Romance book club. We tend to discuss the plot lines and characters anyway. Might as well make it official."

Cleo nodded.

"We'll need T-shirts."

"Of course."

"Did you have a busy week?" I asked. "How'd the meeting with the activewear people go?"

"It went well."

"Excellent."

"I need to show you the update to Photoshop sometime. Some of the new features are fantastic," she said. "And Tore and I decided to book a holiday in Maui after that conference in November."

"A beach vacation? Nice."

"Oh yeah," said Cleo. "By the way, Mom said to tell you she found a pet cemetery that will accept the ashes of your mystery doggo. She said the rates were reasonable."

"That's great. He deserves a nice afterlife. Something better than sitting forgotten in a corner of the basement. I'll text her tomorrow for the details and to say thanks."

Cleo nodded. "Her church group will also take any unwanted items from your boxes for their fundraiser next month. Anything you think they could sell."

"Okay," I said. "I'm actually almost finished. Apart from the attic. Lars is going to help me start bringing things down."

"When you consider what the place looked like last Christmas," she said, taking in the living room, "you've come a long way."

"For you, my love." Tore passed her a glass of wine. The beer in his other hand he raised in a toast. "To burning weird messages from the future and forging your own path."

Lars passed me a gin and tonic. "I'll drink to that."

He knelt in front of the fireplace and carefully lit the kindling. Flames raced up the neat stack of wood in no time. He added a photo of his family to the mantel last week and his belongings were spread through the house. His presence now seemed more real and permanent. I liked it. We were building a life together.

"While I'm down here," he said, retrieving something from his jeans pocket, "might as well give you this." He held out a small black velvet box.

My eyes were wide as the moon. "What is this?"

"Open it and see."

"Holy shit."

He just smiled as he held it out to me.

With trembling fingers, I opened the box. Inside sat a square cut diamond on a platinum band. Simple and perfect, and so damn sparkly. It took my breath away. "Lars, is this you saying yes?"

"Yes," he said.

"Oh my God."

He rose to his feet and took the ring out. "Are we doing this?"

I nodded as tears welled in my eyes. "But you didn't need to buy this. You could have saved the money for the business."

"You're more important. Don't cry," he said, slipping the ring on my finger. "That looks like a good fit."

"Yes, it is." I turned my hand this way and that so the diamond could catch the light. Amazing. "It's beautiful."

"I'm glad you like it." His gaze was so soft and sweet. The expression on his face was full of love. "I love you, Susie."

"I love you too."

He tossed the box onto the coffee table, cupped my face, and kissed me good and hard. Like he was staking his claim. This was heaven. His lips were on mine, and his tongue was in my mouth. His hands firmly held me, and I could feel the heat of his body. I could have happily stayed right there forever.

"Congratulations, guys," said Tore.

"Did you know about this?" I asked with a sniffle.

He just shrugged and smiled. The man totally knew.

Cleo gave me a hug and her eyes were suspiciously moist.

If anyone told me at the start of the year that I'd be stupidly happy and beside myself to be getting married... I would have called them a liar.

Which left only one thing left to do. One last loose end.

"All righty," I said and headed into the bedroom. "The time has come. This divorce certificate is going down, once and for all."

I pulled open my underwear drawer and pushed aside an assortment of lace thongs and boy shorts. All of my favorite panties. I figured the divorce certificate could use the good vibes. Only, there was nothing there. Just the wooden bottom of the drawer. Next I shoved aside period panties, bras, and a vibrator. But there was still no sign of the damn thing.

"Lars, did you move it?"

He strode into the room. "Why, what's wrong?"

"It's not here."

"I haven't touched it. Are you sure that's where you left it?"

"Yes," I said with a frown.

"Check the other drawers."

"Is there a problem?" asked Cleo.

"I can't find it." Tees and tanks came next. Followed by

scarves and belts and socks. Summer shorts and some pajamas. With jeans, leggings, and a couple of cardigans in the bottom drawer. "Nothing."

"Let's pull all of the drawers out," said Lars. "Make sure it didn't fall down the back or something."

The interior of the set of drawers was empty. Tore and Lars moved the piece of furniture back from the wall. But there was nothing but dust bunnies.

"When was the last time you took it out?" asked Cleo.

"Sunday morning," I said. "Before I went outside to talk to Lars. I put it straight back in the same place."

"Lars?"

"I looked at it a couple of weeks ago," he said. "Haven't gone near it since."

Cleo sighed. "It has to be here somewhere."

"It's definitely got to be in this room," I agreed.

"Okay," she said. "Let's be systematic about this. We'll empty the drawers out onto the bed. Make sure it hasn't been accidentally been tucked away between your shirts or something."

We examined every item in each drawer and repacked it all. Nothing. Then we tore the bed apart. Just to be sure. Along with searching behind and under the frame and the mattress. The same went for every other piece of furniture in the room. And all the while, a weird panic built inside of me. None of it made sense. Where could it have gone?

"I know it was here," I said. "I know it was."

"We'll find it." Lars rubbed my back. "It's got to be somewhere, Princess."

I nodded. "You promise you didn't decide to get rid of it without me? I wouldn't be angry. Well...maybe a little. But I need to know."

"I promise."

"Okay. Let's check out the dining and living rooms. Just in case."

We searched the house for over three hours. Cheese and crackers fueled us through the first half of the hunt. While a sushi delivery provided sustenance for the latter. And all the while, Kat sat on the front door mat watching us with her all-knowing feline eyes.

I couldn't just let it go. The divorce certificate had been a black cloud hanging over our heads for what felt like forever. It had to be in the house somewhere. It couldn't just disappear. Surely. Maybe one of us sleepwalked and hid it somewhere. Or we'd unknowingly been under the influence of a hallu-cinogenic and... I don't know. We rifled through cupboards and checked coat pockets. We examined my office and the kitchen and...nothing. Not a damn thing. Even my purse got upended and inspected.

"It's just gone," I said finally, slumped on the sofa. "How is that possible?"

Lars grunted beside me.

"You're admitting defeat?" asked Tore.

He sat on the ground with Cleo's feet in his lap. His thumbs dug into the soles of her feet. I could use a foot rub. The lift-ing and moving and searching had worn us all out. We'd even checked the attic. Despite there being little chance of it somehow having made its way up there. There were no new footprints in the dust since the last time Lars visited the space months ago. Back when the divorce certificate made its first appearance. Back when this all began.

"We've looked everywhere," said Cleo.

"I just wish I knew what happened." I sighed. "If someone broke in, why only steal that? It makes no sense. My purse and cell and laptop are all still here."

"That thing has never made sense," said Lars.

Cleo sighed too. "No one has benefited from you two seeing that certificate."

"No one but them," added Tore.

"True," Cleo said, and nodded. "They mightn't have gotten together without it."

Kat the cat sauntered over and jumped onto Lars. Curling up in a ball and promptly falling asleep. She was a female who appreciated a good nap. And who could blame her? I would sleep well after all this too. Once we cleared off the bed and put on fresh sheets.

"I don't know," said Lars. "I can't explain it. That thing has always messed with my head."

"Seems it disappeared as mysteriously as it appeared," said Cleo. "What do you think Miss Lillian would say?"

"Hmm." I pondered the question. "Perhaps that its message had been received."

"Like destiny decided it was no longer needed?" asked Cleo.

I nodded. "Yeah. Maybe."

"You fixed fate, huh?" Tore mulled it over. "Makes as much sense as anything. You two have sorted out a lot of shit…"

Lars's gaze changed from determined to bewildered, and back again, over the course of the night. But bewildered won in the end. He picked up my hand and kissed my knuckles. "If you want to keep looking, then that's what we'll do. It's up to you. What do you say, Princess?"

I rested my head on the back of the couch and stared into his eyes. He was the future I wanted. Right there beside me. And I trusted in us far more than I trusted in some cryptic piece of paper. "I say we let it go."

"Are you sure?"

"Yes."

"Okay," he said with a smile. "That's good enough for me."

Epilogue

TEN YEARS LATER
December 4

"Mama," hollered Ingrid. "I'm hungry. Can you give me some cheese?"

"Your child is part mouse. Are you aware of this?" I asked my husband. To our seven-year-old daughter I replied, "I didn't hear a please."

"Puh-lease."

"And you're eating an apple with it."

She groaned and made gagging noises—as you do when you're a small child being threatened with fruit.

"I'll get it." Lars smiled and paused the Seahawks game. "Ingrid, your mother and I would like to know if you're a mouse? What do you think?"

"She does live in the attic," I said. "It's a fair question."

Ingrid giggled and squeaked.

"What do you think? Is your sister part rodent or just overly fascinated with aged dairy products?" I asked the small boy child attached to my left boob. "Look who I'm talking to, your whole life revolves around milk."

As soon as news of the baby reached our eldest child's ears, she started her campaign to relocate to the attic. The nursery took over the second bedroom and my office was now a corner of our bedroom.

The truth was, our family had outgrown this house. While Lars hadn't said a thing, I knew he was waiting for me to broach the subject—and I kept avoiding it. Leaving Aunt Susan's place was going to hurt. It had been my home for a long time, but we didn't necessarily have to move far.

Once Lars delivered a bowl of apple and cheese slices to our daughter, he got resettled in the wingback chair.

"Miss Lillian's old house has three bedrooms," I said, apropos of nothing. "And the principal bedroom is larger than ours. There'd be more room for me to set up an office. More room for all of us."

Lars's gaze rested on me, but he said nothing.

"We know the work done on it was good because it was done by you, Tore, and Mateo."

"I saw they put up a For Sale sign yesterday."

"Just a thought."

"Are you sure you're ready to move?"

I sighed. "Not going to lie. I kind of hate the idea. But we've outgrown this place."

"Yeah."

"Yeah," I agreed.

"I could find you a place with a water view." He smiled. "If you wanted."

"Ingrid wouldn't have to change schools if we stayed nearby. And we like this area."

He nodded. "We do."

"The house also has good vibes."

He chuckled.

"Would you be okay with that?"

"Yes, Princess." He rose out of his chair and pressed a kiss to my forehead. Then a kiss to his son's. And the smile on his face was happy and warm. "I'll give them a call. Set up a time for us to do a walk-through in the next few days."

"You really are ready to move."

"As long as we're all together, I'm good. But you're right. We need more room." He knelt down at my side. "Why don't we rent this place? That way it'll still be yours. We can always think about coming back here once the kids are out of the house."

"I'd like that." I smiled. "I was also thinking, instead of getting divorced today, why don't we order some takeout to share?"

He frowned. Then said, "That is today, isn't it? Damn."

We hadn't completely forgotten the divorce certificate. Though I thought of it less and less over the years. And we never found it either. But we'd won. We were still here. It hurt to imagine what it would have been like if we'd never taken the chance to be together. All of the goodness we would have missed out on in life.

"We did it," he said in a quiet voice.

"Yeah. We sure did."

"Never doubted us. Not once."

Could you burst from happy? It would be messy. But I think it's doable. For the last decade I'd been trying my best to make it happen. My work had grown surely, but steadily. Same went for Lars and Tore's house-flipping business. Cleo and Tore moved into a beautiful houseboat several years ago and were considering attempting to reproduce sometime soon. They'd also done their best to travel the world. Cleo took on work for several magazines and won numerous awards over the years. Life was good.

"We should definitely celebrate with takeout," said Lars. "How about pizza and cupcakes?"

"Have I ever told you how incredibly alluring you are?" I asked.

"Cupcakes?" Ingrid crashed into her father's back. "We're getting cupcakes?"

"Ew," I said. "Who wants smelly yucky cupcakes?"

"Me, me, me."

"I think I know where our daughter gets her food obsessions from," Lars said with a grin. "Why don't you pass him over to me and I'll put him to bed? Then we'll see about some food."

"Sounds good," I said.

The baby in my arms had fallen asleep with a milk-drunk smile on his small face. Not even his sister's shouting could disturb him. His father carefully took him from my arms and carried him to his crib. All the while, Kat watched from her place in front of the fire. And she purred.

★ ★ ★ ★ ★

Turn the page to read the story behind End of Story...

Kylie Scott's prequel novella

Beginning of the End

BEGINNING
OF THE END

One

"You're moving to London?" I asked stupidly for the second time.

"It's a big opportunity for me." Aaron pushed aside the remains of his short rib vermicelli noodles. As if he'd suddenly found them distasteful. This wasn't the first pout he'd pulled on one of our dates. Being an only child, he tended to be used to getting things his own way. Which could be kind of frustrating. We'd been a couple for a while. Long enough for the honeymoon period to be over, apparently. "I thought you'd be happy."

"I, um…yeah. It's just a surprise, you know?"

A frown crossed his handsome face. "I'll only be gone for a year."

Around us, people ate and chatted and enjoyed their Tuesday night out. The Vietnamese café was a popular spot by the water in Ballard, Seattle. It had a high ceiling and cool, modern pendant lights. And the people at the next table had now picked up on my boyfriend's unhappy vibe and terse tone of voice and were not-so-subtly listening to our conversation. Ugh. People. Seriously. If only you could order a cone of silence along with your entrée.

"Of course I'm excited for you," I said.

"Are you?"

After almost a year with Aaron, it was depressing as all hell to know I still wasn't getting this relationship stuff right. Still not supporting him in the way that he wanted. I turned thirty this year. It shouldn't have been this hard. But here we were. Our initial plans for tonight were to have dinner at my place, order some delivery, and relax. Then at the last minute he changed his mind and wanted to go out instead. Call me curious.

"Did you decide to tell me in a restaurant because you were worried I'd get upset?" I blurted out before sanity could stop me. My mouth was like that sometimes: no filter to be found.

"What?" He hesitated for a moment. "No. Of course not."

"Okay."

"Why would you even think that?"

"I don't know…"

"You're my partner, Susie. My girlfriend." He smoothed a hand over his slick dark hair and straightened his tie. "I wanted to go out and celebrate, share this important news with you."

I just nodded. Something inside of me, however, was unsettled. I was not quite convinced. Time to pull up my big-girl panties and ask the big question. "How do you see this affecting us, Aaron?"

"I don't know." He shrugged and slumped back in his seat. Which was not promising. "Why does anything have to change?"

"We'll be living in different countries for a start. That's kind of big."

"Yeah." His gaze skipped around the room. "But like I said, it's temporary."

Sitting on the edge of my seat, I leaned in closer to him, just narrowly avoiding dipping my ample bosom and my new black cashmere sweater in the bowl of spicy lemongrass tofu. "So you're saying you want us to try a long-distance relationship? Is that what you're saying?"

He jerked his chin in a nod. And that was all.

"Okay." I took a deep breath and let it out slowly. "For a minute there I thought you were breaking up with me."

"You and your imagination. You're always so emotional." He reached out and patted my hand with a smile. "We're having fun, aren't we? We're good together?"

"Sure."

"That's what matters." He picked up his beer and downed a mouthful. All while the women at the next table watched on admiringly. It happened all the time. Aaron was movie-star handsome. Six feet tall with dark hair and an athletic build, while I was of average height and weight with pasty skin that refused to tan. We complemented each other, I think. But I digress. Add Aaron's natural confidence and a nice-fitting suit and you had a man who commanded a lot of attention. He basically looked like a modern Prince Charming. So it was a pity he was a little backward about his feelings. However, no one was perfect. I was most certainly not, but still the man chose me. And considering I didn't have the greatest track record with relationships, I counted this as a total win.

The longer I sat there and thought about us being in a long-distance relationship, the more positives came to mind. Things had been a little off between us lately. The last few months, I guess. His tendency to get wrapped up in his work and friends and so on had escalated. Sometimes it seemed as if I wasn't a priority. Like I hadn't made it onto his to-do list. And it had been a while since I had felt like I had his full attention.

The sex had also become a bit hit-or-miss, if I was being

completely honest. Like the last six months or so. Things had become routine, as opposed to the frenzied railing from back in the early days. I tried buying lingerie and setting the scene with candles and mood music. But still, it was perfunctory. He came, and I did not. Or, at least, I didn't come until later when I could take care of business alone.

But every relationship goes through growth periods, right?

I was committed to making this work. When I thought of the future, it was with Aaron at my side. My parents divorced when I was young. Without a doubt, they had not modeled a healthy, loving relationship. It was as if they had long since given up on each other by the time my brother Andrew and I were born. I would not be doing the same. This relationship was my longest ever, and it could and would work.

We'd met outside a bar one night when my car wouldn't start. Aaron and his friend Lars stopped to help. While Aaron and I flirted, Lars figured out I needed a new battery. He even knew a service to call who would bring it around right away. Talk about being handy. Once it was sorted, I bought them a couple of rounds of drinks to say thanks. Aaron was charming and attentive and perfect, really. Just perfect. The man swept me off my feet. He listened when I talked and took me and my thoughts and feelings seriously. And I knew we could get back to that.

If Aaron and I were half a world apart from each other, it might give him more of a chance to miss me and what we had together. At the end of the day, it might be just what we needed. You never know. With time apart, we might build the desire anew. I don't know. It was a working theory.

Then there was the idea of me visiting him in London. How exciting! Oh, the shopping and sightseeing I would do.

"A week isn't long for you to get organized." I tugged on my braid. An old nervous habit. "When did they tell you? When did you decide to accept the position?"

"Not long," he hedged. "A little while. It doesn't matter."

"O-okay." It was time to let my reservations go. The last thing this conversation needed was more tension. Now and then in this relationship, it seemed prudent to let my toxic positivity take over. That bitch could smile through anything. "How about I host a going-away party for you next weekend? Give all of your friends a chance to say bon voyage!"

"That would be great, babe." He finally smiled. "But make it Friday. Mom wants to do something Saturday. Just family. You understand."

"Oh. Right. Of course."

"And let's have it at a restaurant."

I frowned. "That's not much notice to book somewhere."

"Yeah, but you know your roommate and I don't really get along. Having it at your place could be awkward."

"If that's what you want."

"You're the best," he said with a smile. And everything was fine. Totally fine.

"Wait. He's just up and leaving?" Cleo sat opposite me on the couch. "For a whole damn year? Are you serious?"

"Yep."

We had a nice two-bedroom condo on Avalon Way in West Seattle. It was part of a large, newish complex across from the golf course. Though anywhere that was walking distance to Trader Joe's, Thai, Mexican, and barbecue was good with me. Food delivery was my happy place. The kitchen/dining/living area was open plan, and we shared the one bathroom. Considering the amount of makeup and skin care we both owned, this required some organization and compromise. But we'd been hanging together for years. We met through work; she's a photographer, and I am a social-media manager. A great combination. We also shared a love of ice cream and romance books. Our friendship was solid.

"And you're okay with this?" she asked.

"It's his life." I shrugged. "You know how ambitious he is. This move should fast-track him for the corner office he's been dreaming about. You should see how excited he is."

Cleo was already in her pajamas and wearing a red satin sleeping bonnet. "It's your feelings regarding the move I'm worried about."

"I'm fine."

She narrowed her gaze on me. "Are you, Susie? Are you, really?"

"Not going to lie. It threw me at first. It was my own fault for wondering if the last-minute change to our date plans meant he might have been going to ask me to move in with him," I admitted with a wince. "Stupid, I know."

Her lopsided smile was less than supportive. And fair enough.

"Not that it would necessarily be a good idea right now," I said in a rush. "Though, it might have been the impetus for him agreeing to some couples therapy which wouldn't hurt. But I digress... I started thinking about him moving to London for a year and...this could actually be good for us."

"Please explain."

"First, some time apart to test our resolve to stay together. To see if our relationship has what it takes to go the distance."

"Right." She nodded. "What else?"

I unzipped my cool high-heel black leather booties and freed my poor sore feet. "A little distance might make the heart grow fonder."

"You think this move might make him finally appreciate you?"

"He's not that bad. But yeah. Maybe."

Cleo had gone through a hellish divorce a few years back. Her opinion of men and relationships was not great. Though, she finally started seeing someone, a local barista named Josh. It took him months of patience to convince her to give him a chance. She seemed cautiously happy dating the man. Which was beautiful to see.

"I know you love him," she said with a grim smile. "But..."

"Yeah. We've had this talk. It would be nice if you two got along, but not everyone does."

She nodded. "We have had this talk. Many times. Can't help feeling this world would be a better place if our hearts were a little smarter."

"Maybe."

"So you need a restaurant for Saturday night?"

"Friday," I said. "His mom is doing something Saturday. Family only."

She gave me *the look.*

"I know, I know. But they're a tight-knit bunch. I really feel like I'm making inroads with his mom, though. Like I'm on the cusp of getting an invitation to these elusive family-only events."

Cleo just shook her head.

I shrugged. "It's a beautiful dream."

"Family can be complicated as fuck. But I would like the man a whole lot better if he showed the littlest inclination of having your back."

While I tried to be a positive person and stand by my man, I didn't know what to say to that. It had all been said before. Time would tell.

It took approximately five hundred phone calls, but I found a nice local bar and grill for the party. I could catch up on my work over the weekend; making this night good for Aaron was my priority. I wore my long dark hair in a knot and a black body-con dress with bootie heels. The ensemble made the most of my curves to remind my boyfriend what he'd be missing out on. And what he would be coming home to in a year.

When I called my beloved Aunt Susan for some advice

Wednesday night, she recommended I send him away with a smile, thus ensuring he wanted to return ASAP. So that was the plan. Though she had never been married, Aunt Susan was wise in all the ways. After my parents separated, she basically raised me. We talked about everything and anything. But I wasn't sure I wanted to know what her opinion would be on the scene playing out before me now.

Friday night, an hour and a half into the going-away party, Aaron was drunk. Not happy tipsy but spill-your-drink messy. Some friends from his office were buying him shots. They stood at the bar, shouting out the words to some song, and *ugh*. Meanwhile I sat at the long table reserved for our party, playing hostess with a bunch of his other friends and acquaintances. Not awkward at all.

"You okay?" asked Lars.

I pasted on a smile. "Sure."

Lars was blond with tanned skin and lumberjack hot. More mountain man than hipster. He worked as a contractor and had the muscles and general air of unkempt to prove it. Being Aaron's best friend, Lars was often invited along when we went to the movies or out to bars. We'd spent quality time together over the last year. He tended to be quieter and more serious in nature than his bestie. They make for an interesting mix.

And Lars's girlfriend, Jane, was not only stylish but a hoot. She was also bluntly honest. "Can't you talk to him?" she asked Lars, unimpressed.

"Bit late for that," grumbled Lars.

"He's thirty-five. What the fuck is he doing acting like a frat boy?"

I just shrugged. "It's his party. Guess he can get wasted if he wants to."

Lars frowned but kept his mouth shut.

"It's probably the stress of it all, catching up with him," I said. "A lot of organizing things and so on."

"You're a good woman making excuses for him." Jane flipped her hair over her shoulder. "And you look gorgeous tonight, if I haven't said so already. Lars, tell Susie how magnificent she looks."

Lars just shrugged. "She always looks gorgeous."

The warmth that kindled in my chest at their words—I must really have been in need of some kindness. "Thank you."

Lars set down his drink and looked me dead in the eye. "It's just the truth, Susie."

I smiled, and he smiled back at me. And maybe tonight wasn't quite so bad after all.

"You made her smile. Excellent complimenting. Job well done." Jane patted one of his thick shoulders. An attractive young waiter approached the table with our meals, and she gave him a broad smile. "Hello there! This looks delicious! What's your name?"

Suddenly, Lars frowned to the nth degree. I wondered what that was about.

"I'll go tell him dinner is being served." I pushed my chair back and smoothed down the front of my dress. Not that Aaron even noticed the effort I put into looking my best. I'd got a distracted peck on the cheek at the start of the night and that was all. Guess he had a lot on his mind.

He and two of his work buddies made a tight, rowdy group standing at the end of the bar. Drinking this much wasn't normal for Aaron. But then again, it was a momentous occasion. Moving overseas and starting a new job and all. I just had to be patient and understanding. This too would pass. We hadn't made plans yet for his last few days stateside. I was sure, however, that we would get to have some quality alone time. A chance to say goodbye properly. Something involving banging and romance because balance was everything.

"Aaron?" I smiled and slipped my hand into his. "They're serving dinner."

"Huh?"

"Hey. They're serving dinner."

He blinked down at me and frowned. Then he shook me off and said, "We'll be there in a minute, Susie."

"All right."

"C'mon, man." Lars appeared at my side. He slapped Aaron on the back and smiled. "Come and make a speech. Talk to some of your other guests. I've hardly seen you all night."

With a sloppy grin, Aaron followed his best friend back to the table.

I was invisible, I guess. It was the only possible explanation. A knot of tension rolled tighter in my stomach. The thought of eating did not thrill me. But I took a seat at my boyfriend's side and smiled my prettiest smile. Tonight might not be going how I'd hoped it would, but whatever. Aaron was clearly having the time of his life. It would all be fine.

"What did you order?" asked Lars, seated opposite me.

"Crab cakes. What about you?"

"Shrimp and grits."

"Ooh, good choice. We swapping plates halfway through?"

Lars nodded. "Absolutely. Save me some of the lemon."

"You two are so weird with your food thing," said Jane with a laugh.

I shrugged. "Trying more items off the menu is always worthwhile."

Lars was too busy eating to answer.

With a lurch, Aaron got to his feet, a glass of whiskey in hand. Like he needed more. Guess he'd decided to make a speech after all. "Hey, everyone. Thanks for being here tonight."

All twelve or so people who'd come out to wish him bon voyage fell silent. Quite a few had had other plans. But I had managed to get his core group of people from work and the gym and so on. The sound of silverware being set down and the music blasting out of the stereo filled the air. I took a sip of my sparkling water. One of us ought to be sober in case a coherent adult was needed.

And it didn't matter that he didn't thank me for organizing the party. Though, that would have been nice. Instead, he swayed on his feet and said, "Being offered this promotion was a…a real big deal, and I am so happy to get to see you all before I go. Real happy. This is a great night. The job is going to be fucking amazing. I can't wait to get there and get started."

He paused, and a couple of people politely clapped.

"Not finished yet," he slurred. "That's just the professional side of things. Personally, I can't wait to get to London and enjoy *everything*, if you know what I mean." Then he laughed and made a solid attempt at a wink. Which was not wildly dubious. At all.

What in the actual hell? I froze as almost every pair of eyes at the table fixed on me. My skin burned with a mixture of embarrassment and anger. In my lifetime's top-ten most humiliating moments, this was the clear new winner.

Some idiot down at the end of the table shouted out, "Yeah, man! Go get it!"

Next came the sound of bro laughter.

"Did he just…" Jane said with her mouth hanging open in horror. "Holy shit."

Lars gave her hand a squeeze. A silent plea for her to shut up if I ever did see one. Meanwhile, my idiot boyfriend sat down and drunkenly high-fived the two equally inebriated bros down at our end. The silence at the table continued until Lars picked up his fork and recommenced eating, as if nothing had happened. Jane followed his example, and then so did others.

This was not happening to me. Seriously.

I leaned closer to my boyfriend and asked in a low voice, "Aaron?"

"Hmm?"

"What did you mean by *everything* London has to offer?"

He scoffed. "Nothing, babe. Don't worry about it."

"Um. No. It wasn't nothing. And I definitely am worried about it." I licked my lips and chose my words with care. "You said you wanted us to try a long-distance relationship."

"Yeah?"

I tried to offer him a smile, but it didn't happen. My mouth wouldn't tolerate the lie, apparently. "That's what you want? You haven't changed your mind?"

"That's what I said, isn't it?"

"Yes," I agreed. "But you also just insinuated that you're looking forward to fucking around on me. So you can see how I might be a little confused."

He let his fork drop, clattering on his plate. "Dammit, Susie, that's not what I said. And you know I don't like it when you talk like that. Ladies shouldn't use that sort of language."

"Stop being a hypocrite, and answer the fucking question."

He winced as he gazed down the length of the table from beneath dark brows. As if he was worried people were listening to our conversation. "You and your jealousy. You're always jumping to conclusions. To be brutally honest, this is part of why I'm going. To get some space from you."

"*What?*"

"Can we just enjoy ourselves, please?"

I sat back in my chair and stared at him. Studied him, really. The way his shoulders were hunched over and how his jaw was clenched. Like he was hiding a secret or something. "Aaron, look at me."

"What?" He stared at his plate. "Stop it. You're causing a scene."

"Look at me."

"What?" he growled and finally met my eyes.

"Are you planning on cheating on me in London?"

He turned his face away. "Stop being ridiculous. God, you're embarrassing. You're ruining everything."

My back snapped straight. It was like a light bulb had been turned on inside my head. And all of the metaphorical cockroaches scuttling for the shadows were... Whoa. It was heartbreaking and horrible in equal measure. The mess I had made. The familiarity of feeling this way, of knowing something was wrong. Only this time, I wasn't falling for his bullshit that it was all my fault. I wouldn't allow him to turn it around on me. I was well aware of my various issues and neuroses, but it wasn't them leading me astray. It was him.

How had I ignored the signs? What had happened to me? Somewhere along the way I had gone from being kick-ass to wearing a sign that said *Kick me.*

"The problem is, Aaron, you're not as good a liar as you think you are. It just took me a while to see."

"That's enough, Susie," he hissed. "We'll talk about this later."

"No. I think we should discuss it now."

He screwed up his handsome face and hit the table with the flat of his hand, making it shake. Making me jump in my chair. And hell, if everyone hadn't known something was going on before, they sure did now. "That's it," he yelled. "I've had enough. We're through."

"Hey," said Lars in his deep voice. "Calm down."

"Yeah. We're done here." I placed the napkin on the table, stood tall, and squared my shoulders. No way would this asshole see me cry. I refused to give him the satisfaction. "Have a nice life, Aaron."

Two

"I thought I heard someone out here." Aunt Susan, my name-sake, joined me on the front steps of her house. It was a little after nine, the night of Aaron's going-away party.

She owned an old two-bedroom cottage in Ballard. The place had definitely seen better days. But for all intents and pur-poses, it was still my home. As a child, I only ever felt welcome here. Both of my parents were too busy getting on with their lives after the divorce to have time for their kids. Andrew just wanted to go to his friends' houses. Aunt Susan, however, al-ways had time for me. So of course this was where I ran when my life went to shit. This was my safe place. My refuge. Despite it becoming battered and crowded with junk over the years.

"Susie." She tightly wrapped her pink fleece robe around her and tucked a strand of long silver hair behind an ear. "What are you doing sitting out here in the dark?"

"I was working my way up to coming inside. Just wanted to get myself under control first." It was a damn cold night. I huddled down in my woolen coat with my black Alexander

McQueen scarf wrapped tight around my neck and noisily blew my nose into a tissue. "Aaron and I broke up."

"Oh, my love." She wrapped an arm around my shoulders and gave me a squeeze. "I'm so sorry to hear that."

"Neither you nor Cleo even liked him. Which should have been a major red flag yet somehow wasn't. I don't know what the hell I was thinking."

"We can't always help where our heart leads us."

"Yeah." I hiccupped and swiped the tears off my face. My makeup must have been a mess. I probably looked like an ugly clown-woman with a broken heart. It wasn't too far from the truth. Aaron had treated me like a joke for long enough. And I let him—let's not forget that damn salient detail. "I really did have feelings for him. I thought we could make it work. Now, though..."

She said nothing. Just patiently waited for me to pour out my woes. Just like she always had. She smelled of the lavender she picked off the bushes at the front of her house and slipped in among her clothes drawers. Some things never changed.

"He got up and announced at dinner that he couldn't wait to experience *everything* London had to offer," I explained in a husky voice, thanks to my sore throat from crying. "Then he laughed and winked. And then he actually had the audacity to act like it didn't mean anything and accused me of causing a scene when I asked him about it."

"What an idiot." Aunt Susan clicked her tongue. "As I recall, your father used to try to pull the same trick on your mom. Gaslight her to control the story and make her doubt herself. Divorcing my brother was the smartest thing that woman ever did. Apart from letting you spend so much time with me, of course."

"Oh, man." I sniffled and gave her a look. "Are you not-so-subtly telling me I've been searching for my asshole of a father in the men I've been dating?"

"I think I was more subtly telling you that you succeeded."

"Great."

She pressed a kiss to my temple. "Live and learn."

"But I'm thirty now. I should know better!"

"Excuse you. I am almost sixty and still learning new things about myself and my place in this world and whatever is beyond," she chided softly. "Some lessons just take as long as they take. There's no rushing them. And issues left over from childhood can be some of the hardest to grapple with."

"I guess so."

"I'm sorry your heart is hurting. But at least you know you only want him. You don't *need* him."

"I know."

She nodded sagely and said, "It can be hard to be alone sometimes. To not have someone special. Though, he never exactly treated you like you were special, did he?"

I flinched and kept my mouth shut. Which was telling.

"You are wonderful, bright, and so beautiful you blind me. Don't accept less than your due, my love."

"Thank you."

"Anytime," she said. "You want to come in and have a cup of cocoa?"

I shook my head. "No, thanks. I'm going to head home and get some sleep. Give Cleo the good news."

"Fair enough. I should get to bed. Things have been so busy lately, I could use a decent night's sleep." She yawned and gave my shoulder a squeeze. "How about breakfast tomorrow morning? We could make waffles?"

"That would be great."

I let myself into Aunt Susan's house the next morning. After waking with a headache from all of the crying, I applied about a container's worth of concealer, downed some Tylenol, and donned my most comfortable clothing. Baggy jeans with a hoodie and sneakers for the win. Clothes to hide and comfort me. Though, they were still black, because basically everything I owned was black.

Heartache was an utter bitch. But this too would pass. Cleo had been fast asleep when I got home last night. I had texted her the news and woken up to a barrage of supportive messages from her. It was nice to have a friend who had my back.

The cottage was quiet when I arrived a little after nine. Aunt Susan must have decided to sleep in. A car passed outside, but inside the cottage seemed like another world, one unto itself. None of the lights were on, but the winter sun peeked around the edges of the drawn curtains turning the space to shadows. My sleep had been restless and full of bad dreams. But stepping into this house smoothed out the worst of the rough edges. It soothed me. Here I was loved and accepted.

It was just what I needed after waking to voice mail from Aaron. The drunken idiot had called a little after two in the morning. He left a rambling speech offering me the chance to return to his good graces if I agreed to an open relationship and begged his forgiveness for my anger last night.

As fucking if. What a man-child. There would be no second-guessing my decision to walk away from our relationship. Aunt Susan was right: I didn't need him. He'd never treated me like I was special. A hard truth to face, but a fact none the less. I'd wasted a year waiting for an asshole to see my worth when I should have had more respect for myself. Funny how things were always so damn obvious in hindsight. And by funny, I mean *ugh*.

The air inside the house was thick with dust and the scent of lavender. Aunt Susan attempted to keep the place clean. But the sheer amount of stuff she had made it difficult. A Christmas tree stood by the fireplace reminding me that the clock was ticking and I hadn't even started shopping. What the hell had happened to this year?

In the living room, a collection of storage boxes had grown since my last visit. With the basement, attic, and back bedroom full to the brim, space in this place was at a premium. You might say Aunt Susan was a hoarder. And you'd be right. Her dislike of change was further reflected in the dated gold-flecked wallpaper and shag pile carpet, along with the original kitchen and bathroom from way back when. My grandparents, who'd owned the house before Aunt Susan, had a similar frame of mind. Hold onto everything, let go of nothing. The place was like a museum dedicated to things lost and forgotten. Didn't matter. I still loved it here.

I knocked gently on Aunt Susan's bedroom door and pushed it open. Nothing stirred on the bed. No noise was made. No rustling covers or squeaking mattress. Not even the soft in and out of her breathing. Something was wrong. An unwelcome thought crossed my mind, but I shoved it down as hard and fast as I could. I turned on the bedside lamp and a weak wash of light cast long shadows and illuminated the shape of her body beneath the blankets. She was so small she almost seemed like a child. Her eyes were closed, her hand beside her face on the pillow. As if she had been reaching for something when she fell asleep.

Only, she wasn't asleep.

I don't know how I knew. Guess it was the way the cottage was so quiet. Like it was holding its breath. Like it was in mourning. Aunt Susan loved to take up space, to make noise. Even asleep she would mouth-breathe and snore. Now here she lay, small and static. Her expression seemed peaceful, at least. I carefully sat on the edge of the mattress and touched her hand. Her skin was so cold. She must have been dead for hours. To see her this way was bizarre. As if whatever spark of magic that brought her to life had departed. But for some reason, I didn't cry or scream. I just sat there holding her hand.

Grief settled over me like a second skin. There were no suitable words to describe the loss. The weight of her absence. I was here, and she was gone, and that was that. If I had known that last night was my last time with her, I wouldn't have wasted it moaning about Aaron, that's for sure. A hundred and one things came to mind…things I should have asked her. Stories about her and her life that I should have taken the time to hear. It was too late now. And that was a regret that I would carry around for the rest of my life.

I brushed the hair back from her face and said, "I love you, Aunt Susan. Thank you for everything."

That was as close as I could bring myself to saying goodbye.

It stormed the day we buried Aunt Susan. Seattle weather at its finest: an ice-cold wind and angry, gray sky. Though by the time the service finished, the sun appeared, and the mountain was out. It was a Christmas miracle.

I had never carried a coffin before and hopefully would never have to again. But I decided to carry hers after all the years she'd carried me. My insides felt hollow and scraped clean. Like I'd lost too much too quickly.

But losing Aunt Susan certainly didn't make me miss Aaron. It's not like he would have been any help with the funeral. The idiot probably would have raised an eyebrow at my black pantsuit and asked me if I really thought wearing my hair in a ponytail was suitable for the occasion. All of the little ways in which he used to undermine me seemed so obvious now. Love could make you such a fool. Aunt Susan had been right about that.

We had the wake at a neighborhood bar near her house. She'd played Scrabble there every Monday night with a group for years, and they had a small room for private functions. A selection of photos I'd chosen sat on a table in the corner. Aunt

Susan as a baby. Playing at the beach as a child. The bad perm and organza extravaganza from her '80s prom...

"Hey," said Cleo, bumping her shoulder against mine. "How are you doing?"

"I'm okay. Thanks for coming."

"Of course."

I took a sip of beer and glanced around the room.

Some of Aunt Susan's friends sat around a table with lit candles in the center. They appeared to be quietly praying or chanting. My aunt had been active in many local groups, including a pagan group. It was good that there was room for everyone and their beliefs. People told all sorts of stories about her. Ones that made me laugh and cry. Funerals were so weird. It was odd to stand around chatting and drinking to commemorate the sudden absence of linchpins in our lives. But what else could we do?

The medical examiner had confirmed she died of a stroke. That it would have been fast and pain-free. Though, I don't know how much of that was said to put me at ease.

An old song by Heart suddenly blasted out over the stereo. Miss Lillian, a friend of Susan's, gave me a thumbs-up from the bar. She had obviously put a request in for some volume. People seemed to perk up, and the general air of sadness lifted just a little. Now it felt more like a party.

"Aunt Susan would approve," said Cleo.

I nodded. "She loved a good get-together. This is much more her taste."

My brother fussed with the knot of his tie and gave me a brief smile. We were not particularly close. Like our father, Andrew was a workaholic and didn't leave much time for family and friends. The last time I saw him was when mom and her new husband had been in town a few months back.

"I have to get going," he said. "But we should make time soon to talk."

"What about?"

"The inheritance," he said. "When are we seeing her lawyer?"

"I saw her lawyer yesterday."

He narrowed his gaze on me. "Susie, why wasn't I told about this?"

"Because it didn't concern you?"

"What?" He recoiled. "Why would our aunt's estate not concern me?"

"She didn't leave you anything, Andrew. You weren't mentioned. I'm sorry." I tried to be kind. But I doubt it came out that way. The entitlement in his voice was setting me on edge. "I'm surprised you thought you would be. You were never close to her. When Dad used to make us go to her house, you always took off to a friend's place instead."

"She was still my aunt."

"When was the last time you even saw her?"

"That's beside the point."

Cleo shook her head and said nothing. A whole lot of it.

"She left you *everything*? The house too?" he asked, his voice rising to a shout.

It kind of stunned me, to be honest. Which was stupid. Andrew reminded me of our father for all sorts of reasons. When Dad didn't get his way, he was more than happy to get loud. A classic bully maneuver. The kicker was what Aunt Susan had said about my dating proclivities, how I went after men with similar asshole traits. *Ouch and gross.* As soon as we were done here, I was going to sit myself down and have a serious discussion with me about changing my ways. Stat.

"You're selling the house and giving me half, of course," he insisted. "Aren't you?"

"Are you seriously yelling at me about money at a fucking funeral?"

"Susie—"

"This is why you're here today? To get your hands on her house?" I let my head fall back and stared at the ceiling. Wherever Aunt Susan was, if she could hear this, she would have been furious. "Today is about celebrating our aunt's life. Hearing stories about her and taking a moment to be thankful that we knew her. That she was a part of our lives."

"Dad said the estate should be evenly split between us."

"I don't care."

"Mom thought it would be best too."

"I repeat, I don't care. Our parents can think whatever nonsense they like. And throwing a temper tantrum will not get you what you want here."

His face turned ruddy with anger. "She was my aunt too. It's only fair."

"You thought she was a flake. You had no immediate use for her, so you deemed her worthless."

"Susie—"

"I am talking," I interrupted in a loud voice. "And it's so sad. It really is. You missed out, Andrew. Because she was great. Wise and funny and just so wonderful to be around. She had so much love to give, and she cared about us. She really did. When Mom and Dad were too busy, she was the one who made time for me. If you had just given her a chance, taken a moment to get to know her, then you would know what a loss it is to no longer have her here with us. But all today means to you is a chance to try and get your hands on something that isn't yours and that you don't deserve."

"You're being ridiculous."

"Get out. Now."

"Susie—"

"If you had any idea how sick and tired I am of entitled men disapproving of me and getting all up in my face with their self-righteous bullshit..."

"This isn't finished." His chin jerked up, and he gazed down at me. Like he could glare me into submission. Then he marched his idiotic ass out the door.

At which point my shoulders slumped, and I hung my head.

"Well," said Miss Lillian, her abundance of silver bangles clinking together with each move she made. "I feel like we need to sage the place after that."

"How about we do shots instead?" suggested Cleo.

Miss Lillian waggled her brows. "Not that I should be telling you, but Susan was a fiend for tequila back in the day."

I blew out a breath. "Now, that sounds good. Let's do it."

"I can't believe Aunt Susan got arrested for frolicking naked in a city park and never told me." I grinned and swung my purse over my shoulder. All of the tequila, corn chips, and salsa made for a warm buzz in my belly. A melancholy feeling had replaced the pain of grief. For now, at least. "What a legend she was. I'm glad I got to hear about that."

"Sounds like your aunt and Miss Lillian got up to all sorts in college."

"Isn't it nice how they stayed close all these years?"

Cleo bumped my shoulder with her own again. It was her version of a hug. I hardly stumbled at all. I guess I wasn't nearly as drunk as first thought. But Cleo laughed at me just the same.

It had been kind of the bar to let us hang out in the function room drinking and telling stories past the designated couple of hours we paid for. My first-ever time playing Drunk Scrabble. I think Aunt Susan would have approved. Stories had been told, and songs had been sung. While a few tears were shed along the way, it had been, on the whole, more about celebrating her life than commiserating over her loss. There hadn't been a lot of people. But the folk who had been in attendance were fun and kind and full of love for my aunt. You couldn't ask for more.

"I think she would have liked it," said Cleo as we were getting ready to leave.

I buttoned up my black woolen coat as we headed for the door. It was almost eight o'clock, and the main part of the bar was crowded with patrons. An old Soundgarden song played over the speakers, and many sang along. My eye caught a familiar face down at the end of the bar. Lars was hard to miss, all tall and blond. No sign of Aaron, thank goodness. It had already been a day without adding him to it. Though, of course he would have left for London already. Jane sat on a stool laughing at something. Lars smiled down at her. He looked besotted. Totally engrossed in her. And the man had a nice smile. The big dude was masculine-pretty. What really hit me, however, was the way they were interacting. How into each other they were. Just happy to be in each other's company. That's what I wanted. And if I couldn't have that, then I was better off alone.

"What are we looking at?" asked Cleo.

"A couple of Aaron's friends are at the end of the bar."

She licked her lips. Probably still dealing with the remnants of salt from all of the lip-sip-sucking we had been doing. "The big dude? He's handsome. Do you want to go over and say hello?"

"No." I shook my head. "We always got along okay, but… let's go."

"Susie," called a familiar voice. And there was Lars coming after me with his big-ass stride. "Hey."

"Hi," I said. This was not awkward at all.

"I'll just be over here." Cleo wandered off to stare at the

jukebox and give us a moment's privacy. As much privacy as you could have in the middle of a crowded bar.

And his face—he looked so sincere. "How have you been?"

"Fine. You?"

"Good."

I just nodded.

"It's good to see you," he said. "You look...yeah...great."

Seriously awkward as awkward could be. Jane was giving me a finger wave, and I smiled back at her. The people you lost after a breakup was a lot. These two I had definjtely liked. Jane was fun, and Lars was...well, he was Lars.

"Thanks," I said. "You two look like you're on a date. I better let you get back to it."

"Right," he said and stood there and stared at me. "Guess I'll see you around, Susie."

"Sure. See you around, Lars."

I hooked my arm through Cleo's, and we made our way through the crowd to the front door. Outside the sky was clear, the stars shining brightly. A whole universe of them sparkled above our heads. The air was crisp and cold. Holiday lights filled the bar's front windows.

"What did the big guy have to say?" asked Cleo.

"Not much. He's Aaron's best friend. What could he say?"

"True."

"Christmas is going to suck without her," I said, out of nowhere.

"You're coming with me to my mother's place this year. It's already been decided," said Cleo. "She said you're in charge of the wine."

"Thank you."

"Of course."

"Chosen family is a good thing. I'm so lucky to have you." She just smiled.

A woman wearing reindeer antlers walked past arm in arm

with a man. They looked happy. Before she left, Miss Lillian had told us we had a responsibility to go out and be in love with the world. To live our lives to the best of our abilities, because Aunt Susan no longer had the opportunity to do so. And honest to God, I was going to keep trying. Starting with no more men. At least for a while. I needed time to deal with recent events. To figure out myself and why the relationships I chose to be in kept combusting. To show myself some love and understanding. All of which would hopefully lead to me making better choices. A girl could only hope. But dealing with Aunt Susan's house and all of the work it needed would keep me busy for a while. When I thought about the sheer amount of stuff to be dealt with… *Oof.* There'd be no time for worrying about men and such nonsense for a while. Not a bad thing.

"Do you think you'll get another roommate after I move out?" I asked. "Not that it'll be for a while yet. The house is going to take some time to get sorted."

Cleo frowned. "I don't know."

"I'm going to miss not having you to talk to all the time."

"I'm going to miss borrowing your shoes."

I nodded. "I do have great shoes."

"You won't be so far away. We'll still see each other all the time." She smiled. "Feels like life is shaking things up. As if it's time for some changes."

"It does feel like that, doesn't it?"

"Look," said Cleo, pointing at the sky. "It's a falling star. Make a wish."

We both stared at the beauty of the meteor falling through space. Then I asked, "Do you think it's a sign of better days ahead?"

She shrugged. "It could definitely be that."

"Yeah." I smiled. "Let's go home."

★ ★ ★ ★ ★

Acknowledgments

With thanks to my editor, Susan Swinwood, for her endless enthusiasm for this story, and my agent, Amy Tannenbaum, for never giving up. Thank you to all the romance readers out there and especially the reviewers who give so much time and passion to the genre. Also thank you to Sali Benbow-Powers, everyone in my Facebook fan group, Jenn and everyone at Social Butterfly PR, Mish Lewis, everyone at the Jane Rotrosen Agency, Lori Francis, and last but not least, my family for their love, support, and sense of humor.

Kylie's Playlist

"Rebel Girl" by Bikini Kill
"On the Sunny Side of the Street" by Ernestine Anderson &
George Shearing
"Like Me Better" by Parisalexa
"Seasons" by Chris Cornell
"Crimson Wave" by Tacocat
"Something's Gotta Give" by Bing Crosby
"May This Be Love" by Jimi Hendrix
"Crooked Teeth" by Death Cab for Cutie
"About a Girl" by Nirvana
"You Don't Know Me" by Ray Charles
"Crazy on You" by Heart
"Open the Door" by Grace Love
"Yellow Ledbetter" by Pearl Jam
"The Story" by Brandi Carlile